PRAISE FOR MICHAEL ROWE'S *ENTER, NIGHT*

"*Enter, Night* is so rich and assured it's hard to believe it's Michael Rowe's first novel . . . it skillfully brings to mind the classic works of Stephen King and Robert McCammon. But the novel's breathtaking, wholly unexpected and surprisingly moving conclusion heralds the arrival of a major new talent. Michael Rowe is now on my must-read list."

—Christopher Rice, *New York Times* bestselling author of *A Density of Souls, The Moonlit Earth* and *The Heavens Rise*

"A dark masterpiece that virtually burns the pages with bloody incandescence . . . *Enter, Night* will seduce you with its dark lyricism and richly tapestried storyline and then it will gut you with its unrelenting horror. Michael Rowe has written a vampire novel for the ages, one that readers will not soon forget. Remember when you first read Stephen King's *Salem's Lot*? Prepare for a similar experience."

—Paul Goat Allen, BarnesandNoble.com

"With *Enter, Night*, Michael Rowe does the near impossible and rescues the modern vampire novel from its current state of mediocrity with his dead-on portrayal of the gothic small town, rich characters, and deeply frightening story. This is a novel by a writer to watch, starting now. Read *Enter, Night*. With the lights on."

—Susie Moloney, bestselling author of *A Dry Spell, The Dwelling*, and *The Thirteen*

"*Enter, Night* is far and away the best vampire novel I've read in a good while, certainly since *Let The Right One In.* . . . It knows exactly what it's doing."

—Stephen Graham Jones, author of *Demon Theory*

"These are vampires played straight, and set loose on a cast of uncommonly multi-dimensional characters . . . *Enter, Night* is fantastic."

—*The Canadian Science Fiction Review*

"I have no doubt that [*Enter, Night*] will be pointed to and referenced as one of the all-time greats."

—*Horror World*

"[An] outstanding first novel . . . terrific."

—*Outwords*

"An amazing page-turner of a novel. Gripping and gruesome."

—Paul Bellini in *Fab*

[Michael Rowe] has written the vampire novel that I have been waiting for. There is no sparkle in his vampires. They are monstrous . . . they are Evil with a capital E."
—David Nickle in *The Devil's Exercise Yard*

"*Enter, Night* brings back the Bram Stoker and Stephen King days."
—Justine Lewkowicz in *Bookends*

"*Enter, Night* isn't just a great vampire tale, it's a compelling exploration of family, religion (there's some great commentary about the Jesuits that 'civilized' large swaths of Canada), and history written with beauty and intelligence. I can't recommend it enough."
—Adam Cesare in *Brain-Tremors.com*

"Richly textured and filled with complex, convincing personalities, as well as being a truly frightening read, *Enter, Night* is a chilling foray into the emotional, sexual, and ideological horrors we create for one another."
—The 2012 Sunburst Awards Jury

"Rowe manages to do what so many others writing 'vampire fiction' fail to . . . he creates an exceedingly creepy, violent, atmospheric and frightening novel that not only pays tribute to the literary and cinematic past, but also manages to restore the vampire to his former and deserving glory. Highly, highly recommended."
—Paul G. Bens in *Haole Reads*

"Deliciously old-school, Michael Rowe's debut pays tribute to Marv Wolfman's *Tomb of Dracula* comics. Tightly paced and full of lovable, terribly imperiled characters and gloomy, Gothic atmosphere that builds to a crescendo, before letting loose a kick-to-the-heart finale."
—*Rue Morgue*

"Like every great writer toiling within terror, Rowe pays attention to people first, making sure we care about them, know them inside out, and understand their pasts and motivations. . . . Think Stephen King's *Salem's Lot* with a dash of Steve Niles' *30 Days of Night* . . . Rowe is a master teller of tales and his strength lies in the practical beauty of his words. Hugely recommended."
—*Fangoria*

Wild Fell

A GHOST STORY

BY MICHAEL ROWE

ChiZine Publications

Distributed in Canada by
Publishers Group Canada
76 Stafford Street, Unit 300
Toronto, Ontario, M6J 2S1
Toll Free: 800-747-8147
e-mail: info@pgcbooks.ca

Distributed in the U.S. by
Consortium Book Sales & Distribution
34 Thirteenth Avenue, NE, Suite 101
Minneapolis, MN 55413
Phone: (612) 746-2600
e-mail: sales.orders@cbsd.com

Library and Archives Canada Cataloguing in Publication

Rowe, Michael, 1962-, author
    Wild Fell / Michael Rowe.

Issued in print and electronic formats.
ISBN 978-1-77148-159-5 (pbk.).
ISBN 978-1-77148-160-1 (pdf)

I. Title.

    PS8635.O884W56 2013   C813'.6   C2013-905158-9
                  C2013-905159-7

CHIZINE PUBLICATIONS
Toronto, Canada
www.chizinepub.com
info@chizinepub.com

Edited by Brett Savory
Copy edited by Sandra Kasturi
Proofread by Michael Matheson

Canada Council   Conseil des Arts
for the Arts   du Canada

We acknowledge the support of the Canada Council for the Arts which last year invested $20.1 million in writing and publishing throughout Canada.

ONTARIO ARTS COUNCIL
CONSEIL DES ARTS DE L'ONTARIO
50 YEARS OF ONTARIO GOVERNMENT SUPPORT OF THE ARTS
50 ANS DE SOUTIEN DU GOUVERNEMENT DE L'ONTARIO AUX ARTS

Published with the generous assistance of the Ontario Arts Council.

Printed in Canada

For Victor Kleinschmit, the keeper of my ghosts.

And in loving memory of Mark Richard Braun

Home is the sailor, home from the sea,
And the hunter home from the hill.
—Robert Louis Stevenson, "Requiem"

Wild Fell

A Ghost Story

BY MICHAEL ROWE

"The following events occurred on a small island of isolated position in a large Canadian lake, to whose cool waters the inhabitants of Montreal and Toronto flee for rest and recreation in the hot months. It is only to be regretted that events of such peculiar interest to the genuine student of the psychical should be entirely uncorroborated. Such unfortunately, however, is the case."

—Algernon Blackwood, "A Haunted Island"

"A house is never still in darkness to those who listen intently; there is a whispering in distant chambers, an unearthly hand presses the snib of the window, the latch rises. Ghosts were created when the first man woke in the night."

—J. M. Barrie, *The Little Minister*

"Of all ghosts the ghosts of old loves are the worst."

—Arthur Conan Doyle, *The Memoirs of Sherlock Holmes: Volume 3*

Prologue

NIGHTSWIMMING, 1960

"Have you ever seen a ghost?"

Sean "Moose" Schwartz glanced into the rear-view mirror at the dark road behind them, lit only by the red gleam of his taillights and the occasional burst of moonlight when the trees on either side of the road thinned out, then across the passenger seat at Brenda. He half-smiled. "Well, have you? Have you ever seen one?"

Brenda said, "There's no such thing as ghosts." She hesitated. "Have you?"

"Have I what?"

"Have you ever seen a ghost?"

"I thought you said there was no such thing?"

"There isn't," Brenda said. "There's no such thing."

In the road, wisps of late-summer mist spiralled in the yellow headlights and the fecund curve of the full orange moon had slipped out from beneath a quilt of dark blue clouds, clearly visible in the upper left-hand corner of the windshield, shining through the white pine. Brenda had seen the moon when he picked her up at her parents' house and remarked that it was pretty. *Not as pretty as you are*, he'd said as he opened the Chevy's passenger side door for her the way her father always did for her mother. She was wearing tan pedal pushers and a rose-print mandarin collar blouse. The blouse was her favourite because it brought out her tan and colour to her cheeks, and made her blue eyes look bluer. She *felt* pretty tonight. Brenda had blushed at Sean's words. She climbed into the truck, but said nothing.

As they drove, Sean and Brenda made small talk about the summer that was coming to an end, about their friends, about how Brenda's parents weren't crazy about letting her drive around Alvina in Sean's truck because, they said, it was "dangerous," and he was a seventeen-year-old boy and older than she was. The way they said it, he might as well have been a forty-year-old pervert instead of a boy just a year older than she was, an Alvina boy at that.

Sean had asked her out in June, the first week of the summer vacation. This had surprised Brenda, but it also gave her some hope that she wasn't the brown-haired, blue-eyed, plain, unremarkable girl she'd always secretly believed herself to be, the one she'd seen every morning in the mirror over the dresser in her bedroom.

In truth, Brenda Egan was neither pretty nor plain. She hovered in that sphere between those two determinative aesthetic polarities that defined so much of adolescent social life. Her features were regular and even, and when she smiled, people tended to smile back. She had friends, but was not part of any large group. She got good grades, but had no illusions about her curiosity or her intellect. She thought of herself as average, and while she might have wished she were prettier-than-average, or smarter-than-average, she wasn't the sort of girl who lost much sleep over it. When she started noticing boys, however, she was surprised to find herself disappointed that they didn't notice her back right away.

That is until this summer, when Sean Schwartz asked her if she wanted to go swimming with him. She had known of him all her life, in the way of small towns that form their own particular circles within concentric circles, though she didn't know him well. He was a grade ahead of her at Alvina Collegiate. She knew he played hockey all winter with the Alvina Eagles. He was no star, but she'd heard him described as dependable. His primary athletic fame derived from wrestling. He'd been on the junior varsity or varsity team every year since he started high school. From late spring till early October, he worked at his family's marina, pumping gas for the summer people's powerboats, and working on dock repairs with his uncle Vic.

When Brenda first told her mother about Sean Schwartz, Edith Egan had pursed her lips and said, "*Schwartz?* What kind of a name is that? Is he a Jewish boy?"

Brenda said she didn't know. Edith pursed her lips again and frowned.

Brenda heard her mother make a phone call late that night. She heard her mother mention Sean's name. The conversation wasn't a long one. Whatever Edith Egan found out must have satisfied her, because she never asked if Sean was Jewish again and she seemed to have no particular objection to Sean asking Brenda out, so all was well that ended well.

Alvina, Ontario was the year-round home to some 3,205 souls, a population that nearly doubled in the shimmering blue and green days between the end of May and the end of August, when summer people from the cities drove north to lake country and temporarily took up residence in their cottages and summer houses on the rocky beaches and promontories around Devil's Lake, which was not actually a lake at all, but rather a lake-sized basin of Georgian Bay, itself part of Lake Huron.

Alvina people tended to keep to each other's company, except when they had to move beyond it. It wasn't a question of hostility, mutual or otherwise. It was just the way things were done, the way they had always been done during the more than a century that Devil's Lake had been a destination for the rich from Toronto and Montreal—or even farther, as far away as the United States. The people of Alvina had provided the labour for the building and the service in the various businesses that catered to the summer people. It was a relationship that suited both sides admirably and had never been questioned.

Every once in a blue moon, some ill-fated teenage romance embarrassed the families on both sides of the equation, but these instances were rare, and even more rarely discussed when the dust settled afterwards. It was common knowledge, for instance, that sometime in the '40s, some snobby girl from Toronto had a summer fling with one of the local Alvina men and had gotten herself knocked up. That had been the Toronto family's last summer on Devil's Lake. By the next summer, the cottage had been sold to new owners, and the young man in question had bought an expensive new truck, even though he never had two pennies to rub together and hadn't worked in months. Eyebrows were raised, but no one talked about it, except to say what Brenda had heard her own mother say at the beginning of every summer season since Brenda was thirteen—when Alvina people mixed with summer people, nothing good ever came of it.

Sean was a classic Alvina boy, one who had moved through his seventeen years as unobtrusively as Brenda had moved though her own sixteen. In Brenda's eyes this made him more desirable than any movie star because it validated her own place in the natural order of things as a classic Alvina girl.

During the hot weeks of the summer, they'd gone swimming in Devil's Lake after Sean's shifts at the marina were finished. They'd gone to the movies in Collingwood, taking the long route home through the fragrant summer dark. When Sean had kissed her that first time, she marvelled at how soft a boy's lips could be, because she'd always imagined they would feel rough and hard and foreign. Brenda had returned his kisses, clumsily at first, but then with an ardour that surprised her as much as her discovery of the softness of Sean's lips. She explored the bulk of his body, the planes of his chest and back muscles beneath the t-shirt, inhaling the scent of cotton and warm skin that smelled like soap and light, clean sweat.

The night he had reached up under her shirt and touched her breasts, she had told him she wasn't ready. He had acquiesced with a grace that relieved her, and it occurred to her for the first time that perhaps being in love meant feeling safe. Sean never tried again, though even with all her inexperience, Brenda could tell he wanted to, and this sure knowledge thrilled her.

Beneath the wheels of the Chevy, the crackle of gravel and country dirt sounded almost like footsteps in the dark. Sean had skirted Alvina's outer limits and turned onto one of the many dirt roads that led to the shore of Devil's Lake. But he'd kept driving. After a while, Brenda lost track of the number of roads onto which they'd turned and admitted to herself that if she'd had to find her way home by herself, she likely wouldn't be able to do so. But she was with Sean, so who cared? Still, it was odd.

I'm lost in my own town, she thought. *How weird.*

Then, out of nowhere, Sean had asked that bizarre question about whether or not she believed in ghosts.

Sean said, "Well then, if there's no such thing as ghosts, let's get my uncle's boat and row out to Blackmore Island. Let's spend the night there. Let's go to the house."

"Yeah, right. My parents would kill me if I spent the night anywhere with you. And if my dad found out that you'd even suggested it, this town would have a new ghost story—yours."

"Chicken," he mocked softly. "*Bawk-bawk-bawk.*"

"You're such a *jerk.*" She frowned. "I thought this was a date. I thought we were going down to the lake to watch the moon? Why are you talking about rowing out to that place? If there *is* any such house on any such island, it's almost a mile offshore. If this is what you were planning, you should probably take me home."

"It's not a mile offshore from every point in the county. You just need to look for the right spot." He paused. "Have you ever been out there?"

"No," she admitted. "Besides, I don't believe there's any such house. It's probably just a wreck of an old cottage. It's just a story grownups—adults—" she corrected herself, "tell little kids to scare them. And I'm not a little kid, Sean."

"Bren, do you really not believe in ghosts? Or do you just not believe in them during the day? Do you believe in them at night?"

Brenda ignored the question. "My mom isn't going to let me keep going out with you like this once school starts, you know." She was trying to sound bored and was almost succeeding. "Are you sure you want to waste our last Saturday night of the summer this way, acting like an idiot? Or do you want to go down to the beach and watch the moon with me?"

She laid her hand on Sean's leg and caressed it, feeling the thick muscles tense beneath the soft cotton of his chinos. His thighs shifted, spread slightly apart. He leaned back in his seat, gripping the steering wheel tightly. She flexed her grip almost imperceptibly, using her nails this time, running them lightly along the inside of his thigh. Now it was Brenda's turn to smile. She knew what she would find if she slid her hand higher up his leg, to the place where the fly of his khakis was now straining against the cotton fabric. She'd heard all about it from other girls. She was grateful for the darkness inside the pickup's cab. This power was new and unfamiliar to Brenda. She was still testing its boundaries, but didn't move her hand any higher.

She was likewise conscious of rising warmth in her own body. *That* warmth was no longer unfamiliar, though still new, still uncharted.

But at this moment, she was more than prepared to use that power or any other to make Sean forget about his stupid idea to row out to some old ruined house on Blackmore Island at night, a house she'd heard about her whole life but had never actually seen.

They drove in silence through the dark for a while under the full orange moon.

Finally Brenda spoke. "There's no such thing as ghosts."

"Are you telling yourself, or are you telling me?"

"There isn't. *Aren't*," she corrected herself. "There aren't any such things as ghosts."

"There are, too," Sean said. "I've seen one."

"Oh, pull the other one. You have not."

"I have. I'm serious."

"Okay," she said. "When?"

"When I was about nine. I was riding home from Midland with my uncle Vic. It was October, not too long before Halloween—"

Brenda sighed. "Of course it was. Of course it was just before Halloween."

"Do you want to hear this or not?"

"I'm listening."

"So, I was falling asleep in the back seat, not asleep yet, but dozy, you know? I was nine. I was just this little kid. Uncle Vic had an out-of-town roofing job and my folks said I could go with him if I wanted to and if he didn't mind. So he took me. The people he was doing the job for were nice. They let me watch TV inside while he worked, and the lady fed me dinner. When the sun went down, it got cold, and it got really, really foggy. I mean, this was fog like I've never *seen* before."

"Where does the ghost come in?" Brenda said, bored. "Is there a point to this? Because in case you're wondering, I'm not scared yet."

Sean was silent. Then he said: "Never mind."

"No, tell me. Really. I really want to hear."

"No, you don't, Brenda. Forget it."

"I'm sorry. Please tell me."

He relented. "We were just past the Bartleby town line, close to Noack. Not far from home. It was about ten at night." He paused again, a beat longer than Brenda expected. The cab of the pickup was suddenly very quiet. She heard Sean take a breath and found herself taking an involuntary one of her own.

"What happened?"

"A woman," Sean said, exhaling. "A woman ran across the road, right in front of us. Right out of the fog. Uncle Vic shouted *Holy shit!* He slammed on the brakes. The car fishtailed right across the road through the fog, and swerved into a ditch."

"Oh my God!" Brenda said, forgetting for a moment that she didn't believe any part of Sean's story. "Did you get hurt? Did you hit the woman?"

"When he was sure I was safe, Uncle Vic told me to stay in the car. He went out to the road to check on the woman. Neither of us had felt her hit the car, but there was no way we could have *not* hit her. We just didn't feel a *thump*."

"Did he find her body? Was she all right?"

"There was no body." Sean's voice sounded hollow. Brenda didn't think he was putting it on for effect. "Uncle Vic didn't find anything. The road was completely empty. There was no one there. Nothing. Just fog."

"That's impossible," Brenda said. "You must have imagined it."

"How could we both have imagined the exact same thing? We both saw her."

This time it was Brenda's turn to be silent. She waited for him to go on.

"But the thing was—and I'll never forget this—I could have *sworn* I saw her face in the headlights through the windshield when the car swerved. The thing is, I couldn't have seen it. There's just no way. I was in the back seat. We couldn't have been that close, or she would have come right through the glass. But I saw it clearly. It was an old lady. Her hair was all around her face, like it was blowing in the wind or something. But there was no wind. The fog was like a wall that night. She was wearing a blouse with some sort of lacy collar, like one of those you see in the old pictures at the United Church in town—high, buttoned up. But her face . . ."

"What about her face?" Brenda asked in a small voice.

"She had no *eyes*, Brenda," Sean said. He shivered. "There were no eyes. Just black holes where eyes should be. Her face was all shrivelled like a mummy. And her mouth was wide open, like she was screaming. I even saw her teeth. They looked like rotted black toadstools. Then the car turned again and we crashed into the ditch. She was gone." Sean splayed the fingers of his right hand in a flicking motion. "*Pffft.* Into thin air. After a bit, Uncle Vic still hadn't come back, and I was pretty shaken up. So I unlocked the passenger-side door and got out. I could barely make him out through the fog, but he was on the other side of the road coming from somewhere farther back. He saw me and shouted at me to stay where I was and not come any closer, to get back in the car. His voice didn't even sound like his voice. I've never seen him like that. He was white as a sheet."

"Why? Had he found her body or something?"

Sean said, "No. There was no body."

"What, then? What was over there? What did he find?"

"An old graveyard," Sean said. "There was nothing over there but an old graveyard surrounded by a tall iron fence. The gate was locked. Uncle Vic said it didn't look like anyone had been there for a hundred years."

Brenda took a deep breath and exhaled slowly. She gazed intently at Sean's face.

"Sean?" she said.

Sean kept his eyes on the road, staring straight ahead. "Yeah?"

"Sean, you are so full of baloney. But I have to admit, that was a pretty good story. You had me going there for a minute. Maybe two."

"It's a true story, Bren." Sean sounded wounded. "It really happened."

She laughed. "Sure it did."

After ten minutes, Sean pulled over to the side of the dirt road and cut the motor and the headlights. Through the open window, Brenda heard the sound of lake water lapping against rock and shore. The full moon was very bright, and through the trees she saw the undulating shimmer of orange light where it struck the water of Devil's Lake.

He reached for her hand. "Do you love me, Bren? Tell me. I really need to know if you love me."

"Yes, I love you. Of course I love you."

"Do you trust me?"

Brenda was silent. Out in the darkness, a loon screamed.

Sean said again, more insistently this time, "Do you *trust* me?"

"Sean—"

He let go of her hand. "I guess you don't. I guess all this talk all summer has been bull. You don't love me, do you? Not really."

"Sean, what's wrong with you?" Her voice jumped an octave. She hated the sound of it—plaintive and whiny even to her own ears. "I *said* I love you. I'm here with *you*, not out with some other guy. I love *you*. But why are you asking me if I trust you? What do I have to trust you with? Where *are* we?" She reached down and patted the tote bag she'd placed at her feet. "I brought food, in case we get hungry. I even stole a bottle of wine from my parents. You know—for after . . . whatever." She squinted in the darkness of the cab to see his face, but saw only outlines and shadows. She sighed. "Okay, I give up. Yes, I trust you. Fine."

He sighed. "Thank you."

"You're welcome. Now, where are we?"

"We're at the lake, of course." He pointed. "There's the beach."

"For Pete's sake, Sean . . ." She peered through the windshield and frowned. "That's not the beach. I know what the beach looks like."

Sean laughed. "Come on, Brenda." He opened his door. The gust of air that blew in from outside was more October than August. "I have something to show you. A special place you've probably never been before."

Brenda reached for the handle of the passenger side and turned it. The door swung open and she stepped out of the truck. "I hope you brought a flashlight," she said with a bravado she didn't feel. "I don't know where we are. And I hope you brought a blanket, because it's darn cold out here. Did you bring your lighter? We could make a fire."

Sean put his arm around her shoulder and pulled her close to his body. "Don't worry," he said. "I'll keep you warm. I'll protect you from ghoulies and ghosties, and long-leggedy beasties." In his other hand, he carried the canvas tote bag with Brenda's purloined wine.

She leaned into his chest, tentatively at first, then yielding against his bulk. "And things that go bump in the night? And old ladies with no eyes?"

"Them, too." Sean kissed her neck. She smiled in the dark. That warmth again, that heat that rose up in her from everywhere and nowhere. The answering heat from his body. The sound of the lake on the shore somewhere beyond the line of trees along the path ahead. The moonlight everywhere, so bright and yellow, so deep she felt she could swim in it, felt she could let it lift her up and carry them both away on the crest of a dark umber breaker.

Beyond the tree line, the loon screamed again, the sound ricocheting across the black water like a skipped stone. There was a violent splash, then silence.

In the end, Sean had indeed taken Brenda to a place she'd never been.

They stood on a promontory above a rise of flat ground overgrown with weeds and ferns and littered with storm-dead driftwood. A patch of rocky beach planed off to the left from where they were standing, and Brenda saw the remnants of someone's bonfire on the beach, ash and burned logs. She was oddly comforted by the idea that they weren't the first to have discovered this place, that others had been there before—others no different than her, probably teenagers from Alvina or one of the surrounding towns. The normalcy of that thought comforted her, though she wondered why in the world she thought she needed comforting. She was with Sean, his arm still around her shoulders.

She stared at the dark mass of island that rose out of the water like a fortress, ninety feet in the distance—no, not rose, it *soared* out of the water, taller than any island she'd seen in her life. She wondered if it might be a trick of the moonlight. While she could generally orient herself by her location relative to the lake, Brenda had to admit she didn't know where she was. This thought, in and of itself, was more than a bit exciting, but she'd rather die than confess that to Sean, who was still a *jerk*, even though she was starting to enjoy herself more than she thought she would.

There was something a bit magical about seeing Alvina, a town she'd never left, and feared she never would—if indeed they were still within the Alvina town lines at all—as a foreign place, a *different* place. It was like travelling to another country without ever leaving home.

"Look," Sean said, pointing. "It's Blackmore. I bet you've never seen it from this angle before. Where we're standing is where the Blackmore family used to have their private dock and marina in the 1800s. The servants used to row it. Can you believe that? That they had *servants* to *row* them? Just like . . . *slaves!*" Sean laughed. "Isn't that the craziest goddamn thing you ever heard in your whole life?"

"Is that really Blackmore Island I'm looking at?"

"Why would I lie? I told you," he said. "The house is there, too." He indicated the highest point of the tree-rise. "It's up there, behind those trees near the top."

"Is there really a house there, Sean? For real?"

"Yes, it's there. There's a bit of a hill on the island, and rocks below it. The house is at the top of the hill brow."

Brenda had heard rumours of the existence of the ruin before tonight, of course, the local "haunted house" that everyone had heard of but no one had seen. Being a practical girl, in the absence of evidence, she had discounted the stories as just that, rumours. It had precious little to do with any lack of imagination. Quite to the contrary: like any girl growing up in a small town like Alvina—a town whose roots stretched back beyond its established history of impeccable 19th-century rectitude—she was the heiress to a store of legend so vast and rich that to separate fact from fiction would have been not only pointless but counterintuitive.

According to local lore, some rich family with political connections in the 1800s had supposedly built a house on one of the many islands that lay scattered across the blue sweep of Devil's Lake. The family had prospered, and then fallen out of prosperity. One legend had it that the house had burned down. Another had it that it was a pile of rubble and overrun with dangerous animals that were drawn to the island for some reason having to do with Indian demons, or devils dating back to the days of the French missionaries and settlers. Still another told of a brother and sister who lived together as husband and wife. When she had been a small girl, she and her friends had frightened each other under the sheets at sleepovers with ghost stories about the haunted islands of Devil's Lake and the creatures that dwelled there.

Her father had once said that Devil's Lake got its name because the Devil himself had stolen a handful of the islands that had been created when the Indian god Kitchewana, painfully in love with a woman named Wanakita, who was promised to another, threw his wedding decorations into the Great Lakes in a rage when she rebuffed him, thereby creating 30,000 islands.

According to Tom Egan, the islands rising out of Devil's Lake were Satan's work, the fruits of a diabolical theft. She'd asked her father how many islands the Devil had stolen to make the ones on Devil's Lake. He told her he didn't know how many, but there sure were a lot of them. *Too many to count*, he'd said.

"The Devil is always a thief, Brenda," he'd told her. "If he'd steal from a god, you can imagine what he'd take from a little girl like you. So you'd better always be good."

And now, here she was, gazing at part of that very theft, with the full moon shining down on it through the trees.

It was beginning to dawn on Brenda that Sean might be less ordinary than she'd been led to believe, less ordinary than she herself had believed. This alone, the fact that he'd taken her somewhere she'd never been, was showing her things she'd never seen, lifted him out of the realm of the ordinary.

In the part of her mind that dealt in abstract images and desires—the most honest part of herself, the part where her deepest desires and fears were more or less inchoate—Brenda wondered if tonight would be the night that she would lose her virginity to Sean. If there was a way for her to lose that guarded treasure without taking a conscious course of action to cause its loss by deliberate actions of her own—not *rape*, of course, which wasn't even part of her intellectual or emotional lexicon—but rather through gently *surrendering to the inevitable*, which was how she imagined lovemaking to be, she would choose that way. She was almost sure she loved him, and he'd already said he loved her.

She heard her father's voice in her head: *You'd better always be good.*

She reached for Sean's hand. "Have you ever been out there? I mean, to the island?"

"I rowed out there once," Sean said. "I didn't get right onto the land itself, but I saw the roof of the house through the treetops. I had binoculars with me. It was more like a tower on a castle than a roof. There was a sort of stone archway leading up to stone steps built into the hill. There was some sort of writing carved over the archway."

"What did it say?"

"*Wild Fall.* Or *Fell.* Something like that. It was pretty worn out, or at least that's how it looked to me from a distance. It didn't make sense. At first I wasn't even sure it was English. I thought maybe there was a word missing or something."

"Why didn't you explore it? How could you get so close and not land?"

"I was alone. I wanted to do it with someone. Maybe even someone special." He smiled. "I left the boat over there, behind that driftwood. Do you want to row out there with me? Right now? It's a full moon. It's bright. It wouldn't take long. I have a flashlight in the truck, and you brought the wine. Come on, Brenda. Let's have an adventure—let's do something we've never done before. Something you'd never dream of doing alone."

She looked across the water at Blackmore Island set like a dark jewel in the moonlight. Then she looked up at Sean, who smiled expectantly, cajolingly. She felt the desire rise up again in her and knew he was feeling it as well. She suddenly felt thrillingly wicked. She was surprised by how much she enjoyed it, this feeling of being someone unlike herself.

"All right," Brenda said. "But just for a few minutes. And we have to get back in time to get me home for my curfew, or my dad is going to kill us both."

Sean reached out to touch her face, lightly running his finger down her cheek. Then he retrieved the rowboat from under the branches, where he'd hidden it that morning in anticipation of his date with Brenda tonight and pushed it across the pebbled shore into the water.

The wind was colder on the water as Sean rowed, cutting sharper than the cooling late-August breeze of earlier in the evening on the mainland. Brenda looked back to the place from which he'd launched his boat, the place beyond which the Chevy was parked. For a moment, it seemed very far away. Brenda was suddenly conscious of the cold, the sound of the oars churning the water, the grinding of the wooden oars in the iron oarlocks, of Sean's occasional grunt as he bent his body to the task of rowing.

Ahead, the island loomed, getting closer with every pull of the oars. Brenda wished she felt like she'd felt fifteen minutes before, thrillingly wicked. But she didn't. Instead, she just felt very far from shore. Above her, the orange moon vanished behind a caul of purple and black clouds, drawing darkness like a curtain across the water, obscuring Blackmore Island completely. In her mind she pictured Kitchewana's rage, the smashed, hurled granite becoming islands for the Devil to steal. In the sudden darkness, the universe around her—the enormous sky, the vast body of water under the tiny rowboat—felt like a chessboard for gods and demons, a place that could hide any sort of malignant entity.

Her voice was small when she spoke. "Sean?"

"What?"

"Can you turn back? I don't want to do this. I want to go back to shore."

"Bren, we're almost there. You're kidding, right?"

"No, I'm not kidding. Please turn the boat around. I want to go back. I don't want to do this tonight. I was wrong. I changed my mind. I'll go with you tomorrow afternoon if you like. But right now, it's too dark, and it's too late, and I don't want to go there."

"Jesus *Christ*, Brenda. You said you wanted to see it with me. You *said*. What are we doing out here in this boat, then?"

"Sean, I'm sorry, but I mean it. Please. I want to go back."

He swore softly under his breath, and sighed. Holding one oar stationary, he used the other to turn the boat in a wide arc till the bow was pointed towards the mainland.

"Sean, I'm sorry," Brenda said. "Really, I am. I just . . . well, I'm just scared."

"Scared of what?" He sounded gruff, but under the gruffness, she heard something soft, or thought she did anyway. "I'm here. I wouldn't have let anything happen to you. You're safe with me. I just wanted to show you that house."

She felt her body relax as the boat drew closer to the mainland. The moon came back out from behind the clouds and she saw the shore. "I know," she said. "I still want to see it with you, just not tonight. Thanks for turning the boat around."

His voice was hopeful. "We could build a fire. We still have the wine, and it's early yet. I'd really like to, if you want to."

"I'd love it," Brenda said, delighted and relieved to actually mean it. The warmth returned and she embraced it. Beneath the boat, she felt the scrape of sand and rock and crushed shells against the rowboat's hull as it came aground.

Sean swung his long legs over the side of the gunwale and jumped onto the beach, almost, but not quite, avoiding the lapping water. He cursed again, but this time he was grinning, which changed everything about the tone of the imprecation and made Brenda laugh out loud. This in turn made Sean laugh. He reached for her hand and helped her out of the boat.

While he collected nearby driftwood and built the fire, Brenda spread the blanket on the beach and laid out the cold chicken sandwiches she'd prepared in secret that afternoon, knowing full well that if her mother had caught her making sandwiches for an evening date with a boy—even an Alvina boy like Sean, whom her parents had met earlier that summer when she'd started dating him, and whom they even seemed to like—there'd be holy hell, and probably grounding. No, not *probably*—definitely.

Brenda eyed the bottle of wine dubiously. She'd never drunk wine before, and she'd certainly never opened a bottle of it. She peered at the cork, tapping it once or twice, then half-heartedly gave the neck of the bottle a couple of useless twists.

"Sean?"

Sean threw another log onto the flames now rising from the pile of logs on the beach. Plumes of smoke drifted over to where Brenda stood. They stung her eyes. "You need a hand with that bottle?"

She held it out to him. "Yes please."

"Did you bring a bottle opener?"

"A what?"

Sean laughed. "Never mind." He reached into his pocket and pulled out a pocketknife. With a few twists of the blade, the cork came out. "How about glasses? Did you remember them?"

Brenda had indeed remembered glasses. Sean poured them both some wine.

They sat down on the blanket and watched the fire. Sean reached for her hand. She felt his fingers brush hers. Not looking at him, Brenda took his hand and held it lightly. She felt his callouses against the softness of her palm and sighed, a shuddering, breathy exhalation that came almost involuntarily. She took a sip of her wine, finding it unexpectedly bitter yet not unpleasant. The wine warmed on her tongue, slid down her throat, adding heat to heat— the heat of the fire, the heat in her belly and below. Brenda closed her eyes. *It's really going to happen this time. Really. Really. It's all been leading up to this.*

Sean put his arms around her and pulled her to him, lowering them both down on the blanket. He kissed her on the mouth, gently at first, but then with insistence. Brenda returned his kisses, clumsily at first, then with an intuitive, instinctive skill she hadn't known she possessed. She felt his pleasing weight on top of her. He cradled her in his arms, not crushing her. She felt protected by it.

She turned her head to the side. "Sean . . . ?"

"Mmmmm?"

"Sean, I've never . . . I mean, is it okay? You'll be careful, right?"

"Yeah," he said. "I know. I will."

"Do you love me, Sean?"

His voice had grown hoarse. "Yeah."

"Say my name. Say, 'I love you, Brenda.'"

"I love you, Brenda."

"Do you *mean* it, Sean?"

"Yes, I mean it."

"Oh, *Sean* . . ." Brenda sighed again, this time in triumph. The terms of the bargain had been fulfilled and completed, and she gave herself up to him without guilt, without trepidation.

She'd heard about girls getting into the family way and was relieved when Sean took a French letter out of his wallet. Brenda wasn't sure exactly how they worked, but she knew that if the boy put one on his *thing*, then the girl never got into trouble.

Brenda closed her eyes, suddenly shy. Strange, she thought, for a girl who had made a decision to go all the way for the very first time to be shy now. But actually watching Sean put the condom on, took what was about to happen out of the realm of the romantic and into the realm of the pragmatic, not a realm she was prepared to contemplate in that moment. Instead, she listened to the sound of rubber against skin as Sean prepared himself.

When the pain came, it was brief, and he held her tightly until it went away, then it felt like her shuddering body had been shot through with stars. She tasted his tongue, the sweat on his arms, and what she thought might have been brief tears on his cheeks. The vast sky overhead, the moonlight on the water, the feeling of his mouth on hers, the unfamiliar intrusion inside her, his body, her body, the heat of the fire—it had become a one-sided surface of sensation with only one boundary component.

Afterwards, Sean asked her if it had been okay, and Brenda nodded shyly. They lay together in each other's arms, not speaking; each lost in their own thoughts. Sean stroked Brenda's hair as they stared at the fire, feeling its warmth on their skin.

When the flames burned lower, Sean got up and walked naked over to the pile of wood and got another log. Wrapped in the blanket, Brenda studied his body with newly appreciative eyes. To her, they did not seem to be the eyes of the girl she had been only an hour ago, nor did Sean seem like the boy who had picked her up at her house in his truck a mere two hours or so before.

Nothing is the same. I'm somewhere I've never been before, and I'm with someone I've never been before. It's like witchcraft. I've shifted my own shape. I'm travelling through the air, above my own life. Then, regretfully: *I'm going to have to come down soon. I'm going to have to go home. I've got to go back to being myself. But . . . not yet. There's still time yet. Don't let the magic end just yet.*

Sean lay down again on the blanket and bundled them both up in it, his arms around her, his legs pulling hers to him. She felt him stir and twitch against her thigh. She giggled.

"Sean!"

"I can't help it. You just make me feel . . . well, you make me feel that way." He laughed self-consciously.

"I do?"

He was blushing. "Yes, you do."

"That's so sweet."

"Do you want to . . . ?"

In reply, she ran her nails along the shelf of his shoulders and pressed her body to his. Sean groaned. This time, she touched it, feeling it grow in her hands. A feeling of unquestioned, queenly prerogative came over her. In Sean's desire for her, she saw her own desirability. In his clear need for her, she saw her own self-worth. She was finally prettier-than-average, smarter-than-average. She was finally . . . special.

Her father's words came back to her, unbidden.

The Devil is always a thief, Brenda. If he'd steal from a god, you can imagine what he'd take from a little girl like you. So you'd better always be good.

She slammed the door to her mind with a defiance that was likewise new to her.

I am good, Daddy. And there's no such thing as the Devil. And even if there was, he's got better things to do than worry about the likes of me, especially tonight. Now, go away.

They made love again, slowly this time and with a tenderness that was as new to her as was sex itself. This time when she cried out his name, Brenda didn't recognize the sound of her own voice.

When they finished, Brenda reminded Sean that she had a curfew. He told her not to worry, that he'd get her home in plenty of time, but that he wanted to just hold her now and watch the fire for a while. She agreed, snuggling against him, surfing bliss.

"Sean, did you ever read *Romeo and Juliet* in grade nine?"

His voice was wary. "Yeah, I think so. I don't remember. Why?"

"There's a scene when Romeo and Juliet are . . . you know, making love. And she doesn't want him to leave, even though she knows he's got to leave before dawn, or her family will murder him. She makes excuses the whole time, saying it's a nightingale he's hearing, not a lark."

Sean said, "Ummm . . . what's a lark?"

"It's a bird that sings in the morning, dummy. If the sound Juliet was hearing were a nightingale, it would mean they had hours ahead of them. If it were a lark, it would mean he had to leave right away. Don't you get it?"

"No, not really. Sorry."

She punched him in the arm, but gently. "Isn't it a bit like this? I mean, isn't this—you and I, here—sort of like Romeo and Juliet waiting for the lark to sing, so we'll know how much time we have?"

"Bren, I don't know what you're talking about. Wait . . . was *Romeo and Juliet* the one with the ghost in it?"

She rolled her eyes. "No, that's *Hamlet*. Oh, never mind. Honestly, you and your ghost stories. I'd rather think about *Romeo and Juliet* right now than think about one of your made-up, weird ghost stories."

"Bren?"

"*Sean?*"

"Bren, that story I told you in the truck? That one about me and my uncle, and what happened that night?"

"Yeah? What?"

"That wasn't a story I made up." He yawned, covering his mouth too late to stifle the sound. "That was true. That really happened."

"Sure it did, Sean. I'm absolutely *positive* that I believe you. Is there any more wine?"

There was, and he fetched it from where the bottle stood against a rock. The wine was fire-warmed. They each had another glass as they watched the flames. Brenda leaned her head on Sean's naked chest. Her eyelids flickered, felt suddenly heavy.

Only for a minute, Brenda promised herself as she drifted on a drowsy river of warm red that flowed smoothly into a darkening cavern behind her eyes, where sleep waited. *We have to get going soon, or I'll be in so much trouble. Just for a minute.*

Brenda woke shivering in the cold. Her closed eyes stung from the smoke of the dead fire trapped behind her eyelids. She sat up, then rubbed her eyes with her knuckles like a crying child in a cartoon. *Sean let the fire go out,* she thought stupidly. *How did the fire go out that quickly? It's only been a couple of minutes. We just dozed off.*

"Sean . . ."

For a moment, Brenda thought she had gone blind, because she couldn't see anything: not the fire, not the lake, not the trees, not the sky. The world as she had known it before she dozed off had simply . . . vanished. She might have woken up in the blackness of space. She knew, without being able to see, that he was not beside her. Brenda felt around with her hands. The blanket had fallen off her shoulders and was gathered around her waist. Her fingers

16

located the pile of clothes next to the fire. She found her sweater and pulled it over her head. It felt damp and slimy against her cold skin, and she felt her waking confusion and disorientation give way to the first stirrings of genuine fear.

She whipped her head around. *Someone is there. I can feel it. Someone is watching me.* This time, Brenda didn't call out Sean's name: she whispered it, suddenly, crazily afraid that if he wasn't close enough to hear her whisper, someone or something else might answer her from the darkness instead of him.

As her eyes grew accustomed to the dark, Brenda realized that the shoreline of Devil's Lake was enveloped in deep fog, the densest fog she had ever seen in all of her sixteen years growing up in Alvina. Sure, there had been fogs before, certainly the sort of mists anyone living near large bodies of water knows well. They came, they went. At worst they were an annoyance for boaters and drivers on roads, especially at night. But this? She had never seen anything like this.

And how much time had passed? Half an hour? An hour? Two?

Brenda looked up and, for a moment, thought she saw stars in the sky through the ceiling of fog. They comforted her, orienting her in relation to a world she knew instead of this murky alien landscape. She ticked off a mental checklist. *Stars are up, the ground is down. Lake is in front of us, car is behind us. Good, good. I know where I am. But where's Sean?* She looked up again, but the stars had vanished and she was in darkness again, damp darkness that felt like the breath of a large predator with infinite patience.

And she felt the eyes again, just out of sight.

The Devil is always a thief, Brenda.

Unbidden, an image eddied in her mind. It was the image from Sean's stupid ghost story about the woman with no eyes who rushed across the road from behind the locked gate of the desolate country cemetery.

This time not caring who heard her, Brenda screamed out, "*Sean! Sean, where are you?*" but her voice was lost in the deadening weight of the heavy fog. The dullness of it mocked her, isolating her with its brutal, forced quieting. She felt her rising fear flip over into the terror zone before she was even able to understand why it had. Brenda started to cry. Had she been further away from the edge of hysteria, she might have wondered why the thought that perhaps Sean was playing a trick on her, or hiding, or going to the bathroom up against a tree hadn't even occurred to her as an outside possibility, a logical conclusion at which to arrive in these circumstances.

No, Brenda knew two things clearly, internally, on a primal level that did not require external verification. Firstly, she knew Sean was nowhere nearby.

She sensed he wasn't hiding, playing a trick, or anything else. He was simply *not there*. His presence had been *cancelled*. Brenda's conscious mind may not have been able to ride that particular horse but her subconscious mind had already processed it. Secondly, she knew just as strongly that she wasn't alone, that whatever she felt peering at her through the fog wasn't Sean.

Brenda groped on the ground at her feet till she found her pedal pushers and her sandals. She dressed herself blindly, frantically, feeling for buttons and zippers. She knew her panties were somewhere nearby but she couldn't find them, and didn't care if she ever did, or if anyone else ever did either. She briefly flirted with feelings of concern for Sean's well-being, but they dissipated as she remembered that this whole stupid idea had been his from the beginning. And if he *was* playing some sort of trick on her, then he deserved whatever he got for getting her in trouble with her folks. All she wanted was to be dressed, to find the keys for Sean's truck, and to be away from Devil's Lake.

She remembered that she couldn't drive the truck, but discarded that realization as quickly as it came to her. She could *try* to drive it, at least. She'd watched her father drive. *Insert the key in the ignition. Turn the key. Press the gas pedal. Reverse. Drive.* How difficult could it be? Or she could sit in the cab and blow the horn until someone heard her. She could lock the door, *both* the doors, and make so much noise with that horn that they'd hear her all the way back to Alvina and send someone to rescue her. She would blow the horn till *God* heard her.

But Brenda knew she was a long way from Alvina, and it was late at night now. No one was coming for her. No one knew where she was. She'd told her parents she was going for a drive with Sean to the town beach with a group of their friends to watch the moon rise. That's where they would look for her, not here. Not wherever *here* was. She remembered her delight in her disorientation as they'd driven to Devil's Lake, her triumphant pleasure at feeling lost, at the absurd notion of travelling without leaving her town.

Weeping, Brenda stumbled, feeling for branches. The branches would mean the edge of the path leading *up*, away from the shoreline, back to the truck, back to safety. Blindly, she flailed her arms, meeting nothing but the empty fog.

And then she distinctly heard a muffled splash behind her. She pivoted on her heel.

"Sean, is that you? Sean?" *It must be him! Who else could it be?* The relief that washed over her nearly brought her to her knees. Another splash came, louder this time. "Sean? Sean! Answer me! I can't see!"

Brenda took a few halting steps towards the sound, then stopped. Her feet were wet. She had been nearer the edge of the shore than she'd realized. Cold water engulfed her toes across the tops of her sandals. She squinted across the water, willing herself with every fibre of her being to be able to see. The ciliary muscles of her eyes tightened and strained, and her temples throbbed with the effort of focussing.

And then, as if the omnipresent fog had abruptly thinned or parted in the gloom, Brenda *could* see. Not clearly, but at least she could see outlines: the bulk of Blackmore Island, darker than the water surrounding it, the edges looking like smaller pine scrub islands of smooth, rounded granite layering in the lake, grey on grey on black.

A sudden subtle shift of shadows on the surface of the lake drew her eye to a place maybe fifteen yards offshore where a figure stood pale and unmoving in the murky starlight. Brenda drew a sharp intake of breath, covering her mouth with her hands to keep from screaming. As she watched, the figure moved deeper into the lake. This time there was no splash, just a susurrating displacement of water. Brenda saw that the figure was male, and nude. Of course it was Sean. Who else would it be? Before tonight, she might not have been able to recognize his body in the dark, but at that moment she still felt its ghost-imprint on her own and she knew it was him.

Again, the impression of *cancellation* came to her. While she could see Sean through the fog, in the water, she could not *feel* Sean. Whatever he was doing in the lake at night, he wasn't swimming. Or if he was swimming, he didn't know it. She could see the tips of his elbows rising whitely out of the surface.

The thought came to her, as clearly as if a voice had spoken in her brain: *Sean is drowning himself. He's committing suicide in the lake, right in front of your eyes.*

Another step deeper, the water now just at his shoulders. The fog began to thicken again, sweeping across the surface of Devil's Lake from the direction of Blackmore Island, the island itself now hidden from sight.

Then she saw the woman strolling across the water.

Brenda blinked, and looked again at what must surely be a trick of the fog, or the residual starlight, or her own exhausted imagination.

Her first instinct was to call out to the woman to save Sean, to pull him out, to wake him up if he was sleepwalking. She was *right there!* But she knew the woman could not be right there, because what she was seeing could not possibly be real, because nobody ever walked on water except maybe Jesus Christ a long time ago, and there was no way in hell this was Jesus Christ. Not out here, not at night, not in this godforsaken place in full sight of Blackmore Island and the house behind the small forest of windswept white pine.

This is not happening, she thought. *I'm not seeing this.*

"Sean! *Sean! Stop!*" Brenda screamed his name over and over, waving her arms to catch his attention. "*Sean, no! Come back!*" She picked up a piece of driftwood at her feet and threw it as hard as she could into the lake in his direction, hoping to hit him with it, to shock him, to wake him up. When she looked again, Sean was alone in the lake. The driftwood landed uselessly in the water not far from where she stood. The sound of the splash was weak, absorbed by the fog.

Then Sean's head disappeared beneath the water.

Brenda screamed again, taking five lurching steps into the water, kicking up waves as she ran. She would swim to him, to where he had disappeared. There was still time. She realized the folly of that as soon as the water reached her knees. It was cold. Terribly, terribly cold. Not August-cold, but cold like it became in late fall when you realized you'd taken one late-season swim too many and the ice of it shocked your heart and made you scream in a high, warbling voice that seemed to come from the top of your throat because everything below your throat was impaled by the chill coming up from the sediment of the lakebed.

She stumbled backward out of the water and fell, twisting her left knee painfully. White-hot bolts of pure agony shot up from her kneecap, pinning her to the ground as surely as if she'd been nailed to it.

The fog came alive around her in a whirling swarm. Something landed on her face. Then another something. Then another, until her entire face was covered with what felt like tiny scabrous feathers crawling across her nose and eyes. Frantically, Brenda scrubbed her face with her hands. They came away covered with moths, some crushed and broken by the movement of her fingers, others still fluttering, crawling with dreadful insectile determination across her wrists and up her arms. They came in relentless numbers till it was impossible for Brenda to tell the moths from the fog, or where one grey miasma ended and the other began. They swarmed across her mouth, crawling inside. The dry, dusty body of one of the moths caught in her throat. She gagged, coughing and spitting, with her fingers in her mouth, scraping the moths from inside her cheeks and along her gums, the roof of her mouth. Her world was reduced to the chirruping sound of what seemed like the thunder of a million insect wings. She swatted them away with her hands. Her only thought was to get the moths off her body. Then it came to her— she would drown them in the lake. She would swim out to where she'd seen Sean, where the water was deep enough, and she would drown the disgusting things. They couldn't swim, but she could.

A good plan, she thought, crawling laboriously across the ground towards the water's edge, feeling lightheaded and weak and teetering on the edge of a different sort of blackness. The edge of her palm struck the water and sank into the sedimentary mud, grainy with ground rock and sand that oozed between her splayed fingers. Pulling her weight with her arms alone, dragging her injured knee behind her, she launched herself into the lake. She fell face-forward. Lake water and sand surged into her nostrils and her mouth, but she still felt the moths wriggling on her wet skin.

When Brenda reached deep enough water, she flopped forward into it weakly, scrubbing herself with her hands beneath the surface. Then she coughed. And coughed again.

That thing is still in my throat, she thought. *Oh sweet Jesus.*

She coughed again and again, trying to dislodge the carapace of the moth that had lodged in her windpipe, or at least swallow it down. Her throat filled with water on the intake. She rose to the surface, and then slipped below again, taking in water through her nose and mouth. Frantically, she clawed her way up, treading water to stay afloat, coughing and inhaling more water involuntarily as she rose, retching. Her larynx constricted, sealing the oxygen channels to her lungs as water entered her airways, driving out consciousness, and Brenda began to drown.

Suddenly, the scent of camphor and dried violets was everywhere. The fragrance reminded her of the sachets in the drawers of her grandmother's mahogany vanity dressing table, in her bedroom at the top of the old house in Stayner. It was the extract of dim hallways with shuttered windows and high ceilings; of dresses of silk and long woolen coats; of sun-warmed wood panelling, candlewax, unwound clocks, years spent indoors—in essence, the attar of time itself sleeping.

Brenda had a sudden, vivid impression of her grandmother's fine and white hands, smooth as bone, gently brushing Brenda's hair out of her eyes as she tucked her in under the duvet and reached over to turn out Brenda's bedside lamp.

The thought was a comforting one, and it even distracted Brenda from the realization that she was dying. It made her smile, even as she felt her grandmother's hands grasp her ankles and pull her beneath the surface of Devil's Lake, her body spiralling downward, her lungs taking in one final deep breath of lake water, driving the last bit of life out of her in a fine spray of bubbles that floated to the surface, then disappeared.

Two days later, accidentally succeeding where volunteer trackers from Alvina and the RCMP had failed, an out-of-town day boater from Toronto named Denis Armellini found the bodies of the missing teenagers everyone had been searching for.

Armellini was coming around the leeward side of Blackmore Island in a Pacific Mariner Stiletto borrowed from the owner of the cottage he was renting. He caught sight of a bright red bag on a deserted stretch of rocky beach. He cut the motor. Through binoculars, he spied a pile of clothing near an overturned rowboat, and the remnants of a campfire. Barely keeping his excitement under control, he made a note of the approximate location, then pointed the Stiletto's bow in the direction of Alvina.

Before he could start the outboard again, Armellini heard the rap of knuckles against the hull of his boat—a sound not unlike a request for entry. He was startled enough to drop his binoculars into the water, cursing his clumsiness and skittishness. He lurched over the side of the boat, scrabbling madly to retrieve them before they sank, and found his fingers entwined with those of Brenda Egan.

At first, Armellini hadn't been sure what he'd touched—poached driftwood perhaps, or a tree branch bleached white by the sun. When he realized it was the waterlogged and puffy hand of a teenage girl he held, the sound of his screams ricocheted across the water, cracking against the smooth rocks and boulders of Blackmore Island like rifle shots. Sufficient gas from bacterial decomposition had built up inside the girl's bloated body to make it buoyant. She floated face down in the water, half-submerged, as though she were the searcher in a game of Fish Out of Water.

Armellini wrenched his hand away and rubbed it frantically against his jeans, but not before noticing that bits of the girl's hand had been torn away, as if by needle-sharp teeth that had been small, vicious, and unrelenting.

Fucking northern pike will eat anything, Armellini thought, then vomited.

The girl appeared to be wrapped in a white gossamer veil but Armellini realized he was looking at the sodden husks of what seemed to be thousands of drowned moths, legs and wings intertwined, clinging one to the other and to the girl's body like a shroud, woven into her hair like interlaced garlands of white graveyard flowers.

Legends begin in small northern towns on the edge of places other people only drive through on their way to somewhere else, in station wagons and vans full of summer gear: Muskoka chairs in bright summer colours, coolers full of beer, canvas bags bursting with swimsuits and shorts and t-shirts, and dogs who slumber on blankets in the back seat and are bored by the entire process of long car trips.

Towns pass by that are the sum of their parts, and their parts are bridges, barns, fields, and roadside stands where home-baked pies or fresh ice cream are sold in the summer, and pumpkins, sweet corn, and Indian corn in the autumn. These towns are for gas stations that are distance markers for exhausted parents, where the kids can have one final bathroom break before the last stretch of highway leading to driveways that in turn lead to front doors and lake views.

But of the lives of the citizens of these towns—the men and women who live and die in them, who carry to the grave entire universes of their history and lore, and the happenings of the century—these urban and suburban transients know nothing, and care even less.

The towns they pass might as well be shell facades, their residents merely extras in a movie called *Our Drive Up North to the Cottage*, a movie with annual sequels whose totality makes up a lifetime of holiday memories.

In 1960, the drowning deaths of Brenda Egan and Sean Schwartz tore Alvina apart and destroyed two families, each of which blamed the other's child for inadvertently luring their own child to his or her death through irresponsibility, wantonness or malice. There was no peace for either side. The psychic wounds each sustained through their losses and their lack of forgiveness would fester for decades, never fully healing. The funerals had been on separate days, and a lifetime of grudges and feuds would spring from jaundiced notations of who in town attended which funeral, not to mention those traitors who attended both.

The tragedy briefly made newspapers across the country, though the story was a smaller and smaller news item the farther away from Georgian Bay it was written or told. After two days it had disappeared from the news altogether. The deaths of two teenagers in a town in northern Ontario no one had ever heard of weren't going to hold anyone's imagination for long.

In Alvina however, the fact that Sean had been found nude, washed up on the landing beach of Blackmore Island, lent a salacious note to the tale, one that ensured its longevity through gossip—at least behind the backs of anyone from the Egan or Schwartz families.

Had the girl been a secret slut in spite of her goody-goody veneer? Had the boy tried to rape her, drowning them both in the attempt? God only knew. Anything was possible. Besides, it happened out there, near *that place*.

The police had apparently searched Blackmore Island. The big house up there had been locked up tight and shuttered, and it looked like it had been so for a very long time. The grounds had been wild and overgrown. No one had been living there, and there was no evidence that anyone had lived there for decades, much less that either of the two had been on the island the night they died.

Still, nothing good had ever happened near *that place*. Not ever. It might not be a haunted island, but it sure was a goddamned unlucky one.

In 1962, Brenda Egan's aunt, a martyr to the deepest possible grief over the loss of her niece, accidentally set herself on fire on Blackmore Island. Gossip had it that she had rowed out to the island to lay flowers there in Brenda's memory, and had died trying to build a campfire to stay warm while she drank herself into a stupor.

The Egan family prevailed on the local newspaper not to print the details due to the grief they had already endured. The editor, a family man who had seen the gruesome media feeding frenzy that had resulted from the original tragedy, took pity on the Egan and Schwartz families and kept the story out of his newspaper, reporting the woman's death only as a heart attack, thereby ensuring that most of the gossip would be stillborn, except for local word of mouth.

After a time, people in town stopped telling Brenda and Sean's story, because it could only be gossip, and it seemed cruel to gloat about the deaths of anyone that young, no matter what they'd been up to out there in the dark when they were supposed to be watching the moonrise on the town beach.

Tom Egan died in 1972, and his wife, Edith, moved back to Selkirk, Manitoba where her people were from. The memories of what she had lost that terrible night were too much to bear alone.

John and Gladys Schwartz lived quietly in their house in Alvina. They kept Sean's room as a shrine. Gladys dusted his wrestling trophies daily and never passed a photograph of her son without touching it. John never set foot in Alvina United Church again after Sean's memorial service. He maintained that no god who'd seen fit to take his beautiful boy was worth more than the shit straight out of his arse, and wouldn't get any worship from him, not in a hundred years of frosty Fridays in hell.

Gladys, on the other hand, became devout. She brought her grief to the Lord and laid it on his shoulders, putting her faith in the comforting notion that there was a plan that she didn't understand yet, and that she would see Sean again someday.

They died within a year of each other, in 1990 and 1991 respectively.

By 1990, thirty years after the tragedy, the story had passed into children's campfire lore, no more or less real than all the other stories about the haunted island "near here," stories of drowned children, mysterious flickering lights in the water, sudden fires, dark ladies, covens of witches and devil worshippers, and so on.

By 2000, Brenda and Sean had become "the boy and the girl" who went skinny dipping after having sex in the woods and had met their deaths at the hands of demons, or a serial killer, depending which version was being told at any given time. Apparently, the house was still out there somewhere on that island, but there were tens of thousands of islands. It could be any one of them, assuming it even existed. Besides, it was almost spookier not to know. In town, no one remembered their names, which most of the old-time residents of Alvina would have said was just fine had anyone asked them. But no one ever did.

Life moved on, and it had all been so very long ago.

And this is how legends begin in small northern towns on the edge of places other people only drive through on their way to somewhere else: with a scream in the dark, and half a century passed in waiting.

Plume moths remove remembering.
Their feathery snowtouch on the eyelids
sifts out thought and will,
leavens facts until they rise
into the air and pop
into oblivion.

Moths' delicate footprints
on the skin, invisible
as sorrows, chase away
longing and desire, chase
knowledge of things.
Of self, of trees and acorns,
glass jars, death and daisies,
gazelles and geodes.

All of it, gone.

—Sandra Kasturi, from "Moth & Memory"

Chapter One

AMANDA IN THE MIRROR

"I will relate to you, my friend, the whole history, from the beginning to—nearly—the end."
—Diana Maria Mulock, "M. Anastasius" (1857)

I want to teach you about fear.

I want to tell you a ghost story. It's not a ghost story like any ghost story you've ever heard. It's *my* ghost story, and it's true. It happened here in the house on Blackmore Island called Wild Fell, in the inland village of Alvina, Ontario on the shores of Devil's Lake. Like any ghost story, it involves the bridges between the past and the present and who, or rather *what*, uses them to cross from the world of the living into the world of the dead.

But I'm getting ahead of my story. I did say the bridge is between the past and the present. Although I'll tell you this story in the present, I would be remiss if I didn't start with the past—specifically *my* past. Time is, or ought to be, linear. Sometimes it's anything *but* linear, which brings us back to ghosts.

Still, one thing at a time, right?

By the time he was gone, my father, a gentle, loving man with a fierce intellect and great wit, had already been gone for a very long time. He had forgotten everything about what had made him my father in the first place. He didn't know himself and he didn't know me. The erasing had been the hardest part for me to watch, harder even than the sure knowledge that he was going to die, and that it would be soon, if not quickly.

My father had always been my memory, the keeper of our family's history, his own past, and even my past. The memories of any child, while vivid, are always subject to the subtle twist and eddy of time and emotional caprice. Which is in part to say, while I believe I remember everything about my childhood, I can only remember from the inside out. The actual events may have been something other than what I remember.

My name is Jameson Browning. In the summer of 1971, when I was nine I went to Camp Manitou, the summer camp deep in rural eastern Ontario where edges of towns yielded to woods and marshes and rolling farmland hills.

I hadn't wanted to go at all. I deeply distrusted boys of my own age, all of whom had proven themselves to be coarse and rough and prone to noise and force. It would be tempting for anyone reading this to imagine a socially isolated, lonely boy with no friends—a loner not so much by choice, but by ostracism or social ineptitude. But the conjured image would be an inaccurate one. I wasn't a lonely boy at all, not by any stretch, though I did indeed love to be alone.

I loved to read. I loved to be outside by myself, especially in the greenbelt near our house, whose trees, in places, were almost dense enough to be considered a small forest and which had a stream running through it.

I had friends, two little girls. One was real, and lived three doors down in a house that looked very much like mine, indeed like everyone else's in our mid-century neighbourhood of elm-shaded, sidewalked streets and neatly tended lawns. The house in Ottawa in which I grew up was a classic 1960s-era suburban one on a tree-lined street, with four floors and a long, low roofline. On the top floor of the house were my parents' bedroom and bathroom, and my father's study. On the main floor were a spacious living room, the dining room, and the kitchen. One floor below that were my bedroom and a guest bedroom I can only ever recall my grandmother using, once, on a visit before she died in 1969. My bathroom, with the cowboys-and-Indians wallpaper, was a short flight of stairs down in the basement, next to the recreation room and the laundry room.

The other girl lived in the wood-framed full-length mirror bolted to the wall in my bedroom. The place *she* dwelt was indistinctly bordered by my imagination and by the infinite possibilities of the worlds-upon-worlds inside the reflected glass.

The real girl's name was Hank Brevard—well, her *actual* name was Lucinda, and she was a tomboy who was as much of a loner as I was. Her father was away a great deal on business and her mother didn't seem to like her very much, and was always at her to "act more ladylike." Hank had short black hair she'd chopped herself, which had earned her a two-week grounding, during which time she'd not been allowed to spend time with me—which she'd found ways to do anyway, sneaking out of her bedroom window while her mother was watching television.

"She's afraid I'll just cut it again if she makes me grow it long," Hank said with satisfaction when her hair started to grow back, ragged as a chrysanthemum. "She's letting me keep it short as long as I promise to let her take me to her hairdresser when it needs trimming."

Hank could cycle faster than any boy I knew, and she liked to catch tadpoles in the spring with me in the creek. When she'd asked me to call her by a boy's name, I readily agreed. It seemed a very small concession for friendship, especially in light of the fact that she looked like a "Hank" and not remotely like a "Lucinda," and we quickly became inseparable. We spent hours together building tree forts. In the spring, we caught tadpoles. In the fall, we threw ourselves into piles of leaves. In the winter, we tracked small animals by their prints in the snow, or pretended to be Arctic explorers.

We had no secrets from each other, except for the one I kept: I never told Hank about Amanda, the little girl who lived in my mirror, the little girl who had my face and spoke in my voice, but who was someone else entirely.

When I was seven years old, I'd begun speaking to my reflection in the mirror the way some children made up imaginary playmates. I named my reflection Mirror Pal and began to think of it as a separate entity.

I told Mirror Pal about my days at school, my teachers, the games I played at recess. When my mother was angry with me—and she was angry with me a lot—I told Mirror Pal about that, too. I spoke back to myself, pretending that my own voice was Mirror Pal's voice, giving the response I wanted and needed at any given time. For instance, if I brought home a drawing with a gold star on it and my parents told me how good it was, Mirror Pal rejoiced with me. If I was sad, Mirror Pal was always sympathetic and agreeable that I was the aggrieved party, no matter the circumstances.

It was a lighthearted game of imagination and mental magic of the most innocent and childlike sort. At least until Amanda appeared a year later, when Terry Dodds stole my new red bike and had the accident.

I had learned to ride a bike the previous year on a battered and rust-veined green Roadmaster cruiser of my father's that had been stored in my grandparents' garage at the time of my grandmother's death. In addition to its sentimental value, my father thought it was the perfect bike to teach me to ride. Learning to ride a bike is usually a painful process for any child, but my sense of balance was remarkably bad. In the beginning, my father held the bike as I pedalled, keeping me steady, running beside me as I wobbled along the sidewalks of our neighbourhood.

The first time he let go of the seat, I crashed badly, skinning both knees. I burst into tears. The pain from my kneecaps was like fire. They were bloody and there were tiny bits of dirt and concrete dust in them. My father held me and let me cry against his shirt. Then, gently, he insisted I get back up on the bike.

"It's important, Jamie. You need to get back up now. I'll clean off your cuts and put some Bactine on them when we get home, but right now you need to climb back up and pedal."

I sniffled. "Why? I don't want to. It hurts, Daddy. My knees sting. Look," I added with dramatic flourish. "They're *bleeding*."

"Because you need to show the bike that it didn't win, Jamie. That's why." His face was grave, that deeply serious expression he always had when he was imparting something vitally important. He rubbed the bridge of his nose where the horn-rimmed glasses he wore always left a red mark. "If we go home now, it will have beaten you. You need to get back up on the seat. You don't need to go far, but you need to make sure that the last thing you remember about today isn't that you fell down, it's that you got back up again. That's what we do when bad things happen to us."

I stuck out my bottom lip. "I don't want to."

Without replying, he lifted me up and put me solidly back on the seat and told me to pedal. Which, of course I did, hating it, but with him walking slowly behind me, holding onto the seat with one hand so I didn't fall, and steadying me with the other. The sidewalk ahead swam in my vision like I was underwater, but as the tears dried, the path in front of me cleared as sure as the pressure of my father's hand on the small of my back. This became our routine over that week, every evening after dinner. In short order, I graduated to him running behind me holding lightly onto the end of the seat.

Every night, I told Mirror Pal about my progress. Mirror Pal confessed that he wasn't sure I would ever learn to ride a bike, and agreed with me that it seemed like a stupid skill to need to master. He also agreed with me, though, that attaining this skill was necessary so I could ride with Hank anytime I wanted, even if the process would probably kill me.

Then, one day, I had pedalled down the half-length of our street before I realized that he was no longer holding on at all. I looked backwards without falling over and saw that my father was clapping, and doing a little dance because that barrier was down, never to rise again, and the bike hadn't won.

My parents presented me with a brand new Schwinn for my eighth birthday. It was gleaming ruby red and chrome silver. It had a metallic gold banana seat and hi-rise bars, just like the ones the big kids rode as they swept by the front of our house on their way to school like alien gods of coolness from some other planet.

And now, I had one. I was going to be cool, too, just like the big kids. My joy knew no bounds.

Hank (who had learned to ride a bike at five) and I spent the next week exploring the length and breadth of our neighbourhood, which looked somehow completely different from this new vantage point of two-wheeler independence. We barrelled down the greenbelt hills and along the wooded paths by the creek. I'd been forbidden to cross Dearborn Road because of the traffic, so Hank showed me a way to approach the greenbelt from the rear, via the safe streets I was allowed on. We were the same age, but sometimes it was like Hank was older. She was already more like a boy than I could ever imagine being. If that made me the *girl* in our friendship, it wouldn't have bothered either of us—if we'd thought of it that way, which we never did.

Two weeks after my birthday, Hank and I decided to have an adventure.

We rode our bikes as far as we could before stopping. We may have gone as far as three or four miles out of the neighbourhood but it's hard to tell. It certainly seemed like that, or even farther. I had a very clear sense of being way outside the bounds of what my parents would have thought of as an acceptable distance at that age. Still, it was exhilarating. We'd packed a lunch we'd made ourselves, in secret: peanut butter and jelly sandwiches, cheese, cookies, and some candy. No fruits or vegetables—and not by accident, either. It was our adventure and it was, in every sense, outside the bounds of adult authority.

We stopped for lunch in a field and ate under the branches of an ancient oak tree. In the near distance, we saw the edge of one of the new subdivisions that were cropping up all over the city. They were different in every way from our neighbourhood, which was old and established. I imagined that the people living there must be just as different.

I was lying on the ground with my eyes closed, enjoying the sun on my face, well satiated after stuffing our faces with sandwiches and the cookies, when Hank said, "Look, here come some big kids. They don't look like nice big kids, either."

Three older boys, larger by far than Hank and me, were making their way across the field toward us. Rather than walk, they *lumbered*. They reminded me of a pack of cartoon jackals.

"Hey kid, nice bike," the largest one said. "It's too big for you. I want it. Give it to me."

"You can't have it, it's mine. I got it for my birthday. My mom and dad bought it for me." This was greeted with coarse guffaws from the three boys. Again I thought of cartoon predators.

The one who addressed me first—the one I would later learn was Terry Dodds—mimicked me. "'You can't have it, I got it for my birthday!' Waaah, waaah, waaah, baby. What are you going to do if I just . . . take it?" He reached down and picked up my Schwinn as though it were a plastic model. "Huh? How ya gonna stop me?"

Hank shouted, "Leave him alone! It's his bike! Why don't you pick on someone your own size, you . . . you *asshole*?" There was a moment of stunned silence at the use of this word by an eight-year-old girl, but they laughed again.

Terry jeered at Hank. "Are you a boy or a girl? You look like a boy. If you're a boy, let's fight. If you're a girl, then your pal is even more of a sissy for letting a girl fight for him." He turned back to me. "Huh, kid? Are you a sissy? You gonna let this little girl do all your fighting for you, or are you going to come and be a man and take this bike away from me? Because otherwise, I'm gonna take it. And if it's too small for me, I'm gonna give it to my kid brother. He needs a bike. That okay with you, kid?" he taunted me. "Huh?" Terry grinned at his friends. "I guess it's all right with him. He didn't say I couldn't, did he?"

"Nope," they chorused. "He didn't say you couldn't."

"Yes I did! I did say you couldn't. It's *my bike*!"

"Too late," Terry taunted. He climbed on the bike, which was ridiculously small for him—and which made him look even more like some sort of monster astride it—then did a quick, jerky circle on it. "Yep, this'll be okay. See you later, kid. Come on guys, let's get out of here."

Hank, who had been standing next to me, fists flexed at her side, abruptly jumped on Terry's back and began to punch him. She even managed to land a few major blows, blows that made him cry out in pain. He shoved her to the ground. She jumped up and went for him again, shouting a strangled war cry that she had probably picked up from a Saturday afternoon adventure film on television. He shoved her down on the ground again, and this time he put his finger in Hank's face and wagged it.

"Stay down, you little bitch," he said. "If you come at me again, I'm going to put you and your little buddy in the hospital. Got it?"

"Why don't you pick on someone your own size?" she said again, but both of us heard the note of defeat in her voice under the shrillness, as did Terry. "He's just a little kid. Give him back his bike!"

"He doesn't have a bike," Terry said. "*I* have a bike. It's *my* bike now. Come on, guys, let's get home and give this bike to my brother." And with that, he pedalled off across the field toward the new subdivision, with his two friends half-walking, half-running to keep up with him.

I burst into tears. I not only felt the loss of my bike, but I felt the guilt of disappointing my father after all those hours of practice and all his patience. The bike had been a gift of love, the consummation of those painful hours of skin scraped against asphalt, banged-up limbs, and blood, and my father's loving attention to helping me learn.

Hank hugged me. "Come on, get on the back. I'll double-ride you home," she said. "Let's go tell your parents."

I tasted the snot running down my upper lip, mixing with the tears. "They're going to be *so mad*. . . . I'm not supposed to be this far from home."

"Don't cry, Jamie," Hank said. "Let's get home and tell your parents. "We'll get your bike back, I promise. I don't know how, but we will."

When we eventually made it home as dusk descended—a rickety, long, difficult ride with me on the back and Hank pumping heroically over the rutted sidewalks and stopping at crosswalks so both of us could dismount and walk safely across the street—my parents were furious. My mother in particular was enraged that we'd ventured so far out of Buena Vista, our neighbourhood, and managed to lose an expensive new bike in the process.

"It wasn't a toy, Jamie." After everything that had happened that afternoon, her voice seemed unbearably harsh in my ears. I had seen my mother angry before, but this seemed to be a level of developing anger that was new and a bit frightening. "It was a very expensive bicycle and now it's gone. You lost it. You should have been more responsible instead of being such a damn *dreamer* all the time. I'm very, very disappointed in you." My mother had wanted my father to spank me, but he'd refused.

"He didn't *lose* it, Alice. It's not *lost*. It was *stolen*. Another kid *stole* Jamie's bike."

"If he'd stayed in our neighbourhood," my mother said, "this would never have happened. This is his fault and I want him to take responsibility for it. If you won't spank him, I will."

My father held up his hand. He, too, was furious, but his anger was directed differently: he seemed mostly angry that an older kid had bullied me into giving up my new bike. "Alice, *please*," he snapped. "One thing at a time. I want to know how this happened. We can discuss the rest later, but right now I want to understand how this took place. I want to know who this kid was, and where this happened." He turned to me and said, "Jamie, can you tell us again how this kid came to take your bike?"

I told the story again, feeling calmer under my father's steady questioning.

He asked me if I could remember the neighbourhood where it took place. I told him no, but that Hank would probably know how to get back to the field. The boys likely lived in the subdivision across from the field, since that was the direction from which they had come.

My father looked glum. "Well, Jamie, let's call Hank's parents and see if she can go for a ride with us tomorrow and see if we can find out who this kid is. We can drive around the neighbourhood and you can see if you recognize him. But I have to admit, it's going to be a bit of a long shot. Your mother is right—this was very irresponsible of you. I hope we can get your bike back, but don't get your hopes up. In the meantime, I'll go call the police and see what the procedure is to file a report."

"I'm sorry, Daddy. Really, I am."

"I know, Jamie," my father said. "But it doesn't really help matters. It doesn't really change things. You should have been more responsible. I think you should go downstairs and get ready for bed. I'll be down in a little while to tuck you in."

In my room, sobbing and in disgrace, I told Mirror Pal about what had happened.

As always, I did both of the voices, mine and Mirror Pal's, and they both sounded like me. Both voices bore the imprimatur of my grief: one bore it plaintively; the other bore it with justifiably loyal outrage.

A casual adult observer who happened to walk in on me would likely have seen an eight-year-old boy, his face red and puffy and streaked with tears, sitting on the edge of his bed talking to himself in the mirror, working himself into a state of near-hysteria, arms flailing and pointing, punctuating the air with angles and jabs. I have a memory of actually slapping the wall beside the mirror and imagining I heard two slaps.

But of course, I could only have heard one slap. I was entirely alone in my bedroom. The only illumination inside the room came from my bedside lamp, a green-glassed brass ship's lantern with a hand-painted shade featuring a rendering of a sailboat at full mast, hard against the wind.

Feeling better for having vented a bit, I turned away to put on my pyjamas and get into bed. I thought I saw something flicker and shift in the depths of the mirror. There was a sudden impression of fluttering, as though a moth had trembled in front of a lamp, wings beating a frantic insectile tarantella in the air. But when I looked again, I was alone in the mirror with my empty bedroom reflected in the glass behind me.

Then suddenly I *wasn't* alone. I *knew* I wasn't alone as surely as I knew my own name, or that my beautiful red bike had been stolen that afternoon, or that I wanted it back at that moment more than I'd ever wanted anything in the world.

I touched the glass and tapped it lightly with my index finger. "Mirror Pal? Are you real?" Even at eight, I realized how ridiculous that question was, but I asked it anyway. I breathed on the glass, running the tip of my index finger through the condensation, bisecting the cloud of moisture with a jagged line of fingernail. "Mirror Pal?"

What happened next was something I *felt* in a way that almost precludes an adult ability to put it into words. As I opened my mouth to form Mirror Pal's answer to my own question, the air inside my room became heavy with something like the weight of the electricity and ozone that presages a summer lightning storm. By reflex, I closed my eyes as though anticipating a thunderclap. There was the burst of the orange-red light that always accompanies a rapid opening and shutting of the eyelids.

An image rose in my mind—or, more accurately, appeared to impress itself on my mind from somewhere outside of my own reckoning—of a young girl of my age whom I had never seen before. She had long dark hair tied up in the sort of bow I had seen in pictures of my grandmother when she was my age. The girl wore some sort of dark-coloured dress rippling like black water caught in a shaft of moonlight. And her name came to me then: Amanda.

Amanda.

When I spoke, it was my voice, of course—Mirror Pal's voice—but this time it was also *not* my voice at all. I had uttered the name without any conscious intent to do so, but I said it as reverently as if it were an invocation. The name seemed to pour out of me of its own volition, shaping and wrapping itself around my vocal cords and calling them to life. I heard it with my ears, but I also heard a double-voice say it in my mind, as though two record players were playing the same single at different speeds, causing a slight overlap.

With my eyes still closed, I reached over and switched off the light on my night table. Then I opened my eyes and looked into the mirror.

Something indefinable had changed in the reflection. It was still my room, but the edges now bled into a general murkiness, a blurring not dissimilar to that of the faded quality of an antique photograph: yellowing, age-burned and cracked at the edges. My reflection, too, had changed in a similarly impalpable way. My eyes were obscured by the shadows of the room, but my shoulders were hunched in a narrowing way that suggested somehow the fey mien of a young girl sitting on the edge of a large antiqued chair that was too big for her. When I instinctively relaxed my shoulders to dispel the illusion, my reflection followed suit, but it seemed to lag just a beat, as though it slyly wanted me to know that it was doing it on sufferance, not because the laws of physics had compelled it to do so because it was my reflection.

My. Mine.

Mine.

I said, "Mirror Pal? Is that you?"

Again, the unbidden response, the weird aural duotone of my own voice echoing in my head.

My name is Amanda.

I was entranced. I'd forgotten that I was speaking to myself, forgot that this illusion was impossible, forgot that I must be speaking in my own voice because there was no possible way my reflection could be addressing me independently. And yet, the name "Amanda" hadn't come from me. I didn't know anyone named Amanda.

Excitedly I asked my reflection, "Is this my imagination, or is this real?"

Maybe it's both. Maybe I live in your head as well as in the mirror. I felt my shoulders involuntarily rise and fall in a mechanical-looking facsimile of a shrug. *It doesn't matter anyway. I'm here now.*

"Who are you?"

I told you. My name is Amanda.

"Where did you come from?"

From your mirror.

"No, before that."

There is no before, there's only now.

"Where's Mirror Pal?"

Mirror Pal has gone away. I'm here now.

"Why haven't I ever seen you before?"

I don't know why you haven't seen me before. I've always been here.

I asked again, "Who are you?"

I already told you who I am. I'm just a girl. Stop asking me that. A pause. *Where's your bike?*

"How do you know about my bike?"

I just know. Where is it?

"A kid stole it. In the park. I was out with Hank and he came and . . . and . . ."

Don't cry. You'll get it back, I promise.

"How do you know?"

I just know. You'll see. You and your dad are going to go driving tomorrow to the place where you lost it. You're going to look around the neighbourhood and see if the kid is there. Or if his brother is there. He has a younger brother, remember? He told you about him. He's going to give his brother your bike as a present, and the brother is going to ride it all around. He'll probably break it, then throw it away. Your bike. Yours.

I felt my fury rise again. "It's my bike! I want it back. My dad gave it to me for my birthday!"

What do you want to have happen to him? The kid who took your bike?

"What do you mean, what do I want to have happen to him? I want him to give my bike back! That's what I want. I . . . I want him to *shut up!* I want him to shut up and stop being so mean to little kids that are smaller than him. I want him to shut his mouth and give me back my bike."

When Amanda spoke again, her voice—for I was now entirely thinking of it as *her* voice, the words choosing *me*, rather than *me* choosing *them*—had chilled perceptibly. But underneath the new frost I thought I heard a cruel sort of excitement, as though she was about to propose her own version of an adventure.

He will. We'll make him shut up, I promise. And we'll get your bike back.

Then the image in the mirror seemed to shimmer and sway. I tried to stand up, but stumbled and fell backward onto the bed. Hank had showed me a trick once: she told me to pinch my nose shut and hold my breath as long as I could. As the oxygen was depleted from my brain my head was full of giddy black stars and I'd felt like I was floating. It was like that now on the bed, except I could breathe easily. And my head wasn't full of black stars, this time, it was full of gold ones, and there was a mighty hum in my brain as though I was lying on the grass beneath a tree alive with a swarm of furious bees hidden by thick branches. The hum rose in crescendo until there was simply nothing else. Near to losing consciousness, I reached for the switch and turned my nightlight on.

With the sudden light came sudden clarity, and with the clarity came silence and the realization that I was quite alone. There was no humming in my head. There was no Amanda. In the mirror I saw myself and no one else. The only room reflected in it was my own—my own, from wall to wall, every corner present and accounted for, every border distinct, impermeable, linear and real.

I felt something wet against my legs and looked down. The front of my pyjama bottoms were soaked with urine. A line of piss tracked down along the inside of my right leg all the way to the ankle.

I pulled my pyjama pants off and wadded them into a ball. After I had used them to blot myself dry, I put them inside a plastic bag on the floor near my closet door. I tied the bag closed and stuffed it under my bed. From the bottom drawer of my dresser, I took out a pair of clean pyjamas and put them on. Then I jumped onto the bed, crawled under the covers, and pulled the sheets and blanket over my head. I listened to the silence of my bedroom on the other side of the blanket, praying I wouldn't suddenly hear that strange double voice, or feel a little girl's icy hand pull the blanket away from my face.

Fifteen minutes later, I heard the sound of my father's footsteps on the stairs and my bedroom door opened. He walked in and came over to the edge of the bed, smiled down at me. Very gently, he tousled my hair.

"Everything all right in here, Jamie? You ready for bed?"

"Yes, Daddy."

He wrinkled his nose. "You smell anything funny, Jamie? You have any accidents you want to tell me about?"

"No, Daddy." Normally, lying to my father would have been unthinkable, even impossible. But tonight, all I wanted was normalcy, ease and light. "I don't smell anything funny."

He shrugged. "Probably just my imagination, never mind."

I took a deep breath. "Daddy?"

"Yes, son?"

"Daddy, I don't like my mirror. Can we get rid of it?"

"What do you mean, get rid of it?" He peered over at the mirror on the wall. "Is it cracked?" He sighed. "You didn't crack it, did you, Jamie? Your mother is going to be furious if you did."

"No, it's not broken, I just . . . well, I don't need it."

"Jameson," my father said. The switch to my full name wasn't lost on me. "Your mirror is fine. I don't know what this is about, but—"

I cut him off, reaching for his hand and squeezing his fingers tightly enough for him to look back at me with an expression of mild surprise. "Daddy, would you stay here with me for a little while? Until I fall asleep? I'm scared."

His face softened. "Jamie, what's wrong? There's nothing to be scared of. Are you upset about the bike? We'll get it back. You shouldn't have gone out of our neighbourhood, but what happened wasn't your fault. Is that what this is about?"

I glanced over at the darkened mirror hanging innocuous and now empty on the wall. "Daddy, just stay with me. Please?"

"All right. But just for a little bit." My father lay down beside me on the bed and put his arm around my shoulders, pulling me in close.

I pressed my face into his shirt and inhaled deeply. I felt my heartbeat slowing as I relaxed into the bulwark of his warm body and his warm scent. In time, I fell asleep safely against my father's chest. He must have left the room at some point when he saw that I was asleep, turning off my bedside lamp and leaving me in the dark.

I dreamed I was astride my red Schwinn on a promontory of land overlooking a vast, dark lake.

From the centre of the black water rose an island encircled with a wild coronet of grey rock and black-green pine trees. On the island was a castle whose turrets rose above the blackened pines. The sky was streaked with thin sunset stripes of hard red, luminous orange, and bright celadon blue.

The vista was a familiar one: I knew every wave, every jutting rock, every arching pine bough stretching up to gouge the bleeding red sky. The landscape was as familiar to me as my street, but even in the dream I knew it was somewhere I had never been.

The air was raw and northern, but wondrously fresh. I was cognizant that it was late because the sun was going down and the temperature was plummeting as I sat there staring at the island. I knew I was a long, long way from my house—much farther than I had ever been before. I felt the comforting solidity of my Schwinn between my legs and I knew I needed to get pedalling or I was going to be in a lot of trouble.

There was someone standing directly behind me, but I didn't turn my head to see who it was. I already knew who it was. Instead I just stared at the darkening twilight lake and said, "It's late. I need to get home."

I felt tiny fingers settle on my shoulder, and I heard a voice like glacier water whisper in my ear.

You are *home*, Amanda said. *This* is *home*.

If I woke screaming, there were no echoes of it in my bedroom when my eyes snapped open in the dark and it disturbed no one in the silent house. There were no footsteps on the floors above—either the living room directly above my bedroom, or my parents' bedroom above the living room—no heavy adult tread taking the stairs two at a time to save me from any monster that had followed me out of my dreams and into the world.

Instead I woke to broad planks of moonlight on my bedroom floor from the open window on the other side of the room, and to the dreadful silence every child who wakes from a nightmare alone in his bedroom knows. As I lay tangled up in the maze of sweaty sheets and trapped under the suffocating blankets, the only sound in all that quiet was my own heart in my chest, and the pounding of blood in my temples.

Next to my bed, the mirror was black and opaque, as though even the moon was afraid of what it might call to life from the depths of the glass by shining on it.

I lay awake for what seemed like hours. Eventually, the sky began to turn to flush pink. When there was enough light outside to at least bring the contours of my bedroom back into the realm of the safe and the real, I slept, blissfully dreamless this time.

The next morning at breakfast, the phone in the hallway rang. My father looked at the clock and frowned. My mother shrugged and lit her second cigarette of the morning, blowing another plume of smoke into the shimmering blue cloud already hanging over the breakfast table.

My father said, "It's a bit early for callers, isn't it, Alice?"

"Well, it's ringing," my mother replied tautly. "Either answer it or don't answer it. I don't care. But it's ringing." She took another sip of her black coffee. My mother wasn't generally much of a conversationalist at breakfast, at least until she'd had her very own particular breakfast of caffeine and nicotine. All three of us knew it, and neither my father nor I attempted to engage her seriously until after the breakfast dishes were done, preferably by him, preferably with no audible clattering of crockery and silverware in the sink.

My father pushed his chair away from the table and stood up. "So it is," he said. "It *is* ringing. Excuse me, my dear."

Out in the hallway, his voice rose and fell. There was a long pause, then another soft volley of words. Then I heard him hang up the phone. When he returned to the table, his face was ashen. He sat down heavily and rubbed his chin the way he did when he was thinking about how, or whether, to say something painful or difficult.

I put my spoon back in my bowl of Froot Loops. "Who was it, Daddy?"

My father took a deep breath. "Well, Jamie, the police found your bike. We can go over and pick it up after breakfast."

My mother perked up. "Really? Really, Peter? They found Jamie's bike? Where? Did they catch the thief?" She seemed genuinely shocked, as though the prospect of my Schwinn coming home wasn't anything she'd ever seriously entertained. It occurred to me that she sounded disappointed that the long, punitive lesson she'd hoped to teach me about responsibility was now lost to her forever, or at least until my next major cock-up.

My father delicately ignored her question, turning to me instead. "Jamie, you said you don't know the name of the boy who took your bike, right? You'd never seen him before yesterday?"

"Right, Daddy. Was that him on the phone?"

"No, Jamie," my father said slowly. "That was a policeman. I called them yesterday and told them what happened and gave them a description of the bike. The boy . . . well, his name is Terry Dodds. Damnedest thing. His kid brother brought the bike in to the police station this morning and told them Terry had stolen it and he wanted to give it back." Something indefinable in my father's face stayed my euphoria. I waited for him to continue, but my mother cut in before he could.

"His *brother* brought it in?" She exhaled smoke into the air above her. "And he just waltzed into the police station and confessed that his brother *stole* it from Jamie? What on earth would prompt him to do something like that? Not that I'm complaining, but it seems very unlikely."

"His brother is in the hospital, Alice," my father said. "In the intensive care unit. He had some sort of an accident this morning, apparently."

Reflexively she stubbed the cigarette into the saucer of her coffee cup. "A car accident?" She lit another cigarette. "Good Lord. Is he all right?"

"No, not a car. Something . . . well, something else. According to the policeman, this boy was riding the bike around in the field where he stole it from Jamie. They think he must have run over a nest of wasps. Maybe it fell out of a tree or something. In any case, they swarmed. It's pretty bad, apparently. He can't speak."

It was as though all the air was suddenly sucked out of the room. I felt dizzy and the kitchen swayed and dimmed around me. For a moment I thought I might faint. I steadied my hands on the edge of the kitchen table for balance.

We'll make him shut up, I promise. And we'll get your bike back.

When the vertiginous moment passed, my father was still speaking to me. He hadn't noticed that anything was wrong. "The constable asked me if I wanted to press charges," he was saying. "Of course, under the circumstances I said no, of course not." He cleared his throat. "Jamie, the boy's aunt would like to meet you at the hospital. She'd like to have her nephew—the thief's brother—apologize to you on behalf of the family. Her sister, Mrs. Dodd, is with Terry in the ICU. Apparently some of the family is with her. The aunt and the younger boy want to speak with you. How do you feel about that? Shall we go down to the hospital after we pick up your bicycle at the station?"

In a very small voice I said, "Okay."

"Are you sure, Jamie? You're not nervous, are you? They just want to say they're sorry. Apparently the police really gave the young fellow a good what-for about his brother stealing the bike from you. Told him it was your first bike and everything, and that you'd just gotten it for your birthday."

"No, it's okay, Dad. I just feel bad for the kid, even if he did steal my bike."

"You're going to be nice to them, aren't you, Jamie? Even if the boy's brother did take your bike?" My father looked at me hopefully. "They're pretty upset, and it's a hard time for their family, especially the boy's mother. This would be a good time to be kind."

Before I could answer my father, my mother interjected again. "What on earth would have possessed the boy to return the bike on the same day his brother had that accident? I would have thought that's the last thing he'd be thinking about. The whole affair is rather odd. Still, I feel badly for the other boy, even if he's a thief. And his poor mother must be beside herself. On the other hand, how very odd to be worrying about apologizing to Jamie at a time like this. If it were me, that would be the very last thing I'd be concerned about."

I said, "I think it's nice."

"Hmmm," my mother said, lighting another cigarette.

"Bad luck," my father said. He rubbed his chin again. "Bad luck."

"Well, it's certainly more than *bad luck*, Peter, isn't it? It's a rather serious accident, all told. The boy could sustain a brain injury from those stings." My mother could always manage to picture the worst possible outcome for any given situation, with or without the benefit of actual facts.

"No," my father said. "That's not what I mean, Alice. The boy's brother—that's why he brought the bicycle to the police station. He told the policeman at the front desk that it was bad luck. He didn't want it in his house. He was afraid something would happen to him, too."

Later at the hospital, with his Aunt Prudence standing behind him, Stevie Todd said that his brother was sorry for what he'd done.

"Thank you for not bringing charges against my brother," Stevie said in a stilted voice. There was nothing spontaneous or natural in it. He had obviously been coached. Stevie was my age, eight. When Aunt Prudence told him to shake my hand, he started to cry.

"Stevie, shake Jamie's hand," she insisted. Under the harsh, unforgiving whiteness of the hospital's overhead fluorescent lights, Mrs. Dodd's sister's face was puffy and blotched. Her eyes behind thick glasses were swollen and red from crying, bruised with plum-coloured smudges of exhaustion. If this was how her sister looked today, I couldn't imagine how Terry's mother must look. But still, Aunt Prudence pushed Stevie toward me. "I mean it. Come on now. He and his father are being very nice to us by not calling the juvenile authorities about your brother."

"I don't want to!" Stevie wailed. He shrank back from my extended hand as though it were leprous. "I said I was sorry. I don't want to shake his hand. *Why do I have to?*"

"Stop it!" she practically shouted. Roughly, she grabbed Stevie by the shoulder and shoved him towards me. "*Shake Jamie's hand!*"

My father raised his own hands in a gesture of gentle conciliation. "It's all right Mrs. . . . ?"

"*Miss*," Aunt Prudence said. "I'm not married. My name is *Miss* Prudence Rogers."

"Miss Rogers, Stevie doesn't have to shake Jamie's hand. It's fine. More than fine. The boy's obviously upset about his brother. Thank you for inviting us to come and meet you. We don't want to take any more of your time. You should be with your sister and Terry now."

"I'm so sorry." Aunt Prudence's face appeared to fall in on itself. Her voice sounded raw and chapped, almost as though it was bleeding. "We're all so upset. I thought this would be a good idea, you know. That the boys should meet. My nephew . . . Stevie that is, not Terry . . . well, he said he had a bad dream last night that something bad was going to happen. He won't tell me about it. I just thought it would be a good idea for him to . . . to . . ." She began to cry. "My sister—Mrs. Dodd, *Arlene* Dodd—well, her husband passed away last year. It's just she and the two boys, and me. I live with them and try to help out. Terry isn't a bad boy, Mr. Browning, he's just a little lost without his father around. And then this happened this morning. When the ambulance came for him, he was unconscious. Oh God, I'm so worried about my poor sister. If anything happens to Terry, too. His *face* . . ."

"Miss Rogers, please go to your sister. We'll see ourselves out. My wife in particular asked me to send her best wishes for Terry's recovery. I'm so, so sorry. *We're* sorry, I mean. And thank you, Stevie, for being so honest. Your mother and aunt should be very proud of you."

Stevie nodded dumbly and followed his aunt down the hallway toward the elevator to the ICU. Aunt Prudence called out to the two women who were in the elevator just as the doors were beginning to swing shut. One of the women reached out her hand and held the door till they reached it.

Stevie Dodd looked back just once. When our eyes met, his were full of a black dread that aged him beyond his years, far beyond childhood, maybe even further. Then they stepped into the elevator and the doors glided shut.

In the car on the way home, I told my father that I'd changed my mind about the mirror. I said there was nothing wrong with it after all, that I was just spooked last night by having my bike stolen and that I wanted to keep the mirror right where it was.

At first, he told me he didn't know what I was talking about, but then he remembered what I had said the previous night before he tucked me in. He looked at me quizzically, but said he was glad that I'd come to my senses, and he'd never planned to get rid of it anyway. He said we'd already had more than enough disruption and carrying-on to last us quite a while, thank you very much.

When we arrived home after picking up my bicycle from the police station, my father took it out of the back seat and told me to put it in the garage, which I did. He said he was going to go across the street and check on Mrs. Alban's eaves troughs, and that I should see if my mother needed any help in the house.

Mrs. Alban had been widowed earlier that year and my father had been doing the sort of odd jobs around the house that were formerly Mr. Alban's bailiwick. Mrs. Alban always tried to pay him, but my father always refused, as gently as possible. My mother said Mrs. Alban had no sense of the value of money, but my father said she was trying to keep her dignity intact in her widowhood.

That first autumn of her bereavement, I'd caught sight of Mrs. Alban through our living room window trying clumsily to rake the leaves in her front yard in all the brittleness of her old age. It broke my heart to see her fragility. I wished I were old enough to do it for her. When I saw my father do it that first time, a sense that some sort of elemental justice and kindness had been returned to the universe came to me, and I loved my father a bit more for being the instrument of it.

Inside the house, I called out to my mother. There was no answer. I called out again. In the kitchen, there was a note on the table in her rounded, loopy scrawl:

Monica Birdwhistle stopped by for a coffee and some cake. We're off to check out a sale at Ogilvy's at the plaza. She'll drop me home in a bit. There's cold macaroni salad in the fridge for lunch. I will be home later this afternoon. Dinner will be at seven SHARP!

Love, MOM

xoxox

She always signed her notes "Mom," even if they were intended for my father. Some days it seemed as though that was their agreed-upon nomenclature; the rest of the time it seemed calculated to head off the possibility of shocking me with marital familiarity in case I came upon one signed "Alice" by accident. In any case, she wouldn't be home for hours, and for now the house was empty. Silence, general and complete, blanketed the rooms. I felt my heartbeat quicken in my chest.

Downstairs in my bedroom, I closed the door. There was a bolt lock that I had been forbidden to touch, on pain of both spanking and grounding. Neither of my parents believed young boys had any reason to lock their doors. I turned the bolt handle now, hearing the soft *click* as the door locked. Momentarily panicked at my own audacity in flouting this carved-in-stone prohibition, I turned it counterclockwise to make sure it unlocked. When it opened, I sighed with relief. Then I closed and locked it again.

My mother had made my bed while my father and I were at the hospital. The carpet had been freshly vacuumed. I sat down on the navy-blue coverlet and took the room's measure. It was innocuous, full of early-afternoon sunshine. The mirror was still bolted to the wall adjacent to my bed. The glass was faintly streaked, and the ghost-scent of the vinegar she'd wiped it with hung in the air, mixing with the carpet deodorizer.

Briefly I wondered if my mother had caught a glimpse of anything in the glass other than her own reflection when she was cleaning it, but I already knew that Amanda—or whatever I had seen, or imagined I had seen, the night before—would never have shown herself, or *itself*, to my mother.

She'd been waiting for me, and no one else.

Standing in that mellow suburban sunlight, the rational side of my nature, the pre-adult side, told me that the first part of the dream I'd had about standing on the promontory over the lake had started hours earlier that evening, and that I'd very likely dozed off immediately when I came downstairs, then woken when my father entered to tuck me in. But the irrational side of my nature, the part of the nature that connects the open minds of children with magic things unseen and unheard by adults, things of beauty and of horror— what grownups indulgently call "having a vivid imagination"—realized that what I had seen last night had been real. I *had* seen a little girl named Amanda in the mirror. She had used my own voice to talk to me, but they had been her words, not mine. Of that I had not the slightest doubt.

And even if any doubt had remained, the black dread in Stevie Dodd's face at the hospital had told its own story, told it in a language in which both he and I were fluent. I doubted very much that I had been the only dreamer of terrible things last night. Perhaps Stevie had even dreamed of the wasps themselves, dreamed of the swarm of terrible arthropod bodies moving like a yellow-and-black cloud with murderous purpose, stinging Terry's face and mouth over and over till he passed out from the pain of the venom coursing through his bully's body, finally screaming the way I knew he'd made other children scream, while the wasps stung him again and again. He'd finally *shut up*, all right.

The irrational, magical child I was smiled at that. *Good*, I thought. *He stole my bike. He deserved it.*

Then I touched the glass and called softly, "Amanda? I got my bike back, just like you said I would."

After a while, she came out and we spent the afternoon behind that locked bedroom door until I heard the front door open and the sound of my father's footsteps on the floor above.

That year, I spoke with Amanda mostly at night, when the light in my bedroom was dim, or when I switched off my bedside lamp altogether and pulled out and lit the candle that I'd hidden under my bed so my mother couldn't find it. I used the candle mostly when my parents were asleep, because my mother could smell a lit match or candle practically through a wall.

The next summer, my parents thought it would be good for me to get out of the house and interact with some boys my own age.

Their solution was Camp Manitou, which my older cousin Timothy had attended years ago. My aunt Grace told my mother it had done him "a world of good," and that it might help me "learn to fit in a bit."

I pleaded with my mother. "But Mom, why can't I just stay here? Why can't I just spend the summer playing with Hank? Why do I have to go away?"

"Jameson, stop whining," she said. "I don't want you underfoot. It's time you started meeting some normal boys your age. Maybe it'll rub off on you. I've already told you, I don't like you spending so much time with that strange girl. Honestly, what sort of girl calls herself 'Hank'? It's not natural."

"Mom, she's my best friend."

"Well, you need to make a new best friend. For heaven's sake. A boy shouldn't have a *girl* as a best friend. When you're older you can date, then someday you'll marry some nice girl who'll become your wife. But boys and girls aren't supposed to be friends. Aunt Grace says Camp Manitou is full of wonderful fellows. You'll have a new best friend in three shakes of a lamb's tail. When you come home, you won't even be thinking about Hank. *Lucinda*," she corrected herself. "*Lucinda*."

I called Hank on the telephone to tell her that I was going away for the summer.

"I wish it was just going to be you and me for the whole summer," I said miserably.

"Your mom would hate that," Hank replied. "You know she wishes you and I weren't best friends." She sighed. "I wish *I* could go away to camp. I hate it here. There's nothing to do. Boys always get to do the best stuff. You're lucky you get to go. I wish I could go instead of you. I'd love to go away to camp."

"It's a *boys'* camp, Hank," I said. "It's not for girls." I was utterly baffled by her nonchalance. To me it was the theft of our summer together at the hands of my parents. My mother didn't even like her. I briefly considered sharing that dislike with Hank as a way to bring her more in line with my thinking on the injustice of the matter, but I reasoned that it would be unnecessarily cruel.

"So what? I'm more like a boy than you are. You couldn't even climb a tree till I showed you how to do it, Jamie. I'd probably have more fun than you would. I *get* all that stuff. Don't be mad, but you're way more like a girl than I am."

I thought for a moment. There was no malice in Hank's voice. She was simply stating a fact both of us were aware of, one that didn't really bother either of us. She was right—we were an odd pair in our reversals.

"I'm going to hate it. I'm going to *really* hate it."

"Don't be such a baby," Hank commanded, ever the pragmatist. "You'll probably have a great time. And when it's over, you can come home."

I had one last, terrible, burning question. "Hank?"

"What?"

"You won't find a new best friend while I'm away, will you? We'll still be, you know, best friends when I get back?"

"Don't be such a baby," she repeated, but kindly this time.

"Come on, swear?"

"I swear."

"*Pinkie*-swear?"

"We have to be face-to-face for pinkie swear, dummy."

"Okay, let's just *pretend* we pinkie-sweared, then."

Hank sighed. "Okay, Jamie, pretend-pinkie-swear."

"Promise?"

"I promise, Jamie. We'll be best friends till the day we die."

Late that night, after I was sure my parents had gone to bed, I lit the candle in front of the mirror and tried to call Amanda so I could tell her what I had told Hank—that I was going away, even though I wanted to stay home that summer. I wanted to beg her to come with me, to find a mirror somewhere in the camp where I could see her.

"Amanda, it's me. It's Jamie. I have to talk to you." I closed my eyes and relaxed my throat and willed her to speak to me, through me. But no words suggested themselves. I tried again, concentrating harder this time. I squeezed my eyes so tightly shut that I saw purple supernovas exploding behind my eyelids and my head throbbed with the sheer effort of my concentration. I tried again. "Amanda, *please* come out. Don't be mad. I have to go. I don't have any choice. They're *making* me go."

The candle flickered, and then went out.

In the dark, I whispered, "Amanda . . . ? Is that you? Don't be mad . . . please? It's not my fault." But when I switched on my bedside lamp, I was alone in the mirror.

I lit the candle every night for seven nights, but she never came.

A week later, I left for summer camp. In all that time it was as though Amanda had never even existed, as though she had been nothing but a flittering enchantment I had conjured up from the depths of my imagination.

I spent three long, horrible weeks at Manitou as one of the camp's two untouchables. I was in a cabin with five other boys, all of whom had been to Camp Manitou before, and all of whom seemed to be friends already. Worse still, they were friends in that way young boys have of being friends not based necessarily on shared experiences but simply on shared gender. They all spoke the same language, a language with which I had never been naturally fluent. Boys can smell difference at five hundred paces, and whatever they smelled in me, they hated everything about it on sight.

The ringleader was a boy named John Prince. He was a big ugly kid with a forest fire of red hair and a face that was prone to flushing just as hot. He had small, cold fish eyes and fists like hams and, based on my last name, he nicknamed me Brown Nose that first night.

The next night, I was short-sheeted and spent half an hour trying to unmake my bed while the five other boys laughed in the dark at my fumbling because I was too terrified to turn on the light. Finally, in despair, I ripped the rough red blanket off the bed and cried myself to sleep as quietly as possible on the crude pine floor beside the bunk. Two nights later, one of them put a dead squirrel at the foot of my bunk, under the blanket. When I shrieked, they broke into applause and crude laughter.

That night, after everyone else was asleep, I snuck out. I lay in my sleeping bag under a pine tree behind the cabin. After I'd cried all the tears I had to spare, I fell asleep watching a thick cloud of ghostly white moths spin and whirl around the rear exterior light of the cabin. The trembling movement of their beating wings acted as a hypnotic, summoning sleep.

The next morning, when I told one of our cabin counsellors about the dead squirrel, he laughed and said he thought it was a fine prank in the old Manitou spirit. He told me to stop complaining or I'd never make any friends.

The only boy who had it worse than I did was a fat blond boy named Olivier. He had a high, warbling voice and sad eyes set in his face like pale blue poached eggs. He seemed perpetually on the verge of tears. Had we been smarter about it, we might have formed an alliance of sorts, but we despised each other, for each saw in the other some reflection of his own loathsomeness, and we ate alone at opposite ends of the mess hall to avoid attracting the negative attention we would doubtless have attracted sitting together.

One afternoon, during free swim at the pool, Prince purposely jumped off the diving board and landed on my head, driving me underwater, almost to the bottom. My two front teeth buried themselves in the meat of my lower lip as the impact of his feet on my head caused my jaws to snap shut.

Underwater, I almost lost consciousness, but before I passed out, I managed to paddle to the surface, my head full of light and exploding stars. The corner of the pool was red with the blood that gushed from my mouth. The lifeguard took me to the infirmary where the nurse pressed a cold washcloth against my lip to stop the bleeding but deemed stitches unnecessary.

"Just hold the washcloth against your lip," she said. "The blood will clot and it'll stop. Everybody gets war wounds at camp sooner or later. Welcome to Camp Manitou! You're an old warrior now. You've earned it." To denote campers who had passed all the unofficial initiations and were on their second year at Manitou, the camp used the term "old warrior." The nurse beamed at me like she was bestowing a knighthood.

By that evening, my swollen mouth looked like a clown's makeup and almost every movement of my face threatened to open my lip again. When I tried to take a bite of salad and the vinegar in the dressing seared the raw flesh, I nearly screamed in pain and everyone laughed. And no one laughed louder than John Prince and my five cabin-mates.

The upside was that I was excused from most of the camp's outdoor activities for the next two days, which meant that while Prince and the others were out learning to be old warriors, I was left alone to explore the fields and marshes beyond the camp. There was also the camp chapel, which was dark and smelled pleasantly of age and dry wood. It had a piano, which was only slightly out of tune. I played chopsticks for hours, and made up songs that made ample use of the few chords I could play, amplified by the sustaining pedal, which made it sound very symphonic and serious to my ears.

Several times I entered the communal bathroom when I knew it would be empty and stared into the mirrors over the row of sinks, hoping against vain hope that I might catch a glimpse of Amanda. The mirrors were dirty and cracked, and they held no secrets. If Amanda was hiding in their depths, she was well hidden.

But of course, those two days came and went too quickly, and before long I was back in all the camp activities.

I put on a brave face on the one Parents' Day the camp allowed midway through the summer session. I'd shown my father and mother how my diving skills had improved, played the piano for them in the camp's chapel, and introduced them to my counsellors. The counsellors put on convivial faces in front of my parents, even though by then most of them despised me and considered me lazy. That said, I think the counsellors were more worried about my injury reflecting badly on their leadership than they let on, which is why they told my parents what a terrific camper I was and what a great asset I was to Camp Manitou.

For my part, I spoke glowingly about my counsellors in front of my parents, too, even though I feared them and considered them bullies and sadists who exploited my physical weaknesses and pitted the other boys against me till the halfway point had seemed to stretch out like a life sentence of short-sheeting, dunking, and being the one everyone screamed at to *hurry up, asshole!* during those endless hikes under the blazing July sun.

While my mother stood just far enough apart from a group of mothers who were admiring their sons' artwork to let them know that she considered herself a cut above the company, my father asked me to go for a walk with him, to show him where the tuck shop was so he could restock me with "supplies," chocolate bars and the like. Even as he said it, I suspected he wanted to talk, and that it had nothing to do with replenishing my supply of chocolate.

We walked behind the arts and crafts cabin and up the hill overlooking the camp, and sat down on one of the logs that formed the seating boundary at the edge of the campfire pit.

My father reached for my hand, to hold it. I pulled it away sharply. I was horrified at the thought of anyone seeing me walking hand in hand with my father. In light of everything I had already endured, if any of the other campers caught me holding my father's hand, they would see to it that it would be the end of me. I could see that my reaction had hurt him, which hurt me in turn. I didn't like to see my father in pain so when he tried to put his arm around my shoulder instead, I didn't pull away. Instead, I leaned into him. For a moment it felt as though I might burst into tears, but I held it in.

Although my attendance at Camp Manitou had largely been my mother's idea, I also knew my father wanted me to be having a good time and I didn't want to disappoint him. I never wanted to disappoint my father. I wanted him to be proud of me, and right now that meant me not acting like a baby. All it would have taken would have been for me to break down and cry, to tell him what a nightmare it all had been, and he would take me right out of there. I pictured a horrible, loud scene with the counsellors where my father would upbraid them for not taking care of me while my cabin-mates looked on and gloated at what a sissy I was.

My mother would be embarrassed about having a son that couldn't get along with other boys, and I suspected I would pay dearly for that for the rest of the summer, if not longer. When my mother chose to withdraw affection, she could freeze ink with the chill of it.

No, it was better to suck it up and endure the next week and a half. It had to end at some point. In truth, I sensed that my cabin-mates were already getting bored of tormenting me as they developed alliances with other campers like them who had their own targets.

My father smiled and said, "How's it going, Jamie? Are you okay? Are you having a good time at Camp Manitou?"

"It's going great, Dad," I lied. "I love it here."

"Really?"

I tried to meet his eyes, but I couldn't. Instead, I smiled brightly, looking away. "Yup."

He paused. "What happened to your lip? You said it happened in the pool?"

"Roughhousing. It's nothing, Dad. Really. It doesn't even hurt."

"Are you making new friends? Any new buddies you like in particular?"

I shrugged, thinking of the dead squirrel under my sheets and how I'd screamed, and how they'd all laughed. "It's okay, Dad. Everyone's okay."

"You know, your mother and I are very proud of you, Jamie. Your granddad always used to tell me that the wilderness really made a man out of a boy. I guess it's sort of like that for you here, isn't it. You're really growing up."

"I know, Dad. Thanks."

"Are you sure you're okay, Jamie? There's not something you're not telling me, is there? Because you can tell me anything, you know."

I forced a smile at him. Even to me it seemed the smile didn't quite make it to my eyes. But I wanted the conversation to be over, and I didn't want my father to be disappointed in me. "No, Dad. Really. It's fine." I swallowed the thickness in my voice and took a deep breath. "Dad?"

"Yes, son?"

"Would you buy me a mint Aero bar at the tuck shop?"

My father seemed relieved by the innocuousness of the request. "Of course, Jamie." He seemed as relieved as I was to bring this conversation to a close, though I wasn't sure if it was because he suspected more of what was going on than he let on, and that the prospect of dealing with it was too daunting. If so, then my fantasy of him withdrawing me from Camp Manitou if I asked him to really was just a pipe dream. And I didn't want to know that. It was safer not knowing. "Anything else?"

"Dad, would it be okay if we bought some for my cabin-mates?"

It was a sudden, ludicrous burst of inspiration, the notion that chocolate bars might be enough payola to buy, if not the friendship of my cabin-mates— I'd gladly settle for their indifference at that point—at least a reprieve from their bullying. And, as it turned out, it would, for a few hours that evening anyway.

"Of course, son. I'm glad to see you thinking of your buddies."

Then we walked down the hill to where my mother was standing impatiently next to the Mercedes-Benz Estate station wagon she'd insisted my father drive, even though he'd said over and over that he couldn't afford it. My mother didn't look much like she was enjoying Camp Manitou, either.

In any case, it had all come to an end a week and a half later, the day the busses rolled up the gravel drive to the chapel in preparation for the end-of-camp exodus that would to take the boys home and take me to freedom.

But not before I'd found the painted turtle.

It had been sunning itself all that morning on a rock jutting out of the surface of an algae-encrusted, shallow marsh up the road from the chapel—the swampy water bracketed by pussy willows, lily pads, the dead, bleached skeletons of trees, and rotted stumps. With boys milling nearby and shouts ricocheting across the water, it was hard to believe no one else had seen the turtle, which was so beautiful and perfect that I momentarily lost my breath. It was a midland painted turtle, a specific subspecies of painted turtle with a gleaming olive-coloured carapace streaked with bands of red and orange along the sides. Its plastron was yellow, with butterfly-shaped markings along the midline. Its little head and neck, arched as though it were scenting the air, was streaked with thin bands of crimson and gold. The creature shone like a perfect emerald and ruby brooch in the sunlight.

I knew I had to have it. I had to *own* it.

I told myself that I wanted the turtle to be my *friend*, but the truth was I couldn't bear the thought of it not belonging to me. So much of the cruelty of childhood is thoughtless, in the literal sense of the word. When I waded into the swamp and plucked the turtle off the rock, I had no sense that I was kidnapping it, of taking it out of its natural world—indeed, its home—and forcing it into my own.

Terrified, it moved its tiny limbs in frantic protest, and then withdrew its head into its shell. It defecated into the palm of my hand. I wiped my hand on the leg of my khaki shorts, for the first time all summer not caring about how dirty nature was. As gently as I could, I placed the turtle into my pocket and hurried out of the swamp.

Behind the counter in the mess hall, I found a paper sack. I transferred the turtle from my pocket to the sack, carrying it carefully by the bottom with the lip of the bag open to the air so it wouldn't suffocate. The turtle tried frantically to scramble up the sides of the bag. Its head moved from side to side, as though trying to comprehend how one minute it had been basking in the late-July sunlight on a rock in the middle of an eastern Ontario marsh and the next, a prisoner in a brown paper cell.

I felt a flutter of pity. "Shhhhh, little turtle," I murmured. I caressed its drying shell with my index finger, hoping it would feel reassured. "Shhhhh. It'll be okay. You're safe with me. You're coming home with me, to live in my room. We're going to be best friends, you and I. You'll see. I'll feed you and give you water. In the basement, we have a terrarium. I'll wash it out and it can be your new home. I'll watch you grow up. It'll be great. Don't worry."

The turtle's legs kicked more weakly, as though it had finally realized there was no escape. Then they stopped moving, and its head retracted inside its shell again.

In my mind, I had already named the turtle Manitou, after the camp. Even if I had endured three weeks away from everything familiar and comforting, something good would come out of it. My new friend would carry the camp's name. I enjoyed the perversity of that as only a nine-year-old boy can.

For as long as I could, I avoided the counsellors and the other boys. It was fairly easy to do. I'd packed my green canvas duffel bag the night before and delivered it to the dining room where it would then be loaded onto the bus.

I knew that if any of the counsellors saw me, they would confiscate the turtle and let it loose in the marsh. It was expressly forbidden to take wildlife away from the woods and marshes here, even into the camp. At Manitou, we'd done our nature study *in nature*. No snakes, frogs, birds, or turtles were to be captured. The camp organizers were deeply committed to the notion that wild things were wild, and belonged in the wild as their birthright. But what I wanted at that moment more than anything else was to bring the turtle home with me.

I'd received a few sideways glances from boys that had passed me where I sat behind our cabin, and one of them even asked me what I was doing there. The question as usual wasn't really a question at all. It was challenge. But this was the last day of camp, and the challenger was bored enough to accept my stock offering of *nuthin'* without it being a prelude to something that would make me cry out in pain.

When the time came, I climbed aboard the bus and secured the seat two rows behind the driver, Olivier having claimed the seat directly behind him, which was the safest seat of all. Since no one wanted to sit with me, I had both seats to myself—correction; *we* had both seats to *ourselves*, Manitou and I. When I looked into the paper bag to see how he was doing, he appeared to have given up trying to climb out. He looked like he was resting. As quietly as I could, I whispered to him that we were almost home and that I'd let him out of the bag.

The counsellors and the other boys must have assumed I had a snack in the paper bag because no one asked what was inside, at least not until the bus was just outside of Ottawa. Then I felt a rough tap on my shoulder.

"Whatcha got in the bag, Brown Nose?" John Prince had lumbered down the aisle of the bus from the very back where he'd been sitting with his buddies. I'd heard them shouting and laughing almost since we'd left Camp Manitou. He smacked me on the back on my head. "You got food in that bag, Brown Nose? Huh? You got candy?"

I closed the bag and put it to my side and used my body to block access to it. "No," I said. "Nothing. I don't have any food. No candy."

When John Prince laughed, it was a snarling sound full of teeth and phlegm. "Yeah, you're 'know-nuthin' all right, retard. Whatcha got in the bag?" he demanded again. "Show me." Prince shoved me to the side and took the bag in a chapped hand. He opened it and looked in. His eyes widened.

"Hey, it's a fuckin' *turtle*! Brown Nose kidnapped a fuckin' *turtle*!" He laughed again, showing all his yellow teeth. He reached inside and took Manitou out, bringing the small creature right up to his face. For one horrible moment I was sure Prince was going to eat him, was going to tear Manitou's head off with those teeth and crack his shell with his jaws. The turtle's legs were kicking helplessly in the air and its head swayed from side to side in terror. Prince swung Manitou through the air between his thumb and index finger like a child with a model airplane.

"Give him back to me!" I screamed. *"You're* scaring *him! Give him to me!"*

Prince said, "Make me, Brown Nose. I fuckin' dare you. Make me."

The bus driver half-turned. He shouted, "Sit down, you two! Get back to your seats *right now*, or I'll pull this bus right over to the side of the road till the police come, you hear me? And then you'll be headed straight for reform school!"

But of course, it was too late for any of that.

Prince swung Manitou through the air, making *vroom vroom* airplane noises as he did. His friends in the back seat all laughed as though it were the funniest thing they'd ever seen. A few of them started to clap, and one of them—I didn't see which one—said, *Throw it! Let's see if turtles can fly!*

What happened next is still a bit unclear after all these years, but my memory is that I had glanced up at the driver's rear-view mirror and seen nothing in it but clouds.

In one second, the mirror reflected the entire rear aisle of the bus and the faces of forty shouting, jeering prepubescent boys; in the next, it went blank, the view—if it could even be called that—was something akin to looking out the window on one of those mornings in late fall, right before winter, when the fog lies as thickly on the glass as white paint.

Then my vision blurred. I tasted blood in my mouth, and the world was reduced to the sweet music of Prince's screams. I found myself standing up in my seat with a handful of Prince's hair in my fist, smashing his head against the metal bar of the seat. I felt the vibration of the impact thrum up my forearm. I was possessed of a sudden, vicious strength that was so entirely *unlike* me that I felt myself observing the scene as though from a distance. It was a dark and delicious, even voluptuous, violence that lifted me up above myself on black wings.

It occurred to me that Prince sounded much less terrifying with blood from the gash over his eye smearing the chrome and the cheap vinyl upholstery of the bus seat. I loved the sound of his screaming. I *loved* it. I adored it with a barbarism that was entirely alien to my nature. I wanted to lick the air around him and taste that sound. Then I was punching him in the face, hitting his nose, his forehead, and his chin.

The bus swerved as the driver pulled over to the side of the road and the boys were all screaming, *Fight! Fight! Fight!* But there was an undercurrent of awe beneath it all, because someone had changed the rules of dominance, neglecting to tell John Prince or his friends that the impossible had occurred, and Brown Nose was going to kill him unless someone pulled them apart.

At the roadside, the bus diver did just that. He pulled the bus to a stop and broke up the fight, though "fight" was a bit of misnomer: Prince was out cold and his face looked as though someone had swished it around in a tub of blood. It would be closer to the truth to say that the driver pulled me off Prince, and Prince slid to the ground like someone had poured him from a pitcher.

I looked down at his hands: they were empty. The paper bag was crumpled under the seat across the aisle where Prince had kicked it during his struggle. I looked around for Manitou, but I didn't see him anywhere nearby. I shrugged out of the driver's tight grip, kneeled down on the floor of the bus, and looked under the seats.

I stood up and stared at the now dead-silent bus. "Where's my turtle?" Silence answered me. The other boys seemed transfixed by the blood, still trying to reconcile what they had just seen, the utter demolishment of Camp Manitou's Goliath by the unlikeliest possible David. "*Where's my fucking turtle? If anything happened to him, I'll fucking kill you guys!*"

The bus driver shoved me back down into my seat. He pointed his finger at me, then jabbed his finger into my chest for emphasis. It hurt when he did that. "You sit down and shut up, you crazy little freak. You don't move. Boy, you're in some kind of trouble." He looked down at Prince, who was moaning and starting to regain consciousness. Then back at me. His face was a mixture of adult fury, worry, and a grudging sort of admiration. At least it felt like admiration, though I could have been wrong about that, too. "Jesus *fuck*," he said. Then, to the other boys: "Okay, you bozos, what's this about a turtle? Did one of you take his turtle?" He looked back at me. "What the hell . . . was this about a goddamned *turtle*? Seriously? A goddamned *turtle*? Do you two little fucks know how dangerous it is to fight on a bus?"

"The turtle is mine," I said weakly. "He's just a little turtle I found in the swamp. A midland painted turtle." It was as though by naming the turtle's species and genus, I might make it easier for the driver to either locate Manitou on the floor, alive, or else identify his remains if one of these other monsters had done the unspeakable while I was taking apart their leader. I felt everything—the rage, the strength, the fight, the pleasure in the blood and the pain—rise up out of my body and dissipate like vapour. I was lightheaded with it. It was as though an entirely different being had abruptly taken leave of its temporary occupancy of my body and left me with what I had started with before the possession. A sting of tears pricked my eyes. "John was going to hurt him. He took him out of the bag and he was waving him around like an airplane. Manitou was really scared."

"*Manitou!*" The driver gave me a look of fury leavened with frustration, perhaps even sympathy. But when he addressed the bus full of dumbstruck boys in the bus, there was no sympathy, just anger. "Everyone look on the ground, and under your seats. If there is a turtle there, alive or dead, bring him to me right now." The boys all scrambled to obey the driver, obviously grateful for something to do to break the tension. They dove onto the floor of the bus and peered under their seats. "You," he said to me, pointing again. "Don't move a goddamned muscle."

Finally, a boy in the back I didn't recognize shouted out, "Sir, I found him!" He held up Manitou, who kicked his legs in the air. My relief—for I'd had visions of the turtle's crushed shell and limbs—was so all-encompassing that I felt as though the air had been sucked out of me.

"Bring that thing up here," the driver told the boy. "And give it to this kid," he added, pointing at me. "Right now."

The boy hurried up the aisle and handed Manitou to me, not looking me in the eye as he did it. I cupped both hands like a crèche and he deposited the turtle's little body into them. As gently as I could, I retrieved the paper bag and put Manitou back inside. The boy hurried to the back of the bus, still not looking at me.

I could feel, if not actually hear, the collective exhalation of breath when the driver helped Prince to his feet and Prince shrugged him off with a defiant, if bruised *I'm fine, Jesus Christ, leave me alone!* before limping down the aisle back to his friends in the back row. But Prince didn't look at me, either, and no one bothered me on the last forty-five minutes of the bus ride back home.

The bus driver came to my defence at the terminal when Mrs. Prince saw her son's battered face and began to scream. Cold-eyed and red-haired like her son, it was apparent even to me where his splenetic temperament came from. She swept him up in her arms as though he were an injured refugee from a lifeboat suddenly reunited with his lover.

"Your boy started it with this boy, ma'am," the driver said when she wheeled on him and demanded to know what had happened to her baby. I saw Prince wince at the word *baby*, which made me smile in spite of myself. But I was in no way confident enough to laugh at him, however much I wanted to. The driver continued. "He came up behind him and smacked him in the head. And he took this boy's pet turtle away. The boy's reaction was maybe too . . . impulsive. But your boy started the fight. No question about that at all."

"My Johnny is a good boy. He would never have started a fight with this little brat. This boy must have started it—look, he doesn't even have a scratch on him. What kind of camp are you people running anyway? Where are this boy's parents? Where?" Mrs. Prince turned to the throng of parents and called out shrilly, "Who are the parents of this boy?" She plucked the sleeve of a random passing brown-haired man in a madras summer jacket who looked nothing like me. "*You*? Are *you* his father?"

"Excuse me," said the man, looking appalled. He extricated himself from her clutch and hurried away, looking back only once, as if to make sure she wasn't following him.

Turning back to the driver, Mrs. Prince said, "I demand to speak to someone about this *right now!* Do you *hear* me?"

The driver had clearly had enough. A small crowd of parents and boys had gathered nearby. "I expect everyone has, ma'am. I'm not running the camp, I just drive this bus. You can talk to one of the counsellors if you want. Or you can find the boy's parents and complain to them. But if anyone asks me, I'm going to tell them that your son is a bully and a brawler and he picked on this kid for no reason. Now, *good day*, ma'am."

Mrs. Prince wheeled, about to turn her fury on me, when her son abruptly went rigid in her arms and said, "*Mom!* Fucking leave it *alone*. Let's go. I want to get out of here." He looked around at the people staring and lowered his head.

"Johnny, don't curse! And besides, your poor face. You poor baby. We need to get you to the hospital. Then we'll call the police. We'll *sue . . .*"

"Mom, *now*. I mean it. Let's go."

The crowd of parents and boys had grown larger now and were all staring. The mothers in particular, seemed to be taking the measure of the differences in the relative height and weight of Prince and our respective demeanours, as well. In their faces was the beginning of disapproval, though directed not at me but at Prince. They knew a bully when they saw one.

The mother of the boy who had brought Manitou to me in the bus pointed at Prince, and then leaned down to whisper something in her son's ear. When he nodded, she stiffened, hurried him out of the terminal. The boy looked back at me, almost apologetically. For a moment, I thought I saw something like empathy, but by the time I could have been sure, he was already gone. In any case, the summer was over and the time for empathy long past. I looked around for my parents, feeling very alone in the terminal with the paper bag containing my turtle clutched in my hand.

For a moment, it looked like Mrs. Prince was going to say something else, but her son gave his mother a hard, brutal shove toward the exit, picking up his duffel bag from the heap of luggage near the bus door and left the terminal without even a backward glance at me.

From inside the paper bag, I heard Manitou's feeble scratching as he tried to get out of the bag. I opened it and stroked his shell with my index finger, hoping he'd feel some sort of comfort from it. "We'll be home soon, Manitou," I whispered. "We'll be safe from all this stuff soon."

My parents pulled up to the entrance of the bus depot fifteen minutes later. I was waiting for them outside, beside the curb, my duffel bag at my feet and the paper bag in my hand.

I'd caught sight of my own reflection in one of the windows in the terminal and had noticed that I was smeared with Prince's blood. Not only had it spattered all over my white t-shirt, there were droplets of it on my forehead and under one eye. My knuckles were beginning to ache. I ducked into one of the bathroom stalls in the men's room of the terminal and changed into one of the unwashed t-shirts I'd shoved to the bottom for my mother to wash once we got back to the house. It smelled musty, but at least there was no blood on it.

When she stepped out of the car, I saw that my mother wore a dark linen dress. This was a change from the slacks she'd been wearing around the house all summer long. It signalled to me that picking me up was an event, and that she'd missed me. That, at least, was how I chose to interpret the gesture. My parents apologized for their lateness and for not being there to greet me as I stepped off the bus. God knows what image they had in their minds of who, or what, would be greeting them. I'm sure they envisioned their proud, sunburned son, returning home to them from three weeks away, a little closer to manhood now, and proud of his achievements of the summer. The reality is what they'd missed: the apoplexy of Mrs. Prince, the bellowing of the bus driver, and the shame in Prince's eyes. And me, spattered with his blood.

I inhaled the smell of my father's blue cotton broadcloth sport shirt, which smelled like fresh laundry, sun, and Bay Rum aftershave. He held me tight and squeezed me. In my ear he whispered, "Welcome home, Jamie. Did I ever miss you, son. We both did." Then he hugged me again and I collapsed into his arms.

While pleased to see me, my mother was not remotely pleased to see Manitou. When I opened the bag to show her, beaming with pride, she recoiled and took a step backward.

"Jamie, what on *earth* . . . ? What is this? You brought home a turtle? What were you thinking?"

"Mom, his name is Manitou." Her face remained blank. "He's a midland painted turtle," I coaxed. I was hoping that by working up my own level of excitement about the painted turtle, the excitement would become contagious and magically spread to my parents. "I found him on the last day of camp. He was lying on a rock. I'll take care of him, I promise. He'll be my responsibility. You won't have to do anything."

My mother said, "We're going to take that . . . that *thing* right to the pet store on Bank Street and see if they want it. They can sell it. Maybe they'll let you keep part of the money. But you didn't ask permission to bring that turtle home. You know how your father and I feel about pets."

I blinked, feeling tears prick my eyes. Having endured three weeks at Camp Manitou already, let alone the horror of the day that had just been, the turtle was the only decent thing that had come out of it and I felt responsible for him. In many ways, he had come to symbolize everything about the vulnerability and fear I had felt during that three-week eternity. I had a sudden image of him in Prince's hand, his tiny legs kicking in terror as that monster swept him through the air from side to side.

"Mom, please . . . he's so far from home. I'm all he's got right now. And he's so beautiful. Look at him. Mom, please? Let me keep him?"

But she was adamant. "Absolutely not. We're going right to the pet store on the way home. I don't know what you were thinking, Jameson, but you're going to have to learn that sometimes your actions carry consequences. This is as good a time as any to learn that lesson."

"Dad?" I looked imploringly at my father, but he looked away. I had a sudden, dreadful vision of Manitou on display in one of the terrariums at Willard's Pet Shoppe on Bank Street, as far away from the paradise in which he was born and had lived his short, wild life as possible. I pictured children poking him with their grubby fingers, or tapping on the glass walls of his prison trying to get a reaction. I felt a return of some of the rage I felt on the bus when Prince swung him through the air, but there was a new, desolate identification with Manitou that I hadn't felt the last time. I hated my mother then, and wished her dead. "Dad, please. Please? I've never wanted anything more in my life. And if you let me keep him, you never have to give me anything ever again, not even for Christmas, or on my birthday."

My mother said peremptorily, "Don't try to play your father and I off one another, Jameson. You know better than that." She turned to my father. "Peter? Where did you park? Let's get home. After we drop the turtle off, we can all go to Ponderosa to celebrate Jameson's first night back. Would you like that, Jameson? It would be a special treat." You can tell us all about your adventures at Camp Manitou this summer. Wouldn't that be fun?"

Before I could reply, my father said to my mother in a very clear, firm voice, "Alice, I think Jamie's old enough to be responsible for the turtle he's brought home. I think it'll be fine."

My mother stared at my father, open-mouthed. "I *beg* your pardon? The decision has been made, Peter. I'm not having that thing in my clean house. Turtles are messy and they're crawling with disease. I'm not having us all die of salmonella just so Jameson can keep a pet."

"We can talk about it later, Alice, if you like." There was the faintest trace of an edge to his voice, faint but detectable to both my mother and myself. "But I think it'll be fine. What was his name? Manitou? Like Gitche Manitou, the head-honcho Indian spirit? Good name. Jamie will take good care of him, won't you, son? We can use that old terrarium, the one I kept my garter snake in when I was a boy. I think we still have it, don't we, Alice?"

My mother narrowed her eyes and said nothing.

"Yes, Dad, I promise." I turned to my mother pleadingly. "Mom? You'll see. Is it okay? Dad says I can."

She didn't reply to me, either, but she shot my father a look of icy fury. Then she said, "Jameson, take your duffel bag and wait for us outside. I want to have a quick word with your father before we drive home."

I slung my duffel over my shoulder. My parents never raised their voices to each other in public, let alone fought in public, so I knew that this would be settled in a matter of minutes in one of two ways. Either Manitou would be coming home to live with me in a terrarium in my room where I could take care of him, or else we'd be stopping off at Willard's on the way home, in which case I would never forgive my mother as long as I lived. Just before I reached the exit, I turned back and observed my parents.

My mother's face was white with rage and she was speaking to my father in a voice too low for anyone around her to hear. But whatever she was saying was no less furious for its inaudibility. So engrossed was my mother in berating my father that she didn't even notice that he stopped listening to her long enough to give me a brief, almost imperceptible wink.

When he did that, I knew we'd won, at least this round.

My mother sat in the front seat and smoked steadily as she stared out the window. My father tried to make light conversation—with her, at first. When she pointedly ignored him, he tried to engage me instead, but I was too self-conscious to answer beyond monosyllables. Both my father and I were acutely aware of my mother's silence, as we were doubtless intended to be.

Jovially, my father said, "I guess Ponderosa is out of the question, Alice . . . ? Or would you still like to have dinner there? I bet Jamie could use a steak, couldn't you, son? I sure could."

My mother stared straight ahead without replying.

"It's okay, Dad," I said. "I'm not all that hungry."

My father glanced sideways at my mother, then back at me in the rear-view mirror. He sighed. "Well," he said. "Hidey-ho! Home we go!"

As soon as we arrived at our house, my mother went up to their bedroom and slammed the door. Rather than jumping, both of us exhaled our relief simultaneously.

My father grinned and said, "Well. Let's get this little fellow out of that bag and into something more comfortable." He laughed at his joke. I laughed too, more in solidarity with my father than at his joke, which really wasn't all that funny. The love I felt for my father at that moment was profound and all-encompassing. "Put him in the sink, Jameson. Run some water first so the porcelain is a bit moist. It's high enough that he won't be able to get out. Then you and I will get the terrarium out of the garage and get his new home ready." My father reached out and gently squeezed my shoulder. "You like him, don't you? I can tell. Your first pet. Well, well. How about that? Kind of exciting, isn't it?"

"Yeah, it is. Thank you, Dad. You know . . . for making it, you know, okay with Mom."

"I wouldn't say it's okay with Mom," my father said. "But it's okay with me, and she'll get used it, you'll see. Come on now; let's get that sink ready for him. He's been in that paper bag of yours for a very long time."

I ran the water in the sink, then gently took Manitou out of the bag and placed him on the damp porcelain. It could have been my imagination, but the turtle seemed to revive as I watched. He crawled around the perimeter of the sink, not scrabbling hysterically as he had in the bag. If not actually pleased with his temporary quarters in our kitchen sink, he seemed, at least, resigned to it. I felt the first stirrings of something like actual guilt for having taken him home with me. I shuddered to imagine the height from which he must have fallen to have landed on the floor of the bus.

I knew fear. I'd known it for three weeks. I could only imagine what Manitou had felt when he fell from John Prince's hand.

Inside the sink, the turtle circled the perimeter of the porcelain, pausing where the water had puddled, as though he was confused by its presence in a world gone so completely alien in every other way.

I said, "Dad, do you think he'll be okay?"

"What do you mean, son?"

"I mean . . . do you think he'll be okay living here with us? Do you think he's happy?"

My father regarded me thoughtfully. "Jamie, let me ask you a question," he said. "Did you think about any of this when you brought him home? I mean, I know he's beautiful, and I know you wanted to have him as a pet. But did you ask yourself about any of that when you reached for him this morning?"

I thought about it, then shook my head. "No, I guess not."

My father paused. When he spoke again, his tone was gentle but serious. "Well then, son," he said, "it's pretty simple: you made a choice that has impacted this creature's life. You brought him home with you. You took him out of his world and into yours. Now you're responsible for him. Actions have consequences. Your mother was right about that part, even if the way she said it wasn't quite the way she meant it to sound. It's up to you to take care of him now. Do you understand what I'm saying, Jamie?"

"Yes, Dad. I understand." I did, too. What had seemed like a great idea this morning in the swamp now seemed to be a portentous responsibility.

"Jamie?"

"Yes, Dad?"

"I want you to know something." He took my chin in his hand and squeezed it very gently. "I know Camp Manitou was hard for you."

"Dad, it—"

"Jamie, listen to me, I know what it was like. I've been to camp. I saw it in your eyes on Parents' Day when we had that talk. I recognized that look. I know you were putting on a brave face for me, and I know why you were doing it, too. I know you wanted your mother and I to be proud of you. Well, we *are* proud. I just wanted you to know that. That's one of the reasons why I thought you should keep Manitou. You showed me that you could be responsible this summer, and I'm going to trust you now."

My eyes filled with tears, but I was smiling for the first time since I could remember. "Thanks, Dad. I love you."

"I love you, too, sport." His own eyes were slick when he ruffled my hair. "Good," he said. "Now then let's go find that old terrarium of mine. Nobody should have to live in a paper bag as long as Manitou did this afternoon. Or our kitchen sink, either."

Dinner that night was a humourless affair, though less tense than the car ride had been.

After my father and I had set up the terrarium, and filled it with water that would need to be changed daily until we were able to install a filtration system—as well as moss and small gravel rocks for him to rest on—we put Manitou inside.

"I think that'll do it," my father said. "Now I think we need to take a ride to the pet store and pick up some turtle pellets. Then maybe we should stop at the library and check out some books on turtle care so you'll know how to take care of him properly."

At the pet store, my father found a paperback book on the care of reptiles and amphibians. I found one specifically on the care of turtles. My father shrugged his shoulders and bought them both. In the car afterwards, my father and I didn't say much to each other, but that didn't mean we weren't communicating.

When I think back today, that ride home from the pet store was one of the happiest moments of my childhood, full of promise. In retrospect, the wonder of that moment made everything that was to come later all the more cruel.

When we got home, my mother had come out of the bedroom and was cooking dinner. Without turning, she said, "Dinner in fifteen minutes, you two. And wash your hands, for heaven's sake. I know you've been handling that filthy thing."

My mother clearly still resented her edict about the turtle having been overridden by my father, but she was less angry than she had been in the car. Sustaining that level of ire over a long period of time wasn't impossible for her, but it drained her in the same way that leaving a battery outside in sub-zero temperatures would drain its energy. In order to conserve the status quo, my mother must have realized she would have to dial her anger down.

Not for the first time, I looked between my father and my mother at the dining table and wondered why they had ever married in the first place, since she clearly didn't really seem to even like him and he seemed to put up with her out of a sense of loyalty to something other than his love for her.

But in those days, in the early 1970s, divorce was something shameful that "other" people did, the sort of "other" people that people like my family and I had only heard of, but didn't really know. A boy in my class at Buena Vista Public School, Tommy Marx, had divorced parents, a distinction he wore like an affronting port-wine stain birthmark. To the rest of us, Tommy never seemed completely *clean*.

The wife was usually to blame, in popular divorce lore. Even if the husband was the cause of it, it was because of her deficiency in performing her role as a wife and mother. And she passed along her disgrace to her children by alchemical transmutation.

While I had on occasion overheard my mother and her friends refer to divorced men as "cads," or "bounders," whenever the topic of a divorced woman came up, their mouths would set in obdurate lines, their eyes managing to communicate both pity and a kind of flinty resentment that one of their own sex would have let down the team so badly by falling so low. They used the term "broken home," which I found horribly vivid, picturing, as I did, an actual smashed house: shattered walls, jagged spikes of timber beams strewn as though from a great height, deadly shards of glass, rusty nails, everything pointed and lethal—all of it the woman's fault, a failure at the only thing that really mattered in a woman's life.

Still, when I pictured my parents divorcing—something I did with increasing frequency as time went on—I imagined a world composed of my father and me alone, a world which was, if not always joyful, at least always even-tempered and full of simmering love and acceptance. For that, I would have gladly worn the port-wine stain of being the child of a broken home. In those fantasies, my mother was always living somewhere else and my father and I formed a universe of two.

"Mom, is it okay if Hank comes over after dinner so I can introduce her to Manitou?"

It seemed politic to ask permission from my mother rather than my father this time. Even though there was always a better chance of her saying no, I'd been the recipient of enough bounty from my father today that she would forbid me almost anything at this point, just on principle. I waited, resigned to that outcome.

To my surprise, she said, "Yes, Jamie, that would be fine. But she can't stay too late. It's been a long day for you, and for your father and I because of you. And please don't make too much noise. I have a headache. You can play in your room. Do we understand each other, young man?"

"Thanks, Mom." I began to push my chair back in preparation to leave the table. "May I be excused?"

My mother sighed deeply and theatrically, and reached for the pack of cigarettes and the lighter she always kept on the buffet table. She smiled wanly. "You didn't even finish your dinner, Jamie. I can see how glad you are to see me, and how glad you are that I put in all that work to make your favourite dinner to welcome you back home. Oh well, I should be used to that by now. No one in this house appreciates what I do."

Two years before, when I was seven, my mother complained about all the work she did for my father and me, and how no one appreciated the sacrifices she'd endured for our benefit. I'd made the mistake of suggesting to her that if she didn't like housework, she could get a job and hire someone else to do the cooking and cleaning.

I'd thought it was a brilliant idea: in my mind I pictured something glamorous, like being a secretary, or working as a reporter for a newspaper, like Brenda Starr did in the comic strips that came to the house every Saturday in the *Citizen*. I expected a beatific smile and an enthusiastic hug in appreciation for my ingenuity in solving her problem for her. What I'd gotten instead was a spanking, and I was sent to bed without any dinner.

I looked down at the half-eaten plate of spaghetti, the sauce for which I knew she prepared in bulk, then stored in the deep freeze. I also knew there were frozen strawberries from the supermarket in the fridge for dessert. "Mom, it was *so good*!" I said it with as much enthusiasm and sincerity as I could muster. "Thanks! That was the best dinner I've had in weeks! The food at Camp Manitou was—"

She cut me off sharply, moving her hands in a brushing-away motion as though she were shooing away an overly familiar dog. "Go on, Jamie, go call your friend Lucinda. Make sure it's okay with her mother she comes over. And remember what I told you about noise." She looked meaningfully at my father, who stared at some point in the middle-distance but said nothing. "Your father and I have things to talk about."

Hank tapped on the glass wall of the terrarium. "What's he doing in there? He's not even moving." She was about to tap again, but I reached out and took her hand.

"Don't do that," I said. "You'll scare him. Just let him get used to his new home. The book says they need time to acclimatize." I pointed to the paperback on my dresser: *So You're a Turtle Owner Now! How to Take Care of Your Newest Family Member!* On the cover were two blond children; the boy crew cut and ruddy-cheeked, the girl blue-eyed and pigtailed. They were both smiling at a pet painted turtle that looked sicklier, greener, and less vivid than Manitou. It was sunning itself on a rock in their backyard.

Hank frowned. "Acclima-what?"

"Acclimatize. It means 'get used to.' He needs to get used to his new home." I had told Hank the entire story of how Manitou had come to live with me and she was impressed. "He's had a rough day, so I want him to calm down."

"Calm *down*?" Hank looked doubtful. "He's not moving at all in there. He's calm all right. Are you sure he's even alive?"

"Of *course* he's alive." I tried to sound scornful, but I still reached in to the tank with my finger and gave him a little nudge. He moved a few more paces, then stopped, head retracting back into his shell. Manitou had clearly had enough of everyone, including me. "See? He's moving just fine. Geeze, Hank."

"You're lucky," she said. "I wish I had a turtle. When our cat died, my mom said no more animals, period. Me, I'd love a turtle. Or a snake."

"A snake would be cool," I admitted. "But not as cool as this turtle. Maybe if you grew your hair long, your mom would let you get a snake."

"I'd rather eat *worms* than grow my hair long."

"You're right, Hank," I said loyally. "You wouldn't even look like you anymore."

"Hey, do you want to take him to the greenbelt tomorrow afternoon? We could see if he wants to play down by the creek. It would be just like home for him. Bet he'd like that a lot."

"Sure," I said. "But my dad and I are going to build him an outdoor terrarium tomorrow afternoon. We're going to put chicken wire around the sides and the top so he can sun himself outside during the day until it starts getting really cold."

"Yeah, well. Aren't you afraid someone will steal him out there?"

"Who would steal a turtle?"

"I dunno," Hank admitted. "Maybe no one. Probably no one. You're right. You guys have a fence anyway, right?"

"Yeah, that's right." I looked out the window. The sun was going down behind our house. Long shadows reached across the lawn from the edge of the property where the low slats of the redwood fence around the yard were planted. Since Manitou was my first pet, I had never given any thought whatsoever to the notion of a fence as anything except something to keep *me* in the yard. It looked high to me, but who knew? I loved Hank, but I resented her just then for putting that fear in me. "It's pretty high, too."

"You're right," she said again. "Anyway, I gotta get home. I'll meet you in the greenbelt." She wiggled her fingers at the terrarium. Hank was a good friend—I'd asked her not to tap on the walls of Manitou's new home and she'd listened to me. "Bye, Manitou." Hank saluted the turtle. "See you tomorrow."

After Hank left, I felt very tired. My mother had been right—it had been a very, very long day, and it was catching up with me now.

When I'd taken a shower, put on the clean pyjamas my mother had tucked under my pillow, and said goodnight to my parents, I went back downstairs to my room. Before I closed the door, I waited a moment till I was sure my parents were engrossed in their reading—the *Citizen* for my father, my mother flipping through *Family Circle*.

When I was sure they wouldn't come downstairs, I closed the door and turned off my bedside lamp. The only illumination in the room now trickled in weakly through the cedar hedges bordering our yard and the neighbour's from the pole-mounted floodlights around his aboveground swimming pool.

I took off my clothes and sat naked on the bed cross-legged. I stared into the vertical mirror on my wall. In the light of the candle I'd placed on my night table, the image in the mirror was shadow-shaped and ambiguous of gender. I bowed my head as though in prayer, then closed my eyes and whispered: "Come on out, Amanda. Come and talk to me. It's me, Jamie. I'm home."

I felt rather than heard the sigh, and I sensed rather than felt the movement in the air. When I opened my eyes again, I saw my own face in the shadows of the mirror. But it wasn't *really* my face. It *looked* like my face—the same nose, the same mouth, the same prepubescent brow-ridge, and the same pale skin, tanned now from three weeks outdoors at Camp Manitou. It was my face the way an artist of incomparable genius might have replicated it on canvas. The same dark hair as mine, though there was admittedly a suggestion of moving shadows behind the head, as though it were longer hair, a girl's hair.

Yes, *the* head, not *my* head, for by now who, or what, was looking back at me through the glass wasn't me anymore. The eyes were my eyes, but not my eyes.

I felt my lips form the words Amanda spoke in the mirror using my voice. I felt my larynx move, but it was her voice I heard.

Jamie, I missed you. Why did you go away?

"I was at camp, Amanda," I replied. "I told you I had to go. I didn't want to. You know that."

You left me alone here. I was alone for three weeks.

"I hated it, Amanda. They put me in a cabin with five other boys. They were mean to me. They beat me up and made me cry every night. Once, they even put a dead animal in my bed. Why didn't you come to visit me?"

I heard genuine regret in my friend's voice. *No mirror.*

"Not in the cabin, no," I said. I hated the whiny sound of my own voice, but my pique didn't allow me to stop pressing. "But there were mirrors in the washroom. You could've come then. You could've come at night. But you didn't."

I don't live in those mirrors. I live in this one. I felt gentle pressure on my neck as my head turned towards the terrarium. *You brought home a turtle. Why did you do that?*

"I don't know." I shrugged my shoulders. "Everyone keeps asking me that. I guess I just wanted to. He's beautiful. I named him Manitou, after the camp. He's the only good thing that came out of me being there."

Do you like him better than you like me?

"Amanda, he's a turtle. You're my secret friend. Who do you think I like better?"

I don't know. Do you like Hank better than you like me? You talked to her tonight before you talked to me. Which one of us did you miss more?

"You, Amanda. Only you. Always you."

Good. You beat up that boy on the bus, didn't you?

"How did you know about that?"

My secret. Mine.

"No, really, Amanda, how did you know? Did you see it?" I remembered the sudden impression of clouds in the driver's rear-view mirror before I blacked out and came to, seconds later with John Prince's red hair in my fist and his blood spattered on my shirt. "Did you use the mirror over the driver's seat? Did you help me?"

My secret. You beat him up pretty badly. He deserved it.

"Amanda, tell me if that was you. It didn't feel like me. I never beat anyone up in my life. I really hurt him. I didn't want to beat him up; I just wanted him to give Manitou back to me. I didn't want what happened to happen. Tell me, please. Was it you? I won't be mad. Because you just got through telling me that you could only live in this mirror, in my bedroom."

My secret, she said again. A pause, then: *I could have killed him, you know.*

I was suddenly very cold in spite of the humid night and parents who didn't believe in air-conditioning. "What? What did you say?"

I said, 'You could have killed him, you know.'

"That's not what you said, Amanda."

Isn't it? What do you think I said?

"Why are you being like this? Why are you scaring me? We're friends, aren't we?"

Yes, we're friends. But you left me alone here. You're not a very good friend anymore, Jamie. I don't like to be alone. I'm always alone.

"It was only three weeks." My stomach contracted and I felt moisture gather under my arms. "And I told you I didn't want to go to the stupid camp. My parents made me go. It was horrible. I missed being home. I missed you, especially."

Liar. You're a liar, Jamie.

"Goodnight, Amanda. I'm going to blow out the candle and turn on the light now. I want you to leave. I want to go to sleep now. Goodnight, Amanda. Go away."

Don't turn on the light yet, Jamie. Let's play. Let's take your turtle out of the terrarium and play with him. It's dark. Your parents think you're asleep. They won't come down to your room. We can have some fun with him. No one will know.

This new hint of gleeful savagery in the voice terrified me. "I'm going to turn on the light now, Amanda."

Don't. I'm not ready to leave yet. You'll be sorry.

In the dark, I flailed for the switch to my bedside lamp. When the yellow light flooded my room, the only image in the mirror was my own: wild-eyed and pale, a terrified, naked nine-year-old boy whose chest rose and fell in rapid bursts.

I looked around my room, checking to see if anything had shifted or changed. Everything seemed in its place: the sheet and coverlet on my bed were still turned down, the window was still open just enough to admit whatever pathetic breeze might manage to navigate the humid night.

I hurried over to Manitou's terrarium on the table by the window, fearful of what I might find inside, or rather *not* find inside. But Manitou was there, exactly as he was supposed to be, apparently asleep beside the smooth rock we'd brought home from the creek at the greenbelt, thinking it might make him less homesick for the paradise I'd stolen from him.

Impulsively I tore the sheet off my bed and thumbtacked it to the wall over the mirror, covering it. If my mother noticed this at all over the next week (and she must have) she never let on. Since my return from Camp Manitou, her attitude toward me had grown increasingly distant, as though we had decided by mutual consent to stay out of each other's way.

This suited my purposes perfectly. The mirror stayed safely hidden behind the sheet and no one asked me what I was up to, or what I was trying to not see when I looked into it.

In the days following my return from camp, my father had built a custom outdoor pen for Manitou. It was a work of art—basically a larger version of the best terrarium available, complete with a vegetated freshwater pool for him to swim in. The base was padded with moss and bark and grasses, and it was surrounded by strong enough chicken wire to keep predators at bay. In any case, our yard was fenced and we never even had cats roaming the neighbourhood, at least during the day.

The turtle took to it immediately, which delighted my father and me. We wanted him to enjoy the fresh air and warm sun as long as possible until fall and winter set in and we had to bring him back inside. It became my routine to take him outside to the pen at midmorning. I'd make sure the water was fresh, feed him, and leave him there. When I was home, I would check on him every hour or so. When I was away, I'd check him first thing when I came back.

My initial guilt at bringing him home had somewhat abated as we settled into the days and nights together. I never ceased to marvel at how exquisitely beautiful he was with the jewel-toned colouring of his body and the gold streaks veining his neck and head. I was already imagining bringing him for show and tell when school started again in a few weeks.

The day Manitou disappeared, Hank and I had been reading comic books in her basement for most of the afternoon. She had the biggest stack of horror comics in the entire neighbourhood, and when we read them together, we lost ourselves in them.

At four-fifteen, I knew it was time to go home. My mother had told me in no uncertain terms that morning that we were having dinner at five p.m. sharp, because she and my father were going out that night to a party given by someone from his office and she wanted to make sure she had enough time to "dress to the nines."

"Don't you be the reason we're late, young man," my mother had warned me that morning at breakfast. "I'm not kidding. I want you home from Lucinda's by four-thirty so you can do some chores and set the table. Do we understand each other?"

I'd assured her we did, and that had been that.

At four-thirty, I came around the side of the house along the flagstone pathway that led to the backyard and stopped short. The gate was unlatched and stood wide open. I *knew* I had latched it shut and secured it with the circle of wire we used around the handle like a makeshift lock. I vividly remembered that I had done so.

Or had I? With my heart in my mouth, I stepped into the yard.

Manitou's pen was in shambles. The chicken wire had been torn apart and lay littered in jagged shreds all over the yard. Bits of wet moss and vegetation had been flung all around the tangled wreck and all the water had drained into the grass. Hoping that by some miracle I would find Manitou either in the wreckage itself or on the grass nearby, I dropped to the ground and searched. I scoured the length and breadth of the yard; I looked in every one of my mother's flowerbeds, under every plant, all to no avail. There were tears running down my cheeks, blurring my vision, before I even realized I was sobbing. But even with that, it was obvious that the turtle was nowhere in our backyard.

Inside the house, my mother had surprised me with a sudden show of tenderness by holding me close while I cried. There were none of the expected lectures from her about my irresponsibility with regard to the gate. For his part, my father sat me down and told me there was an excellent chance that Manitou had escaped whatever had happened.

"Then where *is* he?" I said, weeping. "I couldn't find him *anywhere* in the yard! Not *anywhere!* If he's safe, why can't I find him?"

"*Think*, Jamie," my father said encouragingly. "Where would he go? He'd go down to the creek in the greenbelt. That's the place that's most like his home. That's where he'd go. That's where you need to think of him being right now."

I turned my tear-stained face to him. "Then let's go look for him. If he's there, we should be able to find him and bring him home where he'll be safe. Please, Daddy, can we go down to the creek and see?"

He looked over my head at my mother. I didn't see what passed between them, but my father sighed and gently squeezed my shoulder.

"Sure we can, Jamie. You know your mother and I have to go out tonight, but let's go down to the creek now, before we have to get dressed, and look for Manitou. But remember something, Jamie," he said. "If we don't find him down there, that doesn't mean he's not there. It just means he's found somewhere new to live, probably with others like him—a place that reminds him of his home. We all want to be at home, don't we? Even turtles. Do you understand?"

WILD FELL

"Yes, Daddy," I said. "I understand." Then I started to cry again.

My father spent an hour with me at the creek looking for Manitou. He got down on his hands and knees with me and looked under rocks and ferns. Even when it started to rain, he kept looking, only taking my hand and telling me it was time to go back to the house when the rain began to sluice down to a degree that made it impossible to keep searching because we could no longer see. Then, hand in hand, we ducked our heads and ran back to the house as lightning flashed in the roiling sky overhead.

Today, of course, I know my father had gone through the charade of looking for Manitou with me out of his love for me, for my peace of mind, because he understood my guilt about having taken the turtle out of its natural world only to meet such a brutal fate in ours. He knew we wouldn't find Manitou, but he'd managed to convince me that we *might*, for at least one night sparing me the heartbreak of the truth.

That night, I was in bed before the babysitter arrived. I hadn't wanted supper, and my mother, again surprisingly, hadn't tried to make me eat something. She'd let me go directly to bed. I'd stayed there until my parents came downstairs to kiss me goodnight before they left for the party.

My mother said, "It'll all feel better in the morning, Jamie, you'll see." She kissed my cheek and switched off the light. The scent of her perfume hung in the darkness after she'd left. I found it oddly comforting that night.

The rain pounded against the roof of the house and ran down the windows in vertical rivers. A sudden flash of lightning from outside lit up the room like daylight. The empty terrarium on the table by the window was like a reproach, but it also comforted me to see it there, to imagine the beautiful little creature whose short life had been entrusted into my hands against its will.

With my cheek lying against the soaking wet pillowcase, I eventually fell into a fitful sleep.

What woke me was the insistent pressure of my bladder.

The room was dark and silent except for the sound of the rain, which continued unabated. I pushed aside the covers and tiptoed past the covered mirror and opened my bedroom door. There was a light on upstairs and I heard the muffled sound of the television through the doors of my father's den. I assumed the babysitter was up there watching it. Opening the door to the basement, where my bathroom was located, I hurried down the stairs. Once there, I relieved myself, remembering to flush the toilet and lower the seat when I was done. I switched off the light and turned to head back up the short flight of steps to my floor.

On the stairs back up to my room, I suddenly stopped and stood completely still. I had not turned on my bedside light when I'd gone downstairs, but there was now a wavering yellow glow coming from inside my room. I blinked rapidly, and then squeezed my eyes shut. But when I opened them again, that quivering light still flickered.

Taking the remaining steps to the landing, I paused in the doorway of my bedroom and peered inside.

Beside my bed was the candle I'd hidden away from my mother's prying eyes under my bed—*Amanda's* candle. Someone had lit it. I smelled the dead plume of waxy candlewick smoke in the air. The sheet I had carefully tacked to the wall to cover the mirror had been torn away. It lay bunched on the floor. In the refraction from the candlelight in the mirror, I saw the dull glint of the two tacks on the rug.

My first thought was that the babysitter was playing some sort of a trick, but almost before the thought was fully formed, I knew otherwise. The babysitter was upstairs, entirely oblivious to what was occurring just under the room where she sat watching television. I heard the loud theme music of some western or other, and the sound of gunshots coming from the television set. No, I knew who had lit the candle and I knew to what purpose.

This had been the inevitable outcome all along. I knew beyond any shadow of a doubt that if I tried to run upstairs to the light and security of the sane, adult world of babysitters and television and light, a world of concrete, impermeable borders, something horrible would happen—either to stop me from reaching that world, or in punishment for reaching it.

I sat down on the edge of my bed and looked into the glass.

"Amanda, come out. I know you lit the candle. I don't know how, but it was you. Come out. Please? I'm sorry about before, but you scared me. Please, let's make peace."

I begged you not to leave me alone, Jamie. I told you you'd be sorry if you did.

"Amanda, did you hurt Manitou? Are you the one who opened the gate?"

No. But maybe you really did leave it open. You know how you get when you're gathering wool, Jamie. You're a dreamer, aren't you?

"I did *so* lock the gate! I did. It was *you!* You did it! You killed Manitou by opening the gate!"

Are you sure? How could I have done that?

"You made the wasps come and they stung Terry Dodd. You made me beat up Prince! You can light candles when you want to! I know it was you!"

Are you sure?

"I didn't do anything! My dad told me Manitou is in the greenbelt. He got away and now he's living with the other turtles down there in the creek!"

Your father is a liar, Jamie. Manitou isn't in the greenbelt. Do you want to see what really happened to your precious turtle? I can show you.

I whimpered, "My dad said . . ."

Touch the glass, Jamie.

Torn between my fear and a growing, dreadful fascination, I reached out and placed the tips of my fingers against the mirror.

When I was three years old, I apparently cut an electrical cord with a pair of metal scissors. My mother told me the force of the electrical jolt threw me across the room and knocked me unconscious. The doctors said it was a miracle I hadn't been killed. The steel blades of the scissors were melted away where they had wrapped themselves around the live wire. I didn't remember it happening, but my mother had saved the scissors as a sort of souvenir. She'd shown me where the steel had dissolved in the crackling electricity.

Had I remembered the event, I likely would recall it as having been like what happened when I touched the mirror. The current that threw me back on the bed wasn't electrical but illusory.

The mirror rippled and shimmered, then my room was flooded with warm afternoon light and the smell of fresh-cut grass.

I was standing in the backyard between the two Dutch elm trees at the farthest edge of the property, near the fence. The back door opened and my mother came out of the house carrying a small clear plastic bag of raw meat. I waved to her but she didn't seem to see me. As I watched, my mother opened the back gate and dropped a piece of the meat on the flagstones, then clapped her hands. Moments later, a large black dog padded into the yard. I recognized the dog at once: it belonged to a family that lived two streets over. It occasionally broke out of its fenced-in backyard and was known to be aggressive. A muzzle order had been imposed on the family by the city after it had attacked a smaller dog in the greenbelt the previous summer, but it was known to escape and roam. And here was my mother, feeding it. She continued to back into the yard, beckoning the dog with her hands. The dog, smelling the meat, followed her, cautiously at first, then with increased confidence. She hand-fed the dog another piece of meat.

Then, when she was standing next to Manitou's pen, my mother dumped the remainder of the meat into the pool of water where my turtle was bathing.

The dog attacked the chicken wire in a fury of teeth and claws, pulling it apart as though it were made of wet leaves. Driven by the scent of cooked flesh, it pushed its nose through the wire until it located the pieces of meat my mother had dropped, then devoured them.

The turtle's terrified scrambling movements as it tried to get out of the dog's way caught the animal's attention. The dog picked Manitou up between owerful jaws and shattered his shell. Flesh, bone and carapace pulped together with a horrible cracking sound, oozing between the dog's teeth and out the side of its mouth as it chewed. As pieces of Manitou's body dropped from its jaws to the grass, the dog leaned down and snatched them up, seeming to swallow them without even chewing.

When there was nothing left of my turtle to devour, the dog licked its lips and wagged its tail at my mother as though begging for more meat.

"Shoo!" my mother said, swatting it on its hindquarters. "Go on, get out of here! Shoo! Shoo! Go away! *Git!*" Startled, the dog backed away from my mother, then turned tail and cantered out of the yard. It looked back once, reproachfully, but she just made a sweeping motion with her arms and hissed, "Shoo! Shoo!" she said again. This time, the dog tucked its tail between its legs and bolted out of the yard.

My mother walked over to the gate and made to close it, but appeared to change her mind. It remained open. She looked back over at the ruins of Manitou's outdoor pen and smiled, a trifle grimly but with no visible remorse. My mother wiped her hands on her apron. Flecks of greasy steak came away on the white starched cotton. Then she went back into the house and shut the back door, the screen door banging behind her.

Your mother killed Manitou, Jamie. Now you know.

I tried to see Amanda's dim shape in the candlelit glass, but my head pulsed with soaring agony, and black stars exploded every time I tried to focus. "That's not what happened! My mother didn't kill Manitou! You're making me see that! That's not what happened! That's not real!"

Are you sure, Jamie? You know your mother hates you, don't you? And she hates your father. I think we should punish her for killing Manitou. I think it would hurt terribly to get eaten alive by a dog, don't you?

In that moment, for the first time since she appeared to me, I was aware that Amanda didn't sound like a little girl at all. She never had, really. All this time she had fooled me, but now she sounded like a grownup woman pretending to be a little girl. I had never really known with whom I had been conversing. And without knowing how, I knew she could make me see things that weren't real. Or *were* they real?

I screamed at her, "What *are* you? Who *are* you?"

I told you. I'm just a little girl.

"No, you're *not* a little girl! You're not even *real!*"

Of course I am, Jamie. I am real. You know who I am. I know you recognize me. Look harder into the mirror and tell me what you see.

"Liar! Liar! *You* killed Manitou, not my mother! You hurt people by magic!

You're bad! You made the gate open and you made the dog come and eat Manitou! I want you to go away!"

Are you sure?

"Yes! Now go away!"

You know what I think, Jamie? I think we should hurt your mother next. And then, when we're finished with your mother, we should punish your father for lying to you about Manitou being in the creek with the other turtles. He's not, you know. The dog that ate him has already shit him out on somebody's lawn.

"GO AWAY, AMANDA!"

I reached for the bedside lamp and swung it as hard as I could against the mirror. The glass shattered with a silvery, wintery resonance that I heard in my brain as well as in my ears—one that I felt, as well. Underlying the cold din of breaking glass, I felt rather than heard the shriek of undulant, malignant rage. It thundered through me, as cold as I'd imagined the lake in my nightmare to be.

But before it did, I felt my larynx flex unbidden and my lips formed Amanda's words one last time before sound and time and memory evaporated into the air above my head and tattered away to nothing but the mirror frame and shattered glass.

I will always find you, Jamie.

When the babysitter rushed into my room, white-faced and in panic at the noise, she found me standing beside my bed holding my bedside lamp in my hand.

I didn't know what in the world it was doing there, or why my feet were bleeding, or how the floor was littered with broken shards of glass. I glanced dumbly at the mirror, then back at the lamp. She gently took the lamp from my hands and laid it on my nightstand.

"What happened, Jamie?"

"I don't know."

"Why did you break the mirror?"

"I don't know."

"Were you dreaming?"

I rubbed my eyes. "I don't know. I guess." My feet were beginning to hurt from the glass I'd stepped in. The sole of my left foot was bleeding. "I want my dad." Then I started to cry.

When I was forty, decades after my parents had divorced, the year my father was diagnosed with mid-stage Alzheimer's and had begun to visibly deteriorate—still three years away from the events at Wild Fell—he asked me if I remembered the boy who had stolen my bike in the summer of 1970, the one who had been attacked by a swarm of wasps the next day and who had succumbed to the venom from thousands of stings three days later, dying in agony at the age of twelve.

I'd stared at my father blankly and told him, *No, I don't remember anything like that happening that year, or ever.* And it was true: I had no such memory.

Privately I'd wondered, at the time, if the disease had already taken hold to the point that he was not only forgetting what had happened, but was also beginning to imagine things happening that never had. But of course I never said anything to him about those suspicions. I knew that what was coming for him was crueller than anything I could imagine in my worst nightmares, and I couldn't bring myself to add to his terror by verbalizing my own fears about the long, dark tunnel of loss into which he was descending, taking me with him, and away from him, at the same time.

As for the little girl in the mirror, I would have no memory of her for more than thirty years, until I bought the house called Wild Fell on Blackmore Island.

Chapter Two

NURSE JACKSON HELPS ME SAY GOODBYE TO MY FATHER

"We must have moths," Nurse Jackson said. "*Moths*, if you can believe it."

She frowned, as though the incidence of the moths might somehow be perceived as a denigration of her nursing abilities, or worse, the quality of her care for her patients, in this case, my father. Nurse Jackson—whose first name was Ardelia—touched my father's cardigan, fingering two small holes in the maroon cashmere sleeve. "Just *look* at his sweater. I never noticed this before." She laid a light hand on my father's arm and smiled with the beatitude I'd come to think of as her special gift, not just to her patients but also the universe. "Peter, what happened here? Your lovely sweater." She turned to me and said, "You bought this sweater for him, didn't you, Jamie? From Brooks Brothers. In New York."

I nodded, my throat suddenly full. My suitcases were stacked just outside the doorway to his room. Their presence struck me like a reproach. But if it was one, I was reproaching myself. I was the one leaving him here in this place where the scrupulous standards of cleanliness of which the MacNeil Institute was justifiably proud couldn't entirely eradicate the perpetual scent of sour urine and pre-made industrial hospital food. The rooms were painted in warm colours in a valiant attempt to offset the sense of loneliness and gloom that permeated the place.

"He told me once," she said kindly. "He said you gave it to him for Christmas."

"That's right, I did. Five years ago. Before . . . well, before this."

She nodded sympathetically, but not with excess sympathy. Ardelia Jackson believed in the value of living and loving in the present, as she never tired of telling relatives of her patients. She never proselytized, nor did she hector. But she was an adamant advocate for her patients. Nurse Jackson said she tried to see everything as a stage of life to be embraced. When I'd broken down in front of her once and wept openly for the loss of my father as I had known him, she reminded me that he was still in there and that he still felt—and needed—my love.

More than anything else, I needed to hear that, and, even more, believe it. When Ardelia Jackson said it, I believed it.

I pointed to the window, where three small white moths fluttered in the sunlight in front of the glass, obviously confused and trying to escape. "Aha! There are your culprits." I walked over to the window and made to kill them with my hands, but Nurse Jackson laid her hand on my arm to stop me. She reached out and unlatched the window and the moths fluttered out of the room, vanishing around the edge of the building into the morning sunlight.

"Jamie, your father would hate that. He's gentle about things like that. Even things like killing insects. He may not notice much most of the time, but he always seems to notice everything that has to do with any living thing. To him, they're all God's creatures. He told me that, too."

"He's always been like that," I said. "He's always been gentle. You've been good to him, Ardelia. I can't tell you how much that's meant to me."

She winked. "I'm not supposed to have favourite patients, but I can't help myself. Peter is special. He's a wonderful gentleman. He always reminds me of my dad. Dad was sweet like Peter is now."

Nurse Jackson had told me one evening that her own father had lost his battle with Alzheimer's when she was a still a little girl. It gave her an affinity, she said, for sons and daughters of fathers suffering from the disease. Her nursing career, which was as much a vocation as a career, was a direct result of watching her mother endure his loss.

My father stared opaquely out the window at the three moths still circling in quivering, mindless flight.

The world in which he now spent most of his days and nights seemed to at least be a peaceful one, for which I tried to be grateful, even if "gratitude" to the merciless illness that had taken us away from each other—not quickly, as death would, but in excruciating increments of days, weeks, and months—was a hard go.

It had been painful enough to watch my father's shame when he couldn't remember my name. Worse still when he didn't know me, even after I told him I was his son, Jamie. By the time my father was actively *afraid* of the bulky, forty-year-old man he didn't recognize as his son—the one who spoke softly to him with filial familiarity, caressed his hand, tried to hug him, called him *Dad*—I realized I'd had an authentic glimpse of hell. The insidious devils that ran the place bore no resemblance to anything Biblical. Their sadism was far too subtle for mere religious mythology. They'd damned my father by siphoning away the memory of his life, taking care that he'd been aware enough to know it, and they'd damned me by forcing me to watch it happen.

The best years of my childhood had been after he and my mother divorced.

I had been ten. Everyone tiptoed around me as though my mother leaving us was supposed to be the most devastating thing imaginable, but after three solid years of increasingly escalated arguments, it was really more of a blessing. Her indifference to me had hurt less than her anger at him, which seemed to come from everywhere and nowhere. On the rare occasions that my mother made me part of their marital psychodrama, it was as part of a rebuke to her husband.

"You *always* take his side," she seethed. "Like when he brought that stupid turtle home. But you didn't listen, and we know how *that* turned out. It's like you're married to him instead of me. Sometimes I think I should just go off and live by myself and let you two live your own lives together."

My father always protested, of course, but after a while it must have seemed like an excellent idea, likely to both of them. In 1972, she did just that, and left.

I said I wanted to live with my father. Since my mother didn't want me, for the sake of form or even spite, there was no fuss over custody. I simply stayed in our house with him and grew up there. At first, we were hesitant with each other, like two survivors of an explosion that had just levelled a city block; but in time, we both realized that our house was calm and quiet all of a sudden, the atmosphere detoxified and clear of the constant anticipation of hostility. Our spines relaxed, our jaws lost the tense set we hadn't realized they'd adopted. We kept waiting for all of that to change for the worse, even for mourning to set in, but it never did. Since my mother was the one who initiated the separation, I could only gauge its effect on my father as the one who had been "abandoned" (a word I picked up from listening to my mother and her friends talking about women who had been left by their husbands—a word I assumed must be similarly applicable to men who had been left by their wives).

When my mother announced that she was moving to Vancouver to stay with her family "for a little while, till I get things sorted out," I breathed a sigh of relief that it would likely be the end of the tense lunches and dinners in restaurants that had become our sole interaction on "her" day. I have no idea what she told her friends, but when neighbours and close friends of both my parents came over to check up on us (or, more accurately, me, the "abandoned" child), they were surprised to see me smiling and calm and happy in my father's company, and under his care.

I overheard an exchange between my father and Mrs. Alban one evening when she'd come over to drop off a cake she'd baked for us. It hadn't been my intention to eavesdrop, but when I heard my name, I paused on the stairs and crouched there, listening to what the adults were saying.

"Alice is a *gadder*, Peter. Some women are just like that," Mrs. Alban said. I heard her sigh. "You'll forgive me for speaking my mind. I don't mean to impugn Alice, and I've always been fond of you both, but some women aren't always made to be wives and mothers. I'm sure she gave it her best shot. How is Jamie doing?"

"I think he's doing fine, Mrs. Alban. I think he misses his mother, but the two of us are doing well. Alice loves him, and I think Jamie knows that. Divorce is never easy on anyone," he added diplomatically. "But we're going to be okay. Alice, too, I suspect."

"I don't mean to intrude in a way that's too personal," Mrs. Alban said, "but while it's unusual for the child to stay with the father rather than the mother, I think it's probably a very good idea in this case."

My father's voice sounded stiff and formal all of a sudden. I could tell that Mrs. Alban had crossed a line without being aware of it. "Thank you, Mrs. Alban," he said. "We think so, too."

And that was that.

For his part, my father felt it was his duty to present both sides of the story to me, lest I harbour any ill will toward my mother later in life. He had never spoken ill of her in my presence, even when it had become obvious that divorce was inevitable. That was the point at which he stopped making excuses for her and simply let her words and actions speak for themselves. That was as judgemental of my mother as he ever got in front of me.

"Jamie," he asked me one evening after she left, "are you angry at your mother?"

"No, Dad."

"Are you angry at me? It's okay if you are, you know. We can talk about it."

"No, Dad."

"You're probably too young to understand what happened between your mother and I, but even if we don't love each other the way we used to, we still love you. And that's the important thing. Do you know what I'm talking about?"

"I know, Dad. It's okay."

"Jamie, do you . . . do you, you know, want to see anybody about this?"

"Like who?"

"You know. Another grownup, maybe? Like a doctor?"

"No," I repeated. "I'm not sick. I'm really okay." And I really was okay, too. It was the last time my father suggested a psychiatrist.

Privately I *did* wonder if there was something wrong with me with regard to why I didn't miss my mother more. I asked Hank about it once right after my mother left. Hank's view was a pragmatic one, a pragmatism that belied the fact that she was only ten.

"It sucks that your mom left, Jamie," she said kindly. "But you know, your dad is nicer than your mom. And he loves you a lot. At least you get to stay with him. You'll get to do all kinds of cool stuff now, and never have to worry about your mom being mad at you for doing it. Also, I don't think she really liked me that much, so I'm not sad she's gone, either."

Still, I worried. "Do you think it's weird that I'm not really sad?"

She shrugged. "Nope. I think it's weirder that your mom wanted to leave you guys. You have a nice house, and your dad is a nice person. As for me, my mom is a pain in the you-know-what. I wish she'd leave, too. I wouldn't be sad if she did. Well, not *that* sad," she qualified. "At least I'd be able to keep my hair short and let the stupid holes in my stupid ears grow over and never have to wear these *stupid* earrings ever again. And nobody would ever call me 'Lucinda Jane' again. I *hate* being a girl."

"You're not a girl to me," I said loyally. "You're just Hank."

"Thanks, Jamie. You're not a boy to me, either. You're just . . ." She paused, thinking it over. "Well, just *you*."

"Thanks, Hank."

When I was thirteen, we left the Ottawa and moved to Toronto because my father got a better job. I missed Hank terribly. We wrote to each other every week and spoke on the phone sometimes late at night when the rates were low. Hank wasn't allowed to rack up long-distance charges so I always called her. My father understood the importance of our bond and encouraged it.

At fourteen, I experienced a growth spurt. My body filled out with new muscle, yielding unfamiliar strength. All traces of the willowy androgyny of my childhood vanished behind a wall of sinew in the space of a year, and I grew five inches, topping out at a solid six-one.

For the first time in my fourteen years, I was the physical superior of all the boys I knew. There was no more bullying from anyone, and there was something in its place: complete equanimity.

My new height and weight caught the attention of the various coaches at my high school. I was encouraged to try out for sports—hockey, football, even wrestling. I resisted at first, of course. None of the experiences I'd had with boys my own age up to then had inclined me toward trust, let alone affection.

But at the coaches' insistence, I tried out for all three. While I had no natural dexterity or ability in either hockey or football, neither the other boys on the team, nor the ones trying out seemed to find anything particularly unusual, let alone abuse-worthy, in my competing on their level. My new physicality seemed to be currency enough; they didn't seem to sense anything different about me the way the boys back home in Ottawa had when I was younger and frailer. If my new physical imposition was my camouflage, it was a perfect illusion. It had erased any traces of who or what I had been. This new Jamie Browning could go anywhere, and did. I finally settled on wrestling. The sport suited my new strength and I responded to the rigours of the training regimen. Best of all, the sport was the perfect conduit for any pent-up aggression I had accumulated over the years. Even if no one I wrestled had any idea who Jamie Browning had been prior to this transformation, they felt the full force of it when I had them pinned under me on the mat.

After graduating from university I became an English teacher at a private school outside of Toronto. I loved teaching and took to it with a naturalness that surprised everyone who knew me, except my father who told me that he'd always envisioned me as a teacher of some kind.

I married a young woman named Ame Millbrook, with whom I'd fallen in love my final year at the University of Toronto. She had beautiful shoulder-length red hair and skin like the inside of a peony petal.

Ame had moved into the Knox College residence after three years of living with two roommates in an apartment on Palmerston Avenue, not far from the university, in the Annex. She had broken up with her boyfriend that summer and had wanted to make a complete break from her previous life while she finished up her history studies. After she received her B.A., she planned to take a year off, she said, to travel.

I swam laps at Hart House every morning before breakfast, and Ame was an early riser so she could study, so we were both usually the first people at breakfast in the dining hall. Early morning small talk at breakfast eventually led to longer talks at lunch and dinner, which eventually led to me working up the courage to ask Ame Millbrook out on a date.

Over Chianti and *pasta puttanesca* at a cheap Italian restaurant near the campus, we each discovered that neither of us was very ready to trust when it came to relationships. Ame had been badly hurt after discovering that her boyfriend had been cheating on her for six months before they broke up. For my part, it appeared that my parents' divorce and my mother's departure had affected me more than I'd thought.

It struck me later as ironic that our very fragility on the topic was the common bond we shared, and that it proved to be the source of our courage to yield to the feelings we were each clearly developing for each other; love in the form of emotional *détente*.

The first night she was nude in my arms, I marvelled at the contrast of her slender whiteness against my own darker skin. Her delicacy against my bulk was shockingly erotic for both of us. In the darkness of the bedroom, I would wrap my arms around her back, cradling it, my back bowed, my weight on my elbows, my hands cupped her shoulder blades as I thrust, both of us slick with sweat. Making love to Ame was a sublime, sensual ritual *pas-de-deux*. I hadn't been a virgin when I met Ame, not by any stretch of the imagination, but somehow, with her, I felt more myself than I ever had.

When I was on top of her, feeling her body react to every movement, I felt somehow as though the act was more than just sex. If I'd believed in souls, I would have said I felt—in my soul—that I was securing the final lock on the door between my childhood and my manhood.

I had no idea why this should be so important to me, nor did I question it any more than I had questioned how this sense of closure was connected to the recurring dreams I'd had off and on since I was nine years old—dreams of a girl in an old-fashioned dress who seemed to grow *alongside* me into womanhood as I grew into young manhood. The girl appeared in different incarnations in different years, always roughly matching my own chronological age, always the same girl in a sequence of old-fashioned dresses and hairstyles, but *always* the same girl.

The night Ame and I got engaged was the last night I dreamed of this girl, now in every sense of the word a mysterious and beguiling young woman, even just in dreams.

In that last dream, she stood on some sort of rocky beach staring out across the water at a point in the distance. When the woman slowly turned her head away from whatever it was she was observing and met my eyes, I knew she recognized me. In the dream, she *knew* me. She smiled at me with a *knowing* that was somehow terrible.

I woke with a jolt, feeling as though I had fallen out of the sky onto the bed. The abrupt movement woke Ame. She murmured comforting words, then took me in her arms and held me until my heartbeat returned to a normal cadence and we both slept, with me dreamless at last.

Naturally, I'd asked Hank to be my best man. It was the right thing to do, and besides, I'd promised.

She'd come out as a very butch lesbian in her second year at Carleton University to no one's surprise, least of all mine.

Hank had called me in Toronto that year and asked if she could take the train up from Ottawa and stay over, because she had something important to tell me. In my dorm room at East House in Knox College, she'd told me that she was gay, and in love with a woman named Cosima, a journalism major. She told me that her life of trying to be what everyone had wanted her to be—a girl named Lucinda Jane—had almost killed her, literally as well as figuratively: she had seriously contemplated suicide when she was sixteen.

"I had the razor blades in the bottom of my sweater drawer. I kept them there, secret. No one knew. Men's razors," she said with a hint of something like pride, or contempt. It was hard to tell which. "Not those fucking pink *lady* razors."

I was horrified. "Why didn't you tell me, Hank? Jesus. All those times we spoke on the phone long-distance. You could have told me. I would have been on the next bus . . ." I trailed off, unable to contemplate what her suicide would have meant. A world without Hank in it was literally incomprehensible to me. "Why? How could you keep something like that to yourself?"

She sighed. "I couldn't, Jamie. I couldn't admit what I was feeling, not even to myself. Telling you would have just made it real, and I wasn't ready for any of it to be real."

Hank confessed that she had finally come to terms with the fact that, in an effort to please everyone else, she hadn't succeeded in pleasing anyone, least of all herself. Her earnestness had moved me, but the news couldn't have been less of a surprise, or less relevant to our friendship, and I told her just that as I held her tight.

Later, as we lay on the floor head to head, very drunk on Jägermeister, staring up at the swirling ceiling of my dorm room, she said she had something to tell me.

"What, Hank?"

"I fucking love you, Jamie." *I fuggen lovezu*

"Me, too, Hank. I love you, too."

"I wish you were my brother."

"I wish you were *my* brother." I started to giggle. "No, I mean, I wish you were my *sister*."

"Not me," she said with drunken solemnity. "I don't want to be anyone's sister. I wish I was your brother, too."

"You are, Hank." Buffeted on the waves of Jäger, it made sense. "You are my brother. Tell you what—if I ever get married, you can be my best man, okay?"

"You getting *married*? To *who*? Why didn't you tell me?"

Now we were both giggling. "No," I said, nearly choking. "I'm not getting married. But . . . *when*."

"And you want me to be your best man? Wow."

The ceiling continued to spin. "Yup. I do."

Hank paused, then reached for my hand, squeezing it tightly. "*Bro*," she said.

The next morning, we weren't sure which of us had passed out first, but we realized two things through the haze of agony: We each had the worst hangovers of our lives. And neither of us could remember having been happier.

In the years since graduation, Hank, having eschewed law school, had become a very successful landscape gardener.

During her undergrad, she had spent her summers planting trees up north and working on outdoor landscaping crews in the city. In the process, she had discovered that she loved the work and, more importantly, that she had a natural affinity for the soil.

Before opening her own small firm in Ottawa, she had worked on various crews for other landscaping companies, first on summer vacations, then full-time upon graduation. She found that her communion with soil and seed was instinctive and unfailingly accurate. Her various employers noticed that she was a hard worker who put in long hours in the sun without complaining. They also noticed that she took an effortless leadership role with the crews, which were usually comprised of men, and that those men accepted her leadership just as effortlessly. Her supervisor, Sid, regularly slapped her on the back and joked that she was "just one of the guys" and "practically a man—and I mean that in a good way, so don't go gettin' all *militant dykey* on me now, eh?"

Hank always assured him she understood exactly what he meant, and laughed right along with him. Sid was still laughing right up until the moment Hank handed in her notice and quit to start her own competing landscaping business. She took two of the company's best workers on the crew with her and, in the process, snapped up a plum condominium maintenance contract her former employers had been too lazy to bother formally renewing with the condo board. Sid had been furious. He'd called her a thieving dyke and promised her he'd blackball her so she'd never get another landscaping job in the city as long as he had breath in his body.

"Do your worst, Sid," Hank said, saluting him as she walked out of the office for the last time. "You're practically a man. And I mean that in a good way."

Ame became less of a free spirit once we were actually engaged, and she wasn't remotely pleased at the idea of a lesbian best man standing next to her fiancé at the end of the aisle in church. When she told me her parents and their friends would be horrified at the idea of a lesbian in their daughter's wedding party, I suggested we elope or marry at City Hall, if she chose, or that her parents stay home. But if we were going to marry in a church, Hank would be my best man.

And so Hank *was* my best man. She was resplendent in a tuxedo that matched mine, her crew cut shining beneath a fresh coat of Brylcreem.

My mother, who flew in from Vancouver, with her second facelift and her third—very rich—husband, was the only person at the reception who called Hank "Lucinda Jane," which Cosima, who'd come as Hank's date, found hilarious.

Before ducking out of the reception, my mother kissed me on both cheeks and gave me a brittle hug.

"I haven't been much of a mother to you all these years, Jamie," my mother said. "I'm sorry about that. I've often regretted not being there. I didn't regret leaving, because I had to find myself. But I regret leaving you. I've always loved you, though, son. I hope you and Ame will be very happy together."

I didn't believe a word of it, but I reached out and kissed her cheek. She stiffened in my arms, but allowed me to kiss her nonetheless, performing the traditional ritual homage to the normal mother and son relationship we'd never had.

"Thank you, Mom," I said as sincerely as I could. "And thank you for coming. You, too, Stan," I added for my second stepfather's benefit. "It means a lot."

My mother, who had studiously avoided my father throughout the service, pressed an envelope into my hand. "A little something for the honeymoon," she said. "I know it's not much, but it made sense to give this to you rather than another silly wedding gift you're just going to throw away, anyway."

When I opened the envelope, it contained a cheque for ten thousand dollars. I briefly thought of tearing it up, but I knew it would be an empty gesture, and ten thousand dollars was ten thousand dollars. If I genuinely didn't bear my mother ill will for having left us, giving my father and me a chance at a happy life together—and I didn't—it seemed hypocritical to throw her gift back in her face.

Ame and I had two good years together before I realized I had ignored the signs that had manifested themselves after we'd gotten engaged, and that I'd married a woman very much like my mother.

We divorced, much more acrimoniously than my own parents. Unlike the departure of my mother, however, the departure of my wife shook me to the core. Through Ame I thought I'd caught a glimpse of what a real marriage could be like, and I discovered that I'd idealized it much more than I'd ever dreamed. And perhaps I *did* catch that glimpse of what it could be like, but you can't build a life together on a glimpse of anything so amorphous.

After my divorce, I moved back in with my father. He protested, of course, citing my youth and my new eligibility, urging me to "get back on that horse" and try again with a new girl.

"I feel guilty," my father confessed, a bit shamefaced. "I believe that your mother and I were a fearful example of marital bliss for you."

"It wasn't you, Dad," I said. "You were a great father to me. I couldn't have asked for a better example of how to be a husband."

"For all the good it did me," he said ruefully. "Look at me. I'm an old man with no wife." He laughed, but there wasn't a lot of regret in that laughter. "No wife, no life."

"Sometimes things just don't work out the way we want them to, Dad." I shrugged. "It happens. As far as I'm concerned, Mom threw away the best thing that ever happened to her. She was a gadder. I don't think she knew what she wanted."

"What did you say?" He sounded shocked, but then he laughed out loud. "Good *Lord*, Jameson. Where on earth did you hear that word?"

"Something I heard Mrs. Alban say one night when you and she were talking, when I was a kid. After Mom left. She said Mom was 'a gadder.' I didn't know what she meant at the time. At first I thought she said 'gander.' I thought that was funny. But you know, I think Mrs. Alban was right. Mom didn't leave you for another man, she left us because she didn't like herself very much and she thought that by leaving us, she could figure out why."

"I don't think she ever did," my father said. "Poor Alice."

"And by the way, you may not have a wife, but you *do* have a life. So don't say that. And you have a son who loves you more than anything."

"That I do," he said gently. "That I do, Jamie. And I'm so proud of you. But I still don't want you to move in with me. I'm far too old, and you've gotten far too bossy."

By the time I moved in with him in May of that year, I had been concerned for some time that things were not entirely right with my father.

It had started off with small things, him repeating himself in conversation with no subsequent memory of having just said what he'd said. At first, he thought I was teasing him when I told him I'd just responded to that very statement a few minutes earlier. When he realized I was genuinely startled, he rubbed his eyes and said, "Well, I guess I'm just getting old-timers."

We both laughed at that. For my part, my laughter was genuine, but my father's carried a trace of something that caused me to look twice. By the second or third time it happened, I was the only one laughing. My father's face had taken on a haunted aspect.

In the weeks and months that followed, my father's memory began to slip slowly, but with what I now realize had been inexorable, murderous determination.

Frequently he would ask me to speak more slowly, though I habitually spoke more slowly than he did. He became enraged at the sound of a radio, or a television, telling me that it was impossible for him to think with all the noise in the house. His confusion became constant, though he did his best to hide it from me. For a while, he managed to do so successfully. But then eventually it became impossible to hide. I begged him to see a doctor about it, but he was adamantly opposed to what he called "a lot of fuss over just getting old."

"This is *my house*," he shouted. "*This* is why I didn't want you to move in with me. I hate all the fussing!" Then, my father, whom I'd never heard swear a day in his life said, "It's one of the reasons I was so glad your *bitch* of a mother moved the *fuck* out of that bastard house in Ottawa. Fucking cold *bitch*."

I was shocked. "Dad?" I reached out to touch him, but he slapped my hand away. "Dad, you're not yourself. This isn't how you talk. This isn't the language you use. You need to see someone. You're scaring me."

"What? *WHAT*? What does everyone want from me? You and that bitch of a mother of yours! Pushy, pushy, *pushy!* Just leave me alone so I can get ready for work, damn you! I'm going to be late for the office. It's *late!*"

It was eleven at night. I stared at him with blank horror, then said the only words that came to mind: "Dad, you're retired. You don't have to get ready for work. Your work is done. And it's late at night." I pointed to the grandfather clock against the wall. "Look, Dad. It's eleven."

My father turned and left the room. I heard his bedroom door slam behind him. When I knocked fifteen minutes later, there was no answer. I pushed it open quietly, taking care not to startle him. My father had fallen asleep across his bed, fully clothed. Only when I pulled a blanket over him did I notice that he was wearing a nylon windbreaker next to his skin, underneath his button-down plaid Viyella sport shirt, and rubber snow galoshes on his feet. Careful not to wake him, I removed the galoshes and put them away in the hall closet.

We tiptoed around each other all the next day in a way we had not since my mother had walked out thirty-odd years before. That evening I was unable to bear the tension any longer and asked my father why he had been so quiet all day.

At first he denied that he had been unusually quiet. He denied it brusquely, but then with increased desperation. When he finally confessed to me that he was afraid to speak because he didn't trust his ability to use the right words to convey what he meant, he broke down and wept tears that sounded like they'd been cut out of his throat with an awl.

The next morning, we made an appointment with Dr. O'Neill, my father's longtime physician, for a full battery of tests. When the results came back, they were exactly what both of us dreaded: mid-stage, progressive Alzheimer's.

"Well," said my father. "Well. My God."

"This is treatable, though, Dr. O'Neill, isn't it?" I was desperate for him to tell me it was, even though everything I had already read on the topic had indicated it wasn't. I'd never wanted more to be wrong about something in my life. "What's the treatment? What do we do? How do we beat this?"

Dr. O'Neill looked pained. "Well, those are two questions, Jamie, I'm sorry to say. For treatment, I'm going to prescribe memantine hydrochloride— Ebixa, it's called. It's an NMDA receptor antagonist, which means it blocks some of the chemicals in the brain that trigger the symptoms of Alzheimer's. It'll help with the memory loss and the confusion. But it's a treatment, not a cure. It's important that you know that. We'll start with twenty milligrams a day—two doses of ten milligrams twice a day. He can take them with or without food, but they have to be swallowed. He can't chew them. It's very important that he swallow them."

My father muttered something under his breath.

"What did you say, Dad? I'm sorry, we didn't hear you."

My father spoke sharply this time. "I said, 'Stop talking about me as though I'm not here.' I'm an old man with an illness, not a child. I'm still your father, Jameson. I'm still an adult."

"I'm sorry, Peter, of course you're right," Dr. O'Neill said. "Please forgive me. That was very insensitive of us."

"Don't condescend to me, either, Dr. O'Neill. Please. I sincerely mean no disrespect, but this is something I'm facing. I need to be spoken to clearly and honestly about it."

"Will the drugs . . . will they cure him?" I couldn't stop asking, even though the doctor had already said no. I wanted there do be a different answer. At that moment, I believed that by asking it again, perhaps there was one the doctor hadn't thought of. "I mean, will they cure my dad?"

Dr. O'Neill took a deep breath. "No, Jamie, they won't. Your father has expressed an understandable desire that I not sugarcoat this for either of you, so I won't. There is no cure for this particular disease. It can be managed with drugs, possibly for a long time. But after a certain point . . ." he trailed off. "Well, after a certain point your lives will be very different than they are now. There will be any number of options at that point. We can discuss them as the situation develops."

My father's laugh was a sharp, dry bark. "I think you mean *deteriorates*, Dr. O'Neill. You should have been an airline pilot, sir. I could easily picture you addressing the passengers of a perpendicular 747 about to crash nose-first into the Atlantic. 'Please listen for further announcements as the situation develops.'"

Dr. O'Neill smiled thinly, but with what appeared to be sincere sadness. He had been my father's doctor for ten extraordinarily healthy years. "I'm sorry, Peter," he said. "I wish there was a better prognosis. But staying as positive as possible is essential."

"I'll work on that, Dr. O'Neill," my father said dryly. "I promise I'll work at staying positive."

My father's downward progression was swift, likely swifter than any of the three of us expected it would be when we left the office that day.

He barely slept at night. Instead, he roamed the house, opening drawers and cupboards and upending the contents. After a while, I stopped turning on the burglar alarm because he set it off every night past midnight when he dropped cutlery and plates on the floor, convinced that it was morning, and I was fifteen years old, and he had to cook me breakfast before I went to wrestling practice.

He was also occasionally convinced that he and my mother were still married, and that we were all living in the old house in Ottawa, and it was still the early 1970s.

He furrowed his brow. "What was the name of that little girl you used to play with, Jamie? What was her name?" Before his illness, my father remembered every detail of my childhood with a sense of recall that was almost eidetic.

"You mean Hank, Dad? Are you talking about Hank?"

He thought about it. "No, that wasn't her name. That's a boy's name, anyway. It was something else. What was her name? You used to spend a lot of time together playing in your room. Come on, damn it. You remember."

"Well, her real name was Lucinda, but no one called her that except Mom. Well, and Hank's mother—she never called her Hank. She was my best friend, remember? She came to my wedding. She was my best man."

He mulled this over. "*Lucinda.*" He tasted the word, closing his eyes, trying to place it in some sort of recollective context. "No, that wasn't her name. I'm sure of it. Damn it. Some other girl."

"Maybe, Dad," I lied. "I had a lot of friends. You're probably thinking of someone else.

I kept a full schedule of classes as long as I possibly could; the house was paid for, I was working, and his savings paid enough for homecare several times a week, but even the rotating home assistance workers who came to help with my father finally admitted that yes, he needed to be watched more than even they and I could manage. But still, I resisted their suggestion of alternate living arrangements for my father.

That remained the case until the rainy Thursday night I got the call from the police telling me they had picked up my father, who had almost been killed wandering in traffic in his pajamas on the Leaside Bridge. When the police arrived, he was stumbling towards the lower railings of the bridge with its deadly forty-five-metre plunge.

The officers had been able to divert traffic long enough to safely rescue him, then calm him down enough to get him into the back of a cruiser. They had been able to identify him by the plastic identification bracelet I'd insisted he wear, one of the few battles regarding his care that he'd given in to with no blowback. The bracelet had his name, our address, and my cell phone number. I was almost hysterical on the telephone, but the female officer's voice at the other end seemed accustomed to dealing with hysterical relatives and soothing them. Mr. Browning was safe and at the station, she told me kindly. He'd said he was hungry, so they'd given him a sandwich—was that all right?

And he was asking that his daughter, Amanda, pick him up at the station and take him home.

When I arrived at the No. 53 Division police station, my father was docile but uncomprehending. He asked me who I was. When I told him, he said he didn't have a son, he had a daughter and her name was Amanda.

"He doesn't have a daughter," I explained to the two constables who had brought my father to the front desk so they could sign him out. "He lives with me. I'm his son. He has Alzheimer's. Aside from the actual disease symptoms, one of the side effects of the drugs he's on is hallucinations and sleep disturbance."

The younger of the two constables looked hard at me. "Who do you think he's asking for? He sounds pretty specific. Do you have a sister, maybe?"

"I'm an only child, officer. I don't have any sisters."

"Could he be asking about his nurses, maybe?"

"His nurses—pardon me, his *ex*-nurses, because I'm going to fire whichever one left him alone long enough for him to get out of the house, then didn't call me immediately—are named Beth-Anne and Florence. I don't know any

Amanda. *We* don't know any Amanda," I corrected. "*We* don't."

The older of the two police officers seemed to intuit the situation more clearly than his colleague, whether by professional or personal experience. He looked at me with a mixture of pity and resignation that led me to believe that he'd seen this before, maybe even up close.

"Mr. Browning," he said. "If you could just step over here and fill out these forms, we can release your dad back into your custody and you can take him home. Please take care of him. At his stage of the illness, he could hurt himself badly—even hurt other people. I don't know what he was doing on that bridge, but I do know that it's always been a magnet for suicides."

"My father would never kill himself," I said automatically. "He's not like that."

The monstrous enormity of that lie shamed me even as I verbalized it. Of *course* he'd kill himself. How many times since the diagnosis had my previously happy father wept in his despair and said he didn't want to wind up as some sort of raving vegetable, dependent on others for everything from feeding him to bathing him to helping him use the toilet? How many times had he slyly asked me (forgetting that he'd already the question a dozen times before) what would happen if the pills he was supposed to swallow were chewed instead?

But I still wasn't prepared to process the notion of my father trying to kill himself by jumping to his death.

"Either way" the officer said. "He's going to need better care, Mr. Browning. Much better than the care he has right now. He could have been killed tonight. I'm not faulting you, sir. This is one of the hardest things anyone has to go through—for both of you, really, in different ways. You only get one dad in this lifetime. Like I said, take care of him."

"I know that," I said. "Believe me, I know it."

I felt my father pluck the sleeve of my raincoat. He reached out and caressed the back of my head, the same way he'd done a thousand times when I was a little boy, under the covers in the dim glow of my nightlight.

"You've cut your hair, Amanda," he said dreamily. "You had the loveliest dark brown hair. Just like your mother."

"I'm *Jamie*, Daddy," I replied, fighting back tears. "I'm your *son*. You don't *have* a daughter. There's no *Amanda*. There never has been. Please, Daddy, stay with me just a little bit longer. Just at least until we can get home and I can call someone to help us. Please, please, please. Just a bit longer."

He sighed ruefully. "You should have waited for me on the bridge, Amanda," he said. "I saw you. I was almost all the way across the road. I was almost there."

That night marked the end of my father as I'd known him. When I got him home, I gave him his medicine and put him to bed. I pulled the blanket up to his chest and tucked it in so he'd be warm enough. He looked up at me from the pillow.

"Jamie," he said in an old man's tentative, tremulous voice. "Would you stay here with me for a little while? Just until I fall asleep? I'm so scared."

"Of course, Dad. Of course I will. Don't be scared. I'm here." I climbed onto the bed and lay down beside him. I put my arm around his shoulders and held him tenderly. In a very short time he was fast asleep in my arms, but I didn't sleep at all that night, even after I'd left his room and gone into the living room and opened the bottle of Canadian Club I'd been given back when Ame and I were still married, but had never touched.

The next day, I brought Dad to the MacNeil Institute, the best private residential facility for Alzheimer's patients in Toronto I could afford. Even today I remember how preternaturally, cruelly bright that sunlight in the parking lot was to my dry, red eyes and how much it stung as we laboriously made our way up the ramp to the front door.

When my father realized I was leaving him there, he cried and pleaded, telling me he didn't want to stay there; he wanted to go home with me.

Of all of the crucifying ordeals my father and I had endured together since his diagnosis, leaving him here, while he begged like a child for me not to abandon him, was first one I had grave doubts about my being able to survive.

And then, at the most desperate moment, like an angel of light, Nurse Ardelia Jackson appeared from behind the swinging doors leading to the locked ward corridor and came over to us.

Without saying anything to me, she linked my father's arm lightly in hers. "There now, Peter," she comfortingly. "What's all this fuss? Everything is fine. It'll be all right, you'll see. Come along now and take a walk with me. Jamie can come along in a bit. Let's get to know each other a little bit, shall we? There now. It's all right. We'll just stroll."

My father calmed at once. It was as though Nurse Jackson had drawn the terror from him like yarrow. As they walked away together down the corridor towards his new home, the place where he would spend the final stages of his life, my father turned back just once. "Jamie," he said. "You go on home, son. I'm going to walk for a bit."

Though my heart was utterly breaking, I still noted with joy that my father had called me *Jamie*, not any other name. He *knew* me again. How long he would know me, I wasn't sure.

But he knew me then, and I *knew* he was aware that he was saying goodbye.

That was three years ago. In the time between that day and today, my father slipped entirely into the hazy, oblique world of his illness.

I visited him at the MacNeil Institute every day, usually after classes, but occasionally also in the morning, before school started.

Then, late one black November night, my world changed once again.

I was driving home from school after staying behind to work with my student actors on the school's production of Arthur Miller's *The Crucible*. I had been teaching the play at the same time the students were acting in it. That afternoon in class, there had been a rousing discussion about small-town sexual hypocrisy and the roiling passions locked away beneath Salem's rigorous façade of pious New England propriety. As a teacher, I had been quietly proud to see that the passion I had been able to get out of my students that afternoon in class had carried through to that night's rehearsal.

It had been raining all day, an early-winter drizzle that began to freeze as evening fell. After sundown, the temperature had steadily dropped until the cold and wet turned the roads and highways slick and black and slippery as wet glass.

In my mind, I had been replaying the scene near the end of the play when Jeff Renwick, who was playing John Proctor, had delivered Proctor's wrenching soliloquy about losing the dignity of his name by confessing to witchcraft when so many of his friends had gone to the gallows rather than besmirch their own with a false confession.

"Because it is my name! Because I cannot have another in my life! Because I lie and sign myself to lies! Because I am not worth the dust on the feet of them that hang! How may I live without my name? I have given you my soul; leave me my name!"

When he had finished, I had tears in my eyes. And I was not the only one in the auditorium who did. The applause had begun slowly, but it reached a crescendo that echoed through the rehearsal auditorium and out into the corridor.

I was smiling at the memory and tapping my fingers on the steering wheel when my car was abruptly sideswiped by a drunken lawyer making an illegal left-hand turn. The impact sent me crashing into a guardrail, or so I was told later.

When I woke from the coma in traction three days later, the attending physician asked me if I knew who I was, or where I was.

My first words to him were, "Leave me my name."

I spent almost six months in hospital recovering from a variety of injuries, including a mild brain trauma that nonetheless left me unable to focus for long periods of time. This particular injury, of all the damage I sustained, effectively ended my teaching career.

On the upside, between the insurance and the money the lawyer's family paid me to avoid me suing them for everything they had, I found myself with more money than I'd ever seen in my life. Certainly it was enough to ensure my father's continued care at the MacNeil Institute. It was also enough money for me to fulfill a dream I'd cherished ever since my divorce: the dream of leaving the city and all its painful memories. I didn't want to be more than a half-day's drive from the MacNeil Institute as long as my father was alive, but as it now stood, I was marking time. I couldn't teach and I was too young for anything resembling a retirement.

So when I came across the advertisement in the *Globe & Mail* for the sale of a turn-of-the-century estate on a private island in Georgian Bay in excellent repair—suitable for a family or as an income property/guesthouse—for a price that was a virtual steal, I did something I'd never done in my entire dogmatically practical, safe, honourable life: I bought the house, sight unseen.

The very act of cutting the cheque felt almost pornographic in its decadence, but it was that very sense of abandon that allowed me to envision a life beyond the grim borders of the one in which I found myself. The point was, I had never done anything like that in my life, and I now could.

On the telephone, when I'd called to tell Hank that I'd bought the house, she'd asked me if perhaps its impulsive purchase was another symptom of the brain injury.

I'd laughed and replied, "No, it's a symptom of having enough money to afford to be able to make mistakes, even big ones. And buying this house—which has a name, by the way, "Wild Fell"—on a crazy impulse is the first fun I've had in years."

I told her about my plans to turn it into a guesthouse, which sounded more than ever like a lark when I related it over the telephone. Hank must have sensed something uncertain in my voice, because she waited till I was finished talking, then asked me the sort of to-the-point question in which she specialized.

"How're you doing, Jamie? Really, though. I don't want to hear bullshit from you. How're you feeling about all of this? Not in general, I mean, but right now, at this moment?"

"Right now, at this moment, I feel guilty, frankly," I told her. "But at the same time, I feel excited, which probably makes me feel even guiltier. I really feel like I needed some distance from everything—the divorce, Dad's diagnosis, the accident. Buying this house and thinking of turning it into a summer bed and breakfast, or guesthouse, might just be a very expensive pipe dream. But I wanted to forget about it all, at least for a while. Does that make sense to you? Do you think I'm crazy?"

Hank snorted. "I've spent a lifetime trying to forget that I was born a girl named Lucinda. What do *you* think? And yes, of course I understand what you're saying. And I agree with you. I've never seen anyone love his father as much as you love yours, Jamie. And it's not like you're leaving the country. You'll be three, maybe four hours away from him. That's nothing. If he needs you, or if you feel like you need to see him, we'll just get in the car and drive."

"Is it really that simple? That's sort of what Nurse Jackson has said, too."

"Yes, Jamie, it's really that simple."

"Then why do I feel sick inside about this?"

She laughed at that. "Because you *are* crazy, Jamie. Just not for the reasons you think you are." That voice with its rawboned, rational practicality could soothe and calm me like no other.

I asked Hank again, "*Do* you think I'm crazy? For buying Wild Fell?"

She paused. I pictured her rubbing her chin as she did when she pondered. "First off, no, I don't think you're remotely crazy. Buying it, especially sight-unseen, might not necessarily have been my first choice when you came into all that money. Me, I might have done some travelling—"

I interrupted her, a bit more brusquely than I might have wanted to. "You know why I can't leave the country."

"*As* I was saying," Hank said patiently. "Whatever I might have done, I'm not you. You took care of your responsibilities with it. You can't teach right now because of your injury, and you don't want to sit around. All of which is a very long and involved way of saying, no, I don't think you're crazy for buying . . . what's it called . . . ?"

"Wild Fell."

"What the hell kind of a name for a cottage is that? What does that even *mean*?"

"'Fell' has at least two meanings," I said. The faintly pompous, lecturing inflection that had become second nature to me after all those years of teaching embarrassed me. It sometimes manifested itself without warning, especially when I felt challenged, as I now did by Hank. "As an adjective, it means 'of terrible evil or ferocity.' But as a noun—which is how I believe it's used in this case—it refers to a hill, or a stretch of high moorland. Alexander Blackmore, the politician who bought the island and built the house in the early-1800s, came to Canada from Cornwall. Unlike most of the islands in the Georgian Bay region, which are flat, this one actually has a rise, like a cliff. It slopes, too. Mrs. Fowler the real estate agent in Alvina, the nearest town, told me was that Mr. Blackmore had been struck by the romantic notion that it reminded him of the moors of his childhood, except it was right in the middle of a Canadian lake. Hence, the 'wild' part. He named the island after himself, and named the house 'Wild Fell' in a sort of romanticized homage to his roots."

"All this fuss over a cottage," Hank mused.

"This is more than a cottage," I said. "You'll understand what I mean when you see it."

"*You* haven't seen it," Hank said dryly. "Did he live there alone?"

"Not from what I understand," I said. "He raised a family there. He had a wife and two children—a son and a daughter."

Hank seemed more curious now. "What happened to them? Who sold the house? Grandchildren? Great-grandchildren?"

"I don't know what happened to the Blackmore children," I said. "Mrs. Fowler didn't say. The house passed from the Blackmore family in Canada to cousins in England who apparently didn't want the bother of its upkeep, or the expense. According to Mrs. Fowler, no one has lived in it for over fifty years."

"Jesus, Jamie, are you kidding? Fifty years? The place is going to be a wreck! What were you thinking?"

"Yeah, I thought that, too," I said. "But they included a home inspection. The results were sort of a surprise."

"What do you mean?"

"I mean, the house doesn't seem to have aged."

She grunted. "Oh, bullshit. You've been totally had, Jamie. Thank God you can afford it."

"No, really," I insisted. "Some fire damage to the exterior of one of the wings, and the usual wear and tear. But other than that, it's in remarkable shape. I read the report, Hank. And for the price I paid for the houswould have been a fool not to buy it."

"'Remarkable shape,'" Hank mimicked. "Jesus. I hope Alvina has a decent hotel for you to stay in once you see this dilapidated wreck."

"You're a landscaper, Hank," I said. "If it's broken, you can fix it, right? You can do anything."

Now it was Hank's turn to sound professorial. "I landscape *outside*, Jamie," she said. "I make award-winning landscapes out of nothing. If you need a *garden* outside this albatross of a house of yours, I can probably do it. But fixing up an uninhabited wreck . . ." Hank trailed off. "Jesus Christ."

"Remember what you said," I teased her. "If it doesn't work out, I can just turn around and go home."

All that was left was for me to close up my dad's house, pack, and leave. I'd briefly thought of selling it, but it was paid up and I favoured the idea of having it to come home to when I visited.

First, though, I had to see him and ask his blessing on my departure, or his forgiveness, even if I knew he couldn't rightly give it. And yet, still, here I was in his room, my suitcases stacked in the hall, trying to say goodbye.

I knelt down next to my father's wheelchair and took his hand in mine. It felt as delicate and dry as a bird's claw. The skin seemed almost translucent, pale veins rising like frozen blue streams in the midst of snow.

"Dad, can you hear me? You know I'm here. I *know* you know." I leaned my cheek against his shoulder, feeling the soft red cashmere against my skin. Even in this awful place, with all its olfactory assaults, I still smelled the sweet scent of my father on the sweater. "Daddy? It's me, Jamie. It's your son. I'm going away for a little while. I'll be back soon to see you, I promise. I swear it. I'm going to go fix up a house. I'm going to turn it into a guesthouse. Maybe you can come and stay with me once it's done." I winced. I hated the sound of my own lie, and I hated how quickly it had come to me. It served to underscore how far away my father was, that I could say almost anything to him and not elicit a reaction.

At that exact moment, I missed the entirety of Peter Browning so much that I felt my heart would shatter from the sheer pressure of the loss.

My father remained silent, his eyes fixed on the window out of which the moths had once flown. In the soft light, he looked younger than his seventy-five years. The disease hadn't robbed him of the aspect of benevolence that was as germane to his face as the planes of skin and bone. While many of the patients at the MacNeil Institute habitually wore looks of confusion, or vacancy, or terror, my father had acquired the beatific patina of an ancient saint in a nineteenth-century Spanish fresco.

"Ah, Jesus," I said. "I feel guilty about leaving. Really, *really* guilty."

"I know you do," Nurse Jackson said. "I understand that. But you shouldn't. He'd want you to live. And you'll be back for regular visits. We'll stay in touch. I'll take good care of your Dad, I promise."

"Do you think he knows I'm going away?"

Nurse Jackson frowned at me. She had a remarkable frown, one that made me feel like I was a bad five-year-old who wasn't paying attention.

"Stop saying you're 'going away,' Jamie," she said crisply. "If you keep saying it, it'll become real to you, and you'll be as lost as your father, in your own way. You're not 'going away' from him. You bought a cottage on an island up north. Think of it *that* way. You're going to make it *into* something. You're not leaving home. You'll be back. Your home is right here, in your father's heart. You're moving to a different spot on that long thread connecting you."

"The house is pretty big to be a called a cottage." I wiped my eyes with the back of my hand, more grateful to her for her blessing in lieu of my father's than I trusted myself able to express. "A white elephant, more likely. I probably should have used the insurance money from my accident on something else. Probably too good to be true."

"Oh, pish-tosh." Nurse Jackson waved away my words with a flick of her plump, soft hands. "It'll be an adventure. If your father weren't there, he'd be in that car with you. Where is it again? The town, I mean? I used to have family up in County Grey."

"Alvina."

"Hmmm, don't know it. Not that that means anything. I never get away from here. Well, not nearly enough, anyway."

I leaned down and kissed my father's cheek. "Goodbye, Dad. I'll see you very soon. I promise. I'll come back to see you in a few weeks. I'll bring pictures of the house for you to see, after we've cleaned it up. It'll be so beautiful, you'll see. You'll be proud of me."

"He's already proud of you, Jamie," Nurse Jackson said. "You know he is. Now, you go and do your work. Life is for the living. It's what your dad would want—*does* want," she corrected herself. "*Does* want."

"Thank you, Ardelia." I handed her a piece of paper. "You already have my cell phone number. I'll have the phone with me. My email address will be the same, obviously. But in case anything happens, or if you can't get through, here's the number of the real estate agency in Alvina and their address. They'll be able to get in touch with me in case Dad . . . well, in case of any sort of emergency."

Impulsively, I reached for Nurse Jackson and kissed her on the cheek. Then I hugged her. When I stepped shyly away, she took both of my hands in hers, as gently as I had just taken my father's.

"You're a good man, Jamie Browning," she said tenderly. "You're a good boy. You're a good *son*. Your father is a lucky man. You just go on." She let go of one of my hands and reached for my father's. She held both of our hands, joining us through the medium of her warm presence. "We'll be fine."

"I'm the lucky one," I said thickly. "To have him. I always was. Goodbye, Ardelia, and thank you again. I'll be in touch as soon as I get settled."

I walked out of my father's room without turning back.

In the hallway, I picked up my suitcases, which seemed much heavier all of a sudden, and carried them down the long corridor to the locked door that would take me out to the foyer, pausing for a moment while the nurse on the other side of the door buzzed it open, unlocking it, then buzzed it closed again, locking my father's world behind me.

Chapter Three

THE ROAD TO WILD FELL

I drove north in my father's boxy Volvo station wagon along a winding sweep of highway that rose and fell as the city faded from sight, replaced by great stretches of highway bordered on either side by a thick green phalanx of spruce pine bracketing occasional glimpses of open fields and rolling farmland. Highway 400, connecting Toronto to Barrie in a two-hour stretch of uninspiring blacktop, abruptly became a wasteland of strip malls and fast-food joints as we approached the city. Past Barrie, I continued north along the west of Georgian Bay, passing Orillia and Midland before continuing to Parry Sound. Then, still farther north. As the 400 became Highway 69, the vista became spectacular.

I'd spent the two-and-a-half-hour drive in a deep, gloomy guilt over having left my father at MacNeil, but the sudden burst of jagged beauty outside shocked me out of my melancholia. I pressed the button that rolled down the Volvo's windows and let the wild northern air surge inside the car, clearing my head and snapping me completely out of my blue funk.

The city I'd left behind had been smothered in a sullen layer of foul brown smog. By contrast, the air rushing past the car windows was almost savage in its lucidity and I could smell the bright cold of Georgian Bay. The terrain itself had been formed from battered ice age granite rock that had been left rounded and smooth by the passage of millennia, forming islands studded with the ubiquitous windswept white pine. From the shoreline, as seen through dense patches of maple, juniper, and birch, the water was impossibly bright, reflecting the argentite sky. I made a right turn off the highway at the outer limits of the town of Adelphi, still fifty kilometres from Alvina. On the side of the road, sunbursts of goldenrod asserted themselves amidst patches of pussy willows and new-growth cedar as the newer highway gave way to the interconnected web of town roads that had bound these rural communities one to the other for a hundred years or more.

The temperature outside gradually dropped from refreshing to chilling as I drove deeper into the countryside, and I rolled the window back up.

The topography also grew bleaker—was that really the word, though? *Bleak*? Perhaps *stark* was a better word, because while the dull green of southern Ontario had given way to the craggy granite vistas made famous by the "Group of Seven" artists, the outlook from the windows of the car was far from unappealing.

In truth, I felt the first genuine flutter of exhilaration, even excitement, since buying the house on Devil's Lake I had yet to even see.

Even more, I had a preposterous anticipatory notion of familiarity, even ownership, as though the terrain outside the window stirred some memory from my childhood of time spent in one of these towns along the shore. But I knew this to be false: I'd never been here before, though I had seen paintings of these scenes in various art galleries over the years. Also, before buying the house, I'd Googled the town of Alvina, and Georgian Bay in general. There was no shortage of photographs of the region online, which was likely one of the reasons I'd felt foolishly comfortable defying logic and practicality for the first time in my life and buying Wild Fell without actually visiting it.

Once the real estate agent, *Mrs*. Velnette Fowler—she had actually insisted on the marital honorific, making the point twice—had been convinced of the sincerity of my inquiry, she had emailed me impressive photographs of the house that had not been included in the advertisement of the listing. They hinted at high ceilings and dark floors, a massive stone fireplace in the centre of what appeared to be the formal living room, still another in the slightly smaller dining room. Inside the house, a hand-carved mahogany circular staircase connected the first and second floors, leading to similarly proportioned rooms upstairs.

Included in the price were the tiny bit of rocky beach on the mainland across from the island and a dock of some sort, apparently constructed by order of the family in England in advance of the sale of the property, from which to launch a small motorboat to get back and forth.

To wit, Wild Fell was, in actual point of fact, far more than a mere "summer cottage." It was a seventeen-room mansion, built with stone that had been locally mined. The same stone had been used to construct the wide steps that led up to the veranda. According to Mrs. Fowler, Wild Fell had been one of the finest houses in three counties, luxurious even by the standards of luxurious houses of the day.

"The gardens," she said. "The gardens were famous. Mrs. Blackmore had more than five hundred varieties of roses in her garden. One variety was the 'black rose' that had been cut and transplanted from the bush that Mary, Queen of Scots slept under, the night before her execution."

"Mary Queen of *Scots*?"

"Nothing was too good for the Blackmore family," Mrs. Fowler said grandly. At that moment she sounded less like a real estate agent and more like a tour guide, or proud servant identifying with the family to whom she'd offered her fealty. "The house was built between 1823 and 1831 at *enormous* cost. It had stained glass windows, the best brocade drapes. Oh, and wallpaper all the way from England. My goodness, it was beautiful. You can see old pictures of it at the historical society. But most of it is still there, except for several pieces of furniture that the family in England insisted we try to sell. But the house is more or less intact. And it is *just glorious.*"

"Like Mary Queen of Scots' rosebush," I said dryly, trying to bring the conversation out of the realm of her gushing. "I find it hard to believe this is all for sale at the price quoted. Is there any possibility there was a mistake?"

There was a pause on the other end of the line, as though I'd offended her, either by my glibness, or by an emphasis on practical matters, like the price. I had dealt with real estate agents in the city, and Mrs. Fowler wasn't like anyone I had ever met. "Mr. Browning, I don't make *mistakes,*" she said. "And while I'm delighted that you find the price reasonable, I must in fairness advise you that it is still not inconsiderable, especially for a house of its size that will require new plumbing and new central heating at some point."

"Now you sound like you're trying to dissuade me, Mrs. Fowler."

"Not at all. I just don't want you to be under any illusions that this is some fire sale wreck. Houses like this one rarely come on the market. I myself would have preferred to offer it for a much higher price, but the family in England insisted that they wanted a fast sale." She sighed. "It's a landmark, and in excellent repair. Frankly, you're the first inquiry, but I expect more of them by this evening, and I expect the house to be sold in a day or so." A cunning note entered her voice. "Two, probably. Tops. There will likely be a feeding frenzy. And it will go to whoever gets there first. Believe me when I tell you, this is a once-in-a-lifetime deal. The family in England wants it gone quickly."

I felt my heart quicken. "Has anyone seen it yet? I mean, potential buyers?"

"As I said, you're the first, Mr. Browning. But when houses like this come up, rich buyers snap them up. Many do so without even seeing the house. We have all the inspection reports on file for anyone to check out. But it won't be on the market long, I guarantee that."

Later, it had occurred to me that she had exaggerated the expected "feeding frenzy," but I asked her to fax over the inspection reports immediately and, flush with the reckless power of my new money, I had called the bank and arranged the transfer of funds. I think even Mrs. Fowler was shocked, but she went into shark realtor mode, all traces of her gushing about wallpaper and rosebushes immediately disappearing behind a volley of figures and process. Less than two days later, the house was mine. That night I promptly got drunk on Jack and Coke, but I wasn't at all sure if I was celebrating my new purchase or processing shock at my foolishness. I'd briefly thought of cancelling the sale, but I realized there wasn't likely any legal basis for it. I had paid cash for the house and I'd signed the papers.

Besides, it felt giddily, ridiculously freeing to make such an absurd purchase. But as time went by, I'd not experienced anything like buyer's remorse, or even anxiety, just a sense of ineffable *rightness*, a rightness I still felt the need to run by Hank to make sure I wasn't actually in the throes of some sort of insanity brought about by my action.

The rest, as the cliché goes, is history.

But at that moment, driving along the weathered, dusty rural roads, half an hour from Devil's Lake, all I felt was that somehow I was coming home.

The thought comforted me as the tiny bullets of gravel spat and ground beneath the wheels of the Volvo and the stark landscape of blue water and granite urged me farther north.

I arrived in Alvina just before dusk under a silver-grey sky layered with a thick scud of topaz-coloured clouds fat with the promise of rain.

The town itself was more or less indistinguishable from all the other towns I had passed through once I had turned off the main highway, except that Alvina looked like it might have been captured in a sepia photograph from another time. It wasn't that it seemed rundown—in fact, far from it. Main Street was smooth under the wheels, and there were boxes of geraniums in stone urns lining the wide sidewalks in between the wrought iron lampposts. Main Street ran through the store-fronted length of what appeared to be the town's old-fashioned commercial district. Several of the storefronts had awnings, old ones with dark pine beams supporting them. Their condition—worn and faded, but not tattered—somehow suggested that they were a regular fixture on the street, not something laid out for the tourists and summer people who thus far seemed indistinguishable one from the other as they meandered along the street, dressed for fall in jeans and flannel. There was a sense of density on each side of Main Street, and I was aware of narrower, winding streets like breakaway arteries lined with smaller commercial buildings, and beyond that, distant lawns and houses. The trees along those streets were old-growth deciduous—maple and elm trees that were nearly pyrotechnic in their sourball-coloured autumnal glory.

I found Fowler Real Estate easily enough, off Main Street and three blocks south of the Alvina United Church, high on the hill brow above the town. The office was nestled in a cluster of buildings that looked as though they had been built in the 1940s, brick and clapboard storefronts and office buildings that bore the scars of decades of Canadian winters in a place where the glacial wind and snow off the bay was cruelly humbling to everything in its path.

I parked the car in front of the agency and stepped out. A damp wind was blowing in from the direction of Devil's Lake. I shivered and opened the car door again to retrieve my maroon nylon windbreaker.

From somewhere in the back of the car, two large white moths rose jerkily into the air, then fluttered out the open door. They hovered for a moment directly in my sightlines, white on white, hard to see in the grey afternoon light, vanishing above my head, carried on the freshening breeze.

I reasoned that they must have been hiding in the folds of my clothes or on the side of my suitcases ever since MacNeil, a thought that faintly revolted me. I peered into the car in case there were any more hiding under the seats or on the floor, but there seemed to be none nestled there among the suitcases and the various items of clothing that had not been safely stowed in the back.

Reflexively I brushed my clothes off before putting on the windbreaker. Nurse Jackson had been correct; they had a moth problem at the home. My father's face rose in my mind and I winced at the sudden pang of guilt. I pushed it firmly down, promising myself—and him, I suppose—that I would call Nurse Jackson as soon as I arrived at Wild Fell and ask her to give my father a hug for me.

The windows of Fowler Real Estate were plastered with printed advertisements for listings, mostly cottages for sale, some for rent. There was a smattering of unprepossessing year-round residential properties for sale, as well. Most were, frankly, ugly. They were clearly intended for families, or perhaps retirees who had chosen to live up north full time. It was difficult to picture any of the photographs Mrs. Fowler had sent me of Wild Fell ever having been placed here among these very ordinary houses; indeed, I wondered what the family in England had been thinking when they engaged

Fowler Real Estate to sell their unoccupied property at all.

I peered through the window at the interior of the office. The glass was streaked and filthy, but I could make out a good-sized room with two clumsy old-fashioned-looking desks placed at complementary angles; a large file cabinet against the far wall, adorned with eleven-by-fourteen photographs of Georgian Bay in all four seasons; and framed photographs of cottages, boats, and families swimming and waterskiing. The photographs were in colour, the hard, flat bright colour of cheap mass-produced commercial photography of the 1960s and before. The families portrayed in the photographs were likewise of that era. The office could have been a period film set piece, or a museum installation. In any case, it appeared to be empty, even though I was expected.

A mechanical bell sounded when I pushed the door open and stepped into the dim office, which smelled like lemon oil and dust.

From a hallway beyond the farthest desk, I heard the sound of high heels on wood and moments later a woman whom I put in her late fifties to early sixties appeared in the doorway. Her hair was done in a dated marcel wave that had already been out of fashion when I was a boy in Ottawa. She wore a lavender pantsuit that had seen many washing cycles and better days. Her face was heavily powdered, and her eyebrows had been plucked almost into nonexistence and darkly pencilled.

The woman, whom I recognized as Velnette Fowler from the reedy voice I'd heard on the telephone, peered at me through the thick lenses of the harlequin glasses hanging on the chain around her neck and said, "Yes, sir, may I help you?"

"Mrs. Fowler? I'm Jameson Browning."

She seemed startled at the sound of my voice, and peered at me again. "Mr. Browning! Of course! I didn't expect you until . . ." She looked down at her watch. "Oh dear, it *was* today, wasn't it. I'm so sorry." She smiled, showing a mouthful of dentures. "I'm Velnette Fowler. Welcome to Alvina. It's so nice to meet you, Mr. Browning." When she stepped forward to shake my hand, I caught a whiff of stale breath, and some sort of inexpensive powdery perfume long past its shelf date. "Did you have a nice drive up? The weatherman's been calling for rain for weeks. We've all been pretty sure it was coming today, but it's already after three in the afternoon and it's not here yet. With any kind of luck it'll hold out till you get to Blackmore and your brand new house."

"Not that new," I said, stepping discreetly backward and tilting my head away in such a way that I hoped wouldn't make my mild revulsion at the various smells obvious. I smiled at her. "More than a hundred years old isn't new. A new house would be one of the cottages on your window there." I pointed to the storefront. "This one is a bit older than that."

"Yes," she said, pursing her lips. My attempt at humour was lost on her, and I was once again reminded of our telephone conversation when she'd bristled at my suggestion that there could possibly be any sort of hidden catch in the sale of a seventeen-room mansion on a private island in Georgian Bay, even for the not-inconsiderable price I'd paid. "Wild Fell is 'a bit older than that,' yes. Obviously you could say that. But I think you'll see that you've made a superb purchase." She peered over my shoulder out the window where I'd parked in front of her office. "Did you bring your wife?"

"I'm not married, Mrs. Fowler. I don't have a wife."

She raised her pencilled eyebrows and pursed her lips. "Oh, I *am* sorry," she said. "I was sure you mentioned that you had a family when we spoke. Wild Fell seems like such a large house for a single man, it never occurred to me that you weren't married." She squinted again. "Do you have children? Forgive my being so nosey, but it seems like just anyone can have children these days, with all the divorces going. You just never know. I wouldn't want to just *assume*. That would be rude of me, you know, to *assume*."

"I have a family," I said, more sharply than I intended. "My father is back in Toronto. He's ill."

"Oh I *am* sorry," she said again. "I *am* sorry. I hope it's nothing serious. Your father, I mean."

"He has Alzheimer's. He's in an assisted-living facility. I may have mentioned that, which may be the source of confusion," I said, knowing I had done no such thing, but wanting to get her off the topic of my private life. Aside from being none of her business, it had been less than four hours since I had abandoned my father at MacNeil. I was too raw to put up with this woman's questions for much longer, and I certainly didn't want to begin my residency in Alvina with an altercation with the local real estate agent. Whatever I didn't know about small-town social hierarchies, I did understand that a woman who was responsible for the buying, selling, and renting of vacation properties in a town whose primary industry appeared to be catering to a summer population would know everyone in town, and be well-connected locally. "But as for a wife and kids," I added with what I hoped was a winning smile, "there's still time, right? You just never know."

"Indeed," she replied. "One never knows what the future brings. And marriage is a serious matter, not something to joke about." Mrs. Fowler pursed her lips again, pausing for a moment before speaking again, as though there was something she wanted to share with me but had ultimately chosen not to. "It's still a very large house for a bachelor, but I suppose you knew that when you bought it, so I'm not telling you anything you don't know."

"I'm not going to be living there, Mrs. Fowler. I'm going to be staying there off and on over the fall and winter, and fixing it up. I plan to open it as a guesthouse next summer. A sort of bed and breakfast-type place."

"Well," she said. "Well, well. That will be interesting. Not much of a call for that sort of thing up here, but there's always room for someone to try something different. Mostly people that don't own cottages here just rent them. From me," she added pointedly. "Still, I suppose it might be good for both of us if we keep in touch about all this."

"How so?"

"Well, if this plan of yours actually takes off—that is, if you're able to make a go of it, you could refer people to our office. You know. In case they want to come back to Alvina and buy, or rent. Likewise, I could let people know about your guesthouse or whatever, in case they want to try a short-term stay. Doesn't that make sense?"

The idea of being bound to Mrs. Fowler in any capacity, business or personal, beyond this afternoon was more than I could imagine, but for the sake of civility, I smiled and told her what an excellent idea it was. The reality of the potential folly of my impulsive purchase washed over me in another wave as I looked around the office; the dated furniture, the yellowed posters, and Mrs. Fowler's garish, clownish hair and makeup—all of it serving to underscore how very far away I was from home. And not just geographically. I felt lonely all of a sudden, and what I wanted more than anything at that exact moment was to get out of that dim, dusty room.

Mercifully, Mrs. Fowler changed the topic, switching back into the present. "Now," she said, "I wish we had more time to chat, but I imagine you'll want to get going before the rain comes." She handed me a slim manila envelope. "These are the names and phone numbers of some of the local contractors you might need to be in touch with in the next few days. We've had the power turned on, but in case you have any problems, the number for the hydro office is in there, as well as the number for the water people. The house was built winterized, and as you saw from the structural reports we sent you, the insulation is top-notch, all things considered. The vendors had a new furnace put in, so everything works along those lines, too. As a precaution, we took the liberty of having some cordwood shipped to the house. You'll find it stacked outside the back door, adjacent to the kitchen porch."

"That was very kind, Mrs. Fowler."

"Not to worry, Mr. Browning. We factored in the cost of the cordwood and added it to your purchase price. It's the least we could do. We wouldn't want you freezing out there on Blackmore Island. Alvina doesn't need any more ghosts."

The phrase struck me as odd, coming as it did from this humourless woman, my interactions with whom had been remarkable for nothing quite as much as their lack of levity. "I'm sorry, I don't understand—'Alvina doesn't need any more ghosts?' What do you mean by that?"

Mrs. Fowler giggled. It was a grotesquely girlish sound, from a woman her age. She covered her mouth with her hand as though suddenly self-conscious about her false teeth. Her face turned bright red under the heavy powder. "Oh, never mind me. I was just making a little joke. Forgive me, it's nothing."

"Yes, but what did you mean? You didn't say *ghosts*, you said *more ghosts*."

"I'm sorry," she said stiffly. "I didn't mean anything by it. And I certainly didn't mean to upset you."

"I'm not upset." I smiled and opened my hands in what I hoped she would read as a conciliatory, welcoming gesture. Adopting as light a tone as I could, I said, "I was just curious. You didn't just sell me the local haunted house, Mrs. Fowler, did you?"

"What a question. Of course not."

I prodded her gently. "So what did you mean?"

"Oh, for heaven's sake. All right, I'll tell you. But it's just the silliest thing to be having a conversation with a grown man about ghosts."

"You raised it, Mrs. Fowler."

"Wild Fell—your house—is very old. Alvina is a very small town. There are all sorts of stories about Devil's Lake, even about Blackmore Island. They've been around forever and no one pays any attention to them."

"Go on," I said. "I'm interested."

"Well, there was a tragedy in the early '60s. My late husband—Mr. Fowler—told me about it. I'm not from here, you see," she confided, as though to separate herself from the specifics of the story she was about to tell, thereby establishing both her distance and her neutrality. "I'm from up Wiarton way. My brother moved here and married a local girl. I was visiting him when I met Mr. Fowler. We settled in Alvina after we married. I wanted to be near my brother and his family. I was very close to my niece. Oh, it was all a long, long time ago. We took over Mr. Fowler's father's family business. Anyway, this young couple drowned not far from the house, from what I heard. It was a bit of a scandal." She lowered her voice, as though the details of this fifty-plus-year-old story were too potentially scandalous to be accidentally overheard. "They were . . . *unmarried*."

"And they drowned at my house?"

"Heavens no. Near there, I think. Devil's Lake is a substantial body of water, you know. And this was a long time ago, as I've already said, so even if they had . . . well, they didn't, in any event. You have nothing to worry about." Mrs. Fowler smiled again, not bothering to cover her mouth this time. "Only one family ever occupied Wild Fell, the Blackmores themselves, and they were very happy, by all accounts. It was a happy house. Mr. and Mrs. Blackmore's son and daughter loved the house so much they lived at Wild Fell their entire lives. Neither of them married, you see. They were deeply, deeply devoted to one another, almost like a husband and wife. Very touching. Yes, Wild Fell was—is—a very happy house," she said again. "The only ghosts you might have to worry about would be happy ones."

"What a relief." I smiled. "Well, maybe I'll call it 'Happy Ghosts Bed and Breakfast.' What do you think? Do you think people would go for that?"

She again ignored my attempt at humour and picked up her vinyl pocketbook from the top of her desk and looped the handle over her arm.

"If we want to get there before the rain comes, we need to get the show on the road. If you'd follow me in your car, Mr. Browning, I'll lead you to the house. Just follow me and you won't get lost. In the envelope I gave you, you'll find both a map that shows you how to get to and from Blackmore Island from downtown Alvina, and also written instructions. But if you pay attention when you're following me now, perhaps you'll learn how to get to and from the island right off the bat."

"I have GPS in my car," I said. "It's pretty reliable. You know, in case I get lost after today."

"Is that so." She smiled thinly. "Well, that's good, I suppose, but I wouldn't want to count on one of those computers, or robots, or whatever they are, especially not out here up north. It's too easy to get lost. It's always better to write things down, I say. Till the day he died, I told Mr. Fowler, *write it down.* He didn't always, you know, but then again, men don't always listen to women, even when it's for their own good. 'GPS.'" She raised her eyebrows and pursed her lips again, and this time her disapproval was unambiguous and implacable. "Just like voodoo, isn't it? Everything is changing so fast."

"I couldn't agree more," I said. "So, I'll follow you. I'm the white Volvo station wagon right here. Let's go. I'm excited to see my house."

I waited until I saw Mrs. Fowler's ancient navy blue 1962 Chevy pull out in front of me from around the back of the real estate office, then I started the Volvo and followed her through downtown, then turned with her onto the first of a series of rural roads lined with red, yellow and orange-leafed trees that took us deeper and deeper into the northern Ontario countryside. Her car picked up a steady cloud of dust and road debris in its wake. Mrs. Fowler drove so slowly that it would have been easy to follow her even without the cloud of dirt, and I kept enough of a distance so that it didn't obscure my vision. I had to smile at her choice of car. While it was apparently in a perfectly fine state of repair, it was of a piece with the rest of the time-warp effect of her presentation. I imagined that she would be considered something of a character in town, and I couldn't conceive that I was the first client of hers to find her a bit bizarre. Certainly to city eyes, she was more like a cartoon small-town Ontario character than anyone real.

It was the second week of October, and the maple and sumac trees bordering the road were already well into their seasonal change. After a while I stopped trying to remember the various twists and turns of the roads, one into another, and focussed on a visual memory of the route. The GPS would do the rest, in conjunction with what I had no doubt were detailed instructions by the fastidious Mrs. Fowler.

My sense was that we were west of Devil's Lake and north of Alvina itself. Every now and again, I caught a glimpse of the lake through the trees, always on the same side of the car. From this I maintained a rough sense of direction without relying too much on anything but the scenery outside the window and Mrs. Fowler's dust devil in front of me. I kept the driver's side window open so that the crisp pungency of the air, particularly pleasing after the staleness of the real estate office, continuously fanned my face as I drove. Slowly, slowly, the sense of euphoria returned in increments as the anxiety I felt in Mrs. Fowler's company receded and I imagined myself in the landscape as an owner, not a visitor—as part of it, not someone in an alien milieu with which he had no connection. When we had been driving for just over forty-five minutes, Mrs. Fowler took a sharp, sudden right turn off the road without signalling.

I cursed her under my breath, but followed her gamely down a narrow road, this one even older and less maintained than the ones we had already travelled.

Here, the flanking pine trees were so thick they actually shuttered the available light. There was a sense of entering an abrupt, dark-green dusk created from natural gloom and road dust. As I followed her car through the piney murk, I had the sudden impression of not moving at all, as though the car was stationary and the alley of trees was creeping past the window.

The effect was disorienting. I shook my head in an attempt to clear it, but the sense of travelling down an otherworldly, lightless corridor persisted. Then, just as suddenly, the trees thinned and the light returned.

Mrs. Fowler parked the Chevy in a flat clearing. Beyond it there was a glimmer of blue through the thick curtain of trees, and I realized we were at the top of a hill leading down a winding path to what I had already come to think of as "my" beach, with "my" dock. There would be an outboard motorboat tied up to it, the boat that had been included in the price of the house, and which would have a full tank of gas.

It's finally real, I thought. *This is where it all begins.*
Wild Fell. My house.

Mrs. Fowler stood beside the Chevy, staring out in the direction of the lake, her back to me. When she turned at my approach, I saw that she held her handbag tightly against her chest, almost like a shield.

She gave me a forced smile and asked me if I'd had any trouble keeping up. "I hope I wasn't going too quickly for you," she said with no discernible irony or sarcasm. "I was trying to go slowly enough that you'd be able to get your bearings. Do you have a sense of where you are in relation to the town? Did you take mental notes?" Before I could answer, she added, "Never mind. In any event, it's all in the papers. We followed the exact route out here that I wrote down on that sheet of paper. You should have no trouble getting back and forth from this point."

"Well, it might take me a bit longer," I replied. "Perhaps when we get out to the house, you can show me where the town is. I imagine the highest point is the tower room, right? I believe I saw a balcony in the photograph. That will probably orient me best."

She looked at me blankly. "When we get out to the house? What do you mean?"

"What do I mean?" I laughed. "I mean, when we get out to Wild Fell and you show me around the house. I assume the boat is just down there." I gestured in the direction of the water. "I'll run you back across afterward, of course, and walk you to your car."

"Mr. Browning, you know how to operate the boat, don't you? Most men do. You don't need me. I don't really have time to take you out to Blackmore. It's just right over there. You can see where it is. Here," she said, fumbling in her purse before extracting a heavy iron key ring to which several keys were attached. She handed it to me. When I didn't take it from her, she jabbed the set in my direction again. "Mr. Browning, these are the keys to Wild Fell. They belong to you. The house is yours now. You don't need me to go out there with you. It's self-explanatory. The various keys have all been photocopied and I have noted which rooms they are for. It's in the packet of notes in the manila envelope."

"Mrs. Fowler, you have *got* to be kidding. You're my real estate agent. You *have* to show me the house. I've never been there before. I have no idea where anything is."

"It's all in the notes," she said stubbornly. "As I said, you can drive an outboard motor, can't you?"

"Yes," I said. "But that's not the point. This is your job. It would be extremely unprofessional for you to leave me stranded out here. You're my real estate agent," I said again, wondering if somehow she hadn't heard or understood me the first time.

High spots of colour had risen on her powdered cheeks and sweat beaded at the base of her hairline. When she answered me, her voice was suddenly shrill. "I am *not* your real estate agent. I am the *house's* real estate agent. That is to say, I represent the family selling the house. Your choice to not engage a real estate agent of your own was your choice. And I'm telling you, I'm not going out to Blackmore Island with you. Not now, not ever. I've been out there. I took the pictures. I got it ready for sale. You bought it. It's yours—the house, and everything in it. *Everything.* Now, take the keys." Again she jabbed the key ring in my direction.

Again I refused to take the keys. "What the hell is wrong with you, Mrs. Fowler? This is the most unprofessional behaviour I have ever seen in my life, from anyone in any job. If you don't accompany me, you leave me no choice but to report you." Even as I said the words I realized how ridiculous they sounded. Who would I report her *to*?

"I said *take the keys*." She flung them at my feet where they landed in the soft earth, leaving a dent and sending up a small cloud of moss spores and pine needles. "And as for reporting me to anyone, Mr. Browning, I think you'll find that it will be my word against yours. I'll simply tell people that you behaved lewdly toward me out here, and that I was frightened. You're an unmarried man, and I'm a widow. I'm *of* this place, through my marriage to Mr. Fowler. His family has lived here for almost as long as this town has existed. You are from away. No one in Alvina is going to begrudge me my unwillingness to set foot on Blackmore Island for one minute longer than I have to, let alone stepping across the threshold of that house. You're not back in Toronto now, sir. Please don't presume to threaten me with reports. You bought this place. No one local would have it, you know. *No one.*"

"This is absurd. Are you mentally unbalanced?"

For a moment, Mrs. Fowler looked as though she were about to say something else, but thought better of it. She straightened up and smoothed the blouse of her pantsuit. Her eyes squinted at me from behind the thick harlequin glasses, but when she spoke, her voice was once again flat calm.

"I think you'll find everything inside the house to be as you expected," she said. "As I may have mentioned, it has been professionally cleaned, and the furnace is running. It's not new, but it works. I assume you brought your own bedding, but in case you didn't, there was some left in the linen closet. It, too, has been cleaned. Three of the bedrooms have been made up—all three on the second floor. If you prefer, you can sleep in that bedding, or use your own sheets."

"Unbelievable," I marvelled. "Just. Fucking. Unbelievable."

"Charming language." She turned and walked toward her car. Before getting in, she said, "Enjoy your new home, Mr. Browning. Good day."

I had barely heard the Chevy's door slam before the car started up and spun around in the direction of the road to Alvina. This time, Mrs. Fowler wasn't driving slowly. I followed the cloud of dirt and rock the Chevy left behind as it sped away until it was lost inside that strange stalled-time alleyway of pine trees and darkness leading to town.

Chapter Four

IN WHICH I MEET MY HOUSE

I bent down and picked up the keys. They were made of iron, big and old-fashioned—the largest of them most likely the key to the front door. I brushed them off even though they weren't dirty, but because the thought of the lunatic real estate agent having even touched them was offensive to me at that moment.

I tucked the keys in my pocket and trudged down the hill through the trees and underbrush to the water. The path was overgrown, but there was evidence to indicate that the various tradesmen who had been engaged by Mrs. Fowler at the previous owners' behest had used it lately. The ground was compacted where feet had walked. In any case, the path could only go in one direction: down toward the water and the dock.

As I walked, I made a mental note to send an email to the family in England about the real estate agent's horrendous and unprofessional behaviour, but even as I thought it, I dismissed it. There wouldn't be any point. *Caveat emptor.* They had my money and the house was mine, lock, stock, and barrel. What had she said? *And everything in it.* If it was a white elephant, it was now *my* white elephant.

On the other hand, if the house was not as it had been represented—to wit, if the safety inspection had been fraudulent, or if the house was not as it had been described in the contract, or something other than how it had appeared in the photographs, I might theoretically have a case against the vendors. But even then, I could easily imagine a judge calling me an idiot for having bought it sight unseen and laughing me out of court.

On the other hand, the woman was obviously unbalanced. I thought of her prattling away in the office about cooperating with each other in terms of sharing tourist prospects as either paying guests for my guesthouse, or potential clients for Fowler Real Estate. I thought of her invasive questions about my marital status and my family, and her rambling about ghosts of drowned couples and haunted houses and small-town legends.

Maybe she had serious mental health issues or maybe it was just general small-town insularity and strangeness. In any case, I felt calmer. Whatever a fool I had been in buying the house, if she were actually crazy, I would only sound sane and reasonable next to her, in court or anywhere else.

And then I pushed around one more copse of trees and Blackmore Island revealed itself to me. At that moment, all thoughts of suing anyone tattered away like smoke, as I stood stock-still and stared at the swath of pine-crowned granite set in the grey inlet, tiered like a stone staircase covered with russet trees. Above the tops of the highest trees, the towers of Wild Fell grasped for the sky.

At the edge of the water was a small wooden dock. On the beach beside it was a Bass Tracker motorboat half-covered with an olive canvas tarp to keep it dry.

A wave of dizziness passed over me and I swayed on my feet. An image stirred somewhere inside my brain, not a memory, exactly, but something more vivid than ordinary *déjà vu*. I had been here before, as a child, I was sure of it. Right here, right on *this* precise spot. I had stared across *this* expanse of water at *this* island. An amorphous vision of my nine-year-old self eddied through my mind, but even as it did, I knew it was impossible. I had never been this far north in my life, not even on infrequent cottage weekends with friends while I was still at university, and certainly never as a child. I shook my head to clear it, but the vertigo, or whatever it was, lingered.

The air had grown very still and heavy. Even the cool, damp wind that had been making the treetops dance and toss their scattering cull of dead maple leaves had stopped blowing. It was as though nature itself was subject to the strange cone of silence that had descended on the spot. Again I shook my head. I swallowed, trying to make my eardrums pop, to hear again, because there was no sound at all, and that was impossible.

And then I was conscious of someone standing directly behind me.

The hairs on the back of my neck stood up, and a prickly flush crept across my shoulders and down my back. I turned around quickly, expecting to see Mrs. Fowler, having come to her senses, finally, and having realized that it was her job to see me directly to my front door.

But when I looked, the beach was empty, as was the path leading up to the flat place where my car was parked.

I called out, "Hello?" but there was no answer. I took a few tentative steps toward the path, unable to rid myself of the notion that there was someone there, that I was being watched. "Hello? Mrs. Fowler? Is anyone there?" And then, boldly, in my new role as the owner of Blackmore Island and Wild Fell— and although it sounded ridiculous to me even before I said it—I shouted, "You're trespassing on private property!"

From somewhere high above me, a bird screamed, shattering the silence. The shrill caw ricocheted across the flat water of Devil's Lake. A few seconds later, I heard the flap of wings in the branches and saw something black fly away into the thicker trees beyond the clearing. I felt the wind off the lake on my face again, and I heard its susurration in the treetops.

Almost immediately, the feeling of being watched vanished. I exhaled my relief. The prickling sensation between my shoulder blades had turned to a trail of sweat that stuck my shirt to my skin under my windbreaker.

I was very conscious that the area was remote and isolated, far from town. While my city-dweller's paranoia about human predators was hard to shake in itself, the companion fear of *non*-human predators was fuelled by the same urban self-preservation instinct. I tried to remember everything I had ever heard about bears and their seasons, about coyotes, wolves, wolf-coyote hybrids and other scavengers of the northern Ontario woods. As it happened, I remembered nothing about any of it, and chastised myself for having been spooked by what was most likely nothing more than a crow.

It was a crow, for God's sake. Get it together, Jamie. Cut this bullshit right now.

Damning Mrs. Fowler again for exacerbating my sense of isolation, as well as a growing fear that I was so far into the bush that my cell phone wouldn't be able to get a signal, I pulled it out of my pocket and punched in Hank's number. I told myself that I was just testing it to make sure I was still in cellular range.

I was convinced at that moment that I was entirely cut off from the human world. After a minute passed, I heard the phone ring. After a few rings, it went directly to Hank's voicemail. I forced a note of joviality into my voice.

"Hey, Hank, it's me, Jamie. Guess where I am right now? I'm standing on the edge of Devil's Lake, looking at my new place. You wouldn't believe how beautiful it is. In a few minutes, I'm going to get into my new boat and cruise on over and check it out. I wish you were here with me. I'm leaving this message because apparently cell reception out there isn't great and I wanted you to know I got here in one piece." I paused. "If you have a minute, would you mind giving Nurse Jackson at MacNeil a call and check in on my dad? I'd appreciate it. I'll call again as soon as I have my bearings, but don't worry, it's all good. And come out here and visit in the next few days. Can't wait to show it all to you. Take care, love you, bro."

I walked down to the boat and pulled off the tarp. Then I took the keys out of my pocket and located the smallest, newest one on the ring. A quick examination confirmed that it was the ignition key to the Bass Tracker. I checked the seats to make sure they were dry. When I was satisfied that the boat would carry me safely across the inlet to Blackmore Island, I climbed back up the hill to where the car was parked.

I opened the Volvo and withdrew the two suitcases of essentials I had brought with me. Carefully I tucked Mrs. Fowler's folder into the side of my overnight tote. These I carried down to the water's edge and loaded into the back seat of the Bass Tracker. The boat was tied to the landing dock, so I leaned my shoulder against the hull and pushed it into the water. When it was floating in enough water to not scrape the bottom, I stepped back onto the beach and then onto the dock. I had soaked my feet in the process, and my shoes left wet footprints.

I untied the boat and climbed in quickly, put the key in the ignition and started up the engine, gradually edging the boat away from the dock and into deeper water. Then I revved the engine to drive-level throttle and pointed the bow toward Blackmore Island. The Tracker pulled away from shore, leaving a wake behind it. I found the mechanical noise of the engine comforting after the lonely silence of the beach.

The boat sliced through the water, bouncing along on its own waves. I looked around me at the corona of forest and the rocky shore that planed around the island like a granite horseshoe, stretching far past any line of demarcation I could see. But while the terrain around Blackmore was vast, the island, now growing closer and closer by the minute as the boat headed to shore, was undiminished by it. Indeed, the island loomed. There was no better word for it. It had seemed large from the shore, but up closer it was majestic.

I cut the engine before landing, and was guided by the orange flags atop a sequence of floating buoys doubtless left by the workmen during the recent back and forth between Alvina and the house.

The boat cruised easily into the berth adjacent to the dock off the rocky shore. The Blackmore dock was older than the new one back on the shore, though it seemed to be in excellent repair. I tied the bowline around one of the posts and stepped onto the beach. I stood there for a moment taking the measure of my surroundings. The dock from which I had launched the boat was a small spot on a shoreline I could barely see. Beyond it, up the hill, hidden completely by the trees, would be my car and the road back to town.

In front of me was a steep stone staircase that appeared to have been carved into the cliff itself, leading up to the house. Also built into the cliff and flanking the staircase on either side was a massive gothic archway, intricately carved with a faded garland of baroque bas-relief Victorian renderings of classic Canadian motifs: roses, trilliums, pine boughs, and what appeared to be wild northern birds of prey—owls, eagles, and ospreys, the latter in flight. In the centre of the archway, cut deeply into the stone, faded by more than a century of violent weather were two words:

WILD FELL

"Home," I whispered to myself, testing the alien word on my tongue. Finding it oddly comforting, even familiar, I said it again: "Home. I'm home."

I began climbing the staircase to the house just as sheet lightning lit up the bruise-coloured sky and cold rain fell—lightly at first, then with increased force.

To steady myself, I kept one hand on the ornate iron bannister running alongside the staircase, which proved to be old but solid, festooned with delicately twisted strands of thick copper that had been welded into the shape of ivy vines, complete with filigreed iron leaves that curled around the slats as though alive. The effect was doubly striking because the copper had turned green with age in places, lending vivacity to the effect that may or may not have been the original intention when the railing had been built.

Looking down from the vantage point of the stairs as I hurried up, I wondered how many accidents had occurred here over the years, and what the Blackmore family had been thinking when they constructed it this way. There were wide, empty spaces between the railings, certainly wide enough that a dog, or even a child, could slip through and fall, perhaps fatally, to the rocky beach below.

The wind picked up a new violence, and the clouds descended in earnest, bringing more rain, and near-complete early-evening obscurity settled on the entire island in a matter of minutes. I put my head down to keep the rain out of my eyes and kept climbing. My suitcases—one slung over my chest by a long strap, the other clutched in my left hand—seemed unbearably heavy. My right foot slipped on a patch of murderously smooth wet step, and for a horrible moment I was sure I was going to fall. I righted myself and put my foot carefully on the next step, then the next.

And then, suddenly, I was at the top of the staircase, standing on the edge of a two hundred acre plot of land bordered with still more trees and surrounded by overgrown gardens and wild, tall grass. Even wild and untended, there was a sense of formality and symmetry to the grounds: elegant bones beneath the untidy riot of unkempt vegetation and trees. They had obviously been carefully planned at one point and must have been exquisite.

The rain was surging now, frankly a gale by any standard of the word, and it was through this translucent wall of water that I saw Wild Fell for the first time, separated from the gloom and general obscurity of the deluge by two successive flashes of lightning that lifted it away from the storm's darkness, creating the illusion of the house appearing to step forward to greet me.

I ran toward it as yet another bolt of lightning shattered the sky in a jagged streak that left a bluish afterimage seared behind my eyelids as it struck a tree twenty-five yards from the front of the house. There was a loud, sharp crack as the tree burst into flame and crashed to the ground. I felt rooted where I stood, gaping at the fire, but the rain was quickly dousing it, leaving only the smell of woodsmoke.

Before the last bit of flame went out, I saw something that must have been a trick of wind and rain making the trees sway.

A figure was standing fifteen yards from the far end of the house under a copse of white pine, not far from the burning tree, as though warming itself by the fire. The figure appeared to be female, though aside from its slight stature, I would have been hard-pressed to say exactly what it was that had communicated gender, since I could make out no details, such as body shape, face, let alone clothes.

I squinted into the shadows, trying to focus on the figure, but when lightning flashed again in the next few seconds, there was no one standing under the white pine and the doused fire from the burned tree was smoking in the rain, which continued to fall, even harder now than before.

Jesus fucking Christ! Get a grip. This is the second time today. You're going to drown in this shitstorm looking for people who aren't even there. Get out of the goddamn rain and into the house.

I hurried up the large stone steps to the shelter of the covered veranda and put my suitcases down. Feeling in my windbreaker pocket for the keys, I located the largest one by touch and fumbled for the lock on the massive oak door. I inserted the key and turned it. The door swung open inward, perhaps pushed harder by the wind. Then I stepped over the threshold and into the house.

The blackness that swam toward me from the open door was huge and absolute. There was an immediate sense of vastness and space, a dimensional illusion created, no doubt, by the absolute lack of light coming from anywhere inside or outside of the house—except for the occasional flashes of lightning, which did nothing to illuminate the interior, even when they touched the panes of the high stained glass windows deeper inside. When I closed my eyes, there was no discernible change in the comparative depth of the dark. By instinct, I felt along the wall near the front door until I located the hard ridge of what could only be an antiquated light switch. It was stiff with age, but it yielded to pressure, and suddenly there was light.

I stood in a hallway of dark panelled walnut or mahogany, and not for the first time did I wonder by what fluke or error I had been successful in purchasing something this ridiculously grand, even out here on an island in the middle of nowhere. Maybe Mrs. Fowler really had been insane and had sold me this house in error, leaving an extra zero, or a comma, off the purchase price.

I walked slowly down the dim hallway, taking its measure, turning on light switches wherever I found them until the downstairs was reasonably illuminated—at least enough for me to inspect. Directly in front of me was another carved arch of the same rich dark wood as the panelled hallway walls. This one was blazoned with an exquisitely rendered coat of arms that I assumed belonged to the Blackmore family.

To my left was a well-proportioned room, also panelled, that must have been a stately library in its day. The numerous shelves were mostly empty, but here and there were bunches of ancient books: first-edition nineteenth-century novels, I discovered.

I took one of the books off the shelf, an octavo of Wordsworth's poetry bound in burgundy calf. Opening it carefully, I saw that it bore a bookplate on the inside left cover. In an ornate design of intertwined roses were engraved the words *Ex Libris Rosa Blackmore*.

On a long trestle table was arrayed a stack of magazines with names like *Anglo-American*, *The Canadian Journal*, *The Literary Garland*, and *British Colonial* mixed in with more easily recognizable antique copies of American periodicals like *Harper's New Monthly Magazine* and *Punchinello*. With the exception of the empty shelves, the library looked as though it had remained almost completely untouched during the entire duration of its vacancy. There was no sense of rot, decay, or any sort of degradation or neglect. Mrs. Fowler had said that the house didn't age. At the time I had put it down to part of her theatrical sales pitch, but I could see now that she had a point: there was nothing here to suggest that the true owners of Wild Fell weren't merely on holiday, or that a light turn of the house and some fresh flowers wouldn't bring it immediately back to its genteel state of habitability.

Against another wall, there was a fireplace with reading chairs grouped around it in an inviting way. Oddly, there was a mirror hanging over the fireplace, unusual for a library, I thought, which would normally have some sort of landscape or portrait.

To the right of the hallway was the parlour. Unlike the library, this room had been painted in some light colour rather than panelled in wood, and it was completely furnished, though dustcovers had been carefully draped over every piece in the room. I tugged on one of the covers. It fell away, exposing a richly brocaded wingback chair. I pulled away another cover, then another. I marvelled at what was revealed. Not only were these superb examples of period furniture, but they were also in excellent condition, like everything else I had seen so far. Next to the fireplace stood an elaborate grandfather clock, its hands frozen at three o'clock.

Here, also, was a mirror over the fireplace. The glass was the exception to the rule of agelessness. It was dark with years. Fine spiderweb cracks were visible in the glass around the gilding, and the surface was veined with brown and grey lines.

Along the walls were lightened sections where paintings had once hung. The outlines were clearly visible. I counted four of them, large vertical rectangles that suggested portraits. I frowned, and glanced around the room to see if they had been lined up against the lower walls, but there was no sign of them anywhere. I considered that the family in England might have had them sent to them when they were preparing to sell the house, which I found a bit odd considering that so much other personal furniture had been left behind.

Farther along the hallway, on the same side as the parlour, was the dining room. Like the library, this room had been panelled, and there was a long dining room table with six chairs and a sideboard at the head of the table.

Here, as well, like the two previous rooms, there was a mirror—a rectangular one hanging horizontally above the sideboard, framed in the same mahogany, decorated with gold maple leaves at each corner.

A discreet swinging door at the far end of the room led to a large kitchen and pantry with a set of servants' stairs leading to the upper regions of the house. I glanced up the stairs to the hallway above. Since it was dark and I could find no light switch anywhere nearby, I decided to leave it till the next day, and instead exited through the kitchen and back into the dining room, then out into the hallway.

Between the dining room and the parlour was the staircase I had seen in the photographs Mrs. Fowler sent. It led to the four main bedrooms upstairs and the three servants' bedrooms at the opposite end of the house.

On the second floor, I explored each of the bedrooms. The master bedroom was of lordly proportions, obviously the bedroom of a husband

and wife of wealth and position. Here, as in the parlour, there were superb pieces of mahogany furniture crafted in the Victorian style under the dust covers, which I removed. As was the custom, the room was decorated with an eye to the feminine tastes of the lady of the house. Although the bed and the adjacent chest of drawers were heavily proportioned, there was also an elegant vanity table at the opposite end of the room with a bevelled mirror and a brocade chair. At the other end of the room was a sort of dressing room off the attached bathroom. All the shuttered windows had heavy burgundy velvet curtains with gold-fringed tassel.

There were two other furnished bedrooms, also large, but smaller than the master suite. One of them, obviously a young man's room, was decorated in a bachelor style—bulky masculine furniture, a washstand, a commodious single bed and a floor-to-ceiling mirror. The walls were hung with small oil paintings of northern landscapes, maps, and military-themed prints. Here, as in the master bedroom, all the curtains were burgundy velvet.

The third bedroom, much smaller than either of the other two, had clearly belonged to a young woman. This room had been painted yellow. Originally, it had likely been a sunny buttercup colour, but it had darkened over the years to deep saffron. The curtains here were deep green velvet and the furniture— the bed, a writing desk, a framed full-length mirror, and a vanity table— appeared to have been crafted from white ash, or fine light oak. Beneath the dustcovers, the bed was draped with a substantial quilt in patches of pale rose and violet. I touched the quilt: it was cold and stiff with age, but nonetheless soft and relatively clean. As with the other two bedrooms, there was a fireplace against the far wall.

Over the fireplace was hung a framed collection of what at first I took to be butterflies, but on closer inspection appeared to be moths, all expertly mounted on board and beautifully preserved. There appeared to be more than two dozen, all of them dazzling samples of a variety of the insects, many of which I knew to be indigenous to Ontario, but also many that seemed far too large, colourful, or exotic to be local. Beneath each sample, in exquisite feminine penmanship, was the species name. The ink was too faded to be entirely clear in each case, but I was nevertheless able to read some of the names: *Luna, Polyphemous, Emperor's Gum, Cabbage, Deathshead Hawk, Cecropia, Comet, Blotched Emerald.*

On the mantelpiece directly beneath the framed collection of pinned moths was a rectangular wooden box in a marquetry design of a moth in flight. I opened the box, releasing into the air a dusty, spicy floral scent like very old potpourri or flowers just before they turn after too long in a vase. There was some sort of inscription carved into the inner lid. In the dimness

I strained to make out the three words carved there: *Moths for Forgetfulness*. Underneath the odd phrase were three letters, likely a monogram: *RAB*. I closed the box and replaced it on the mantelpiece.

The overall impression given off by this room, unlike the others, was one of intimacy, even if not actually warmth. But from a purely practical standpoint, I decided to install myself there. Its relatively small size would mean I could maximize the heat from the fireplace. I was soaking wet from the rain and the house was cold. If the heat had been turned on, as I had been told it had, there was precious little evidence of it.

On the covered porch behind the kitchen, the promised cord of wood was stacked carefully beside the door, with a smaller pile of kindling next to it. If the fireplaces worked—I prayed they would—then I would be able to heat some of the rooms in the house before I froze.

It was already past eight o'clock. The long drive, the concerns about my father, and the strange altercations with Mrs. Fowler leading up to my arrival had begun to take their toll. My eyelids felt heavy and my vision was beginning to blur. I needed to sleep, but before I could, I had to make myself warm and dry. I realized I should probably be hungry, but I wasn't. There were some protein bars in my suitcases, which would tide me over in case I needed them. If I didn't need them, they'd make a passable breakfast tomorrow and I'd take the boat back across Devil's Lake and drive to Alvina to pick up some provisions.

I lit two fires, one in the parlour and one in the yellow bedroom upstairs.

The parlour fireplace was massive and the fire I'd built was substantial. To my delight I found that the heat it generated quickly spread through the room and even out into the hallway. This cheered me up immensely and I briefly considered sleeping in a chair in front of it, covered with a blanket from one of the rooms upstairs. I decided against that, reasoning that the room's size would mean it wouldn't hold the heat over the long term, while the smaller room upstairs would likely hold it all night long. I stripped off my wet clothes and laid them on a chair in front of the fireplace, then dressed in dry jeans, a t-shirt, and a flannel shirt over that. When I was sufficiently warm, I left the fire to die down in the parlour and stepped into the hallway and climbed the stairs to the yellow bedroom.

By now the room was warm and inviting, both in terms of the temperature and the ambience. The ruddiness of the fire's glow warmed the yellow walls and the dark green velvet curtains and, for the first time since arriving in Alvina, I had the sense of being in my own time and place. The room was beautiful, and even if it didn't have the twenty-first-century conveniences to which I was accustomed, tonight it didn't matter.

At that moment there was no thought that I was sleeping in a dead woman's bed, in a dead woman's sheets—only that I was the first guest in my own guest house. My eyelids fluttered. I yawned, pulled back the quilt, and climbed into bed without even undressing. The last thing I saw before the whole day faded into nothingness was the sight of my own reflection in the full-length mirror at the foot of the lovely white ash bed. I have no recollection of falling asleep, so complete was my exhaustion.

There was someone in my bed with me, someone erotically skilled and deeply desirable, someone with hands that deftly unbuttoned my flannel shirt and caressed the skin of my chest, pinching my nipples until they stood up like points. I heard someone call my name as though from a great distance, but the room was dark and anything was possible and I didn't want her—for it must have been a woman? *Ame, perhaps?*—to stop, not ever. I felt fingers unbuttoning the fly of my jeans, pulling them down and taking out my penis, which felt enormous, rampant and hard, and squeezing it, teasing the tip till the place where the fingers met the tip of my cock had become the centre of my entire world.

The air around me was awash in some floral scent—roses, perhaps, or violets, and I knew without knowing that it was coming off the smooth, cool skin of the woman who was even now taking my cock in her mouth and tonguing it with long, languorous strokes inside her mouth.

I groaned and thrust upwards, gently, so as not to bruise her throat or her lovely mouth, or do anything that might bring this moment to anything but the perfect climax I knew we both wanted. When she drew her mouth away from my cock, licking the shaft, I cried out in protest. I felt lips against my ear, tasting the inside of it with her tongue.

But when my invisible lover spoke, the voice was not Ame's voice, or indeed any other woman's voice. It was a man's voice, deep and rough with lechery and it carried the weight of a dreadful, lascivious urgency.

Show me your cunt, daughter.

I opened my eyes to my naked father on top of me, straddling my thighs, grinding his buttocks into my midsection. I felt the sharp skeleton pressure of his bare knees digging into my sides. His face was slack with his disease, but his eyes were alive with malignant focus and foul pleasure; his smile was wolfish and hungry and he leaned down and kissed me with lips like raw liver, reeking of sour bourbon. I felt his cold tongue exploring the inside of my mouth.

I tried to scream but he'd sealed my mouth with his own. I struggled under his weight, trying to free myself from his implacable grip on my wrists.

I shoved hard, as hard as I could, and then—

—the impact of falling to the hard floor woke me, still thrashing, still trying to throw off my nude father. I blinked, gasping for air, unable to breathe.

All around me was pitch darkness and, for a moment, it was unclear to me where I'd landed. I was pinned to the floor and thrashed about on the hard wood trying to free myself from the tangle of sheets that had restrained my arms and legs. Then I remembered that I was in the yellow bedroom at Wild Fell. I was on Blackmore Island, in Alvina, and I'd just had the worst nightmare of my life. But if I'd just had a nightmare, then it seemed to have followed me out, because I'd gone blind. Then I realized why. The fire in the grate had gone out, and the room was full of thick black smoke from the fireplace. Choking, eyes watering, I struggled to disentangle myself from the sheets and quilt. I stumbled over to the window and opened it wide, leaning out over the sill and taking in great heaving breaths of air.

My eyes streamed with tears from the smoke. When I found I could open them again, when I was able to focus, I saw that the storm had stopped and an enormous moon had risen above Devil's Lake, and that the water beyond the overgrown lawn was smooth as glass.

Just beyond the lawn, closer to the stairs leading down to the water, the figure of the woman I thought I had seen earlier that day stood motionless, as though watching. When I rubbed my stinging eyes again with the back of my hand, she had gone.

I turned back to the bed and shrieked aloud at the sight of the naked man with the lunatic's rolling eyes standing in the yellow moonlight beside my bed.

But only when he also screamed did I realize that the terrified man was me, and that I was looking at my own reflection in the full-length mirror at the foot of the bed.

Chapter Five

MEETING THE FAMILY

I gathered up my clothes where I found them bunched up at the foot of the bed, tangled up under the sheets and the quilt. I dressed quickly and hurried out of the room. The nightmare of my father straddling me had been too horrible and vivid for me to even consider returning to the bed in the yellow room that night, let alone fall asleep there. Remembering the chill of the lower part of the house, I stepped back into the moonlit room and retrieved the quilt from the floor. I took care to close the door behind me, though God only knew who, or what, I thought I was locking in that room. I left the window open so that the rest of the smoke could escape and give the room a good airing at the same time.

The upstairs corridor of Wild Fell was unearthly quiet, but I found the staircase and made my way carefully downstairs. The Oriental runner on the stairs under my bare feet was soft and worn, but cold like the rest of the house.

The fire I'd left burning in the parlour fireplace had died down to embers, but with very little effort I was able to coax it back to life. I threw on more logs and settled into a chair to think. My throat was still raw from the smoke, but I had no intention of leaving this room until the sun came up, not even the short distance to the kitchen for a glass of water. Instead, I sat and watched the flames and tried to deconstruct what had occurred in the yellow bedroom.

First point: I fell asleep fully dressed, but I had woken nude. The explanation for that was simple enough: I had undressed in my sleep. The room had grown too hot, and I had been uncomfortable. Then, the smoke had woken me, and all of it was mixed up in those images of unspeakable, unnatural foulness.

Second point: The erotic dream had obviously been a dream of Ame. While I hadn't thought of her consciously for a very long time, perhaps I had been suppressing feelings of loss—the loss of our marriage, the loss of those months I'd spent in the hospital recovering from the car crash that took away part of my memory; the loss of my father's memories to Alzheimer's; and mostly, my loss of *him* to the disease, and my abandonment of him to come here to Wild Fell, to chase some entirely ludicrous fantasy of opening a summerhouse in the middle of Georgian Bay. The dream was a synthesis of those various intertwined lusts and guilts. Likewise, the figure I thought I'd seen outside the window.

As for the scents, which were as clear to me in the dream as the voice and the outrageous presence of my father in that perverted context—the violets, the liquor, the warm flesh—these could only have been preambles to my brain identifying the smell of smoke.

Also smoke-related had to be my imagining that I had seen the figure standing on the lawn. My eyes had been streaming with tears, my vision had been blurred. My brain had simply plucked another fantasy from my distraught state earlier that evening when I arrived at the house and replayed it. In both cases, what I thought I'd seen proved to be an illusion on second glance. There was no woman standing on the lawn of Wild Fell either this evening, or half an hour ago. I was alone on Blackmore Island and alone in the vast house.

Thank you, Herr Doktor Freud. Very comforting.

But I was not comforted, not at all.

I *knew* I hadn't woken because of the smell of smoke; I had woken because of the sound of a man's voice in my ear muttering obscene carnality and from the weight of my father, who, though more than four hundred kilometres away, was somehow on top of me, trying to fuck me. The sensation of the tongue in my ear had been so vivid that even remembering it caused me to reach inside with my index finger to dry it or to wipe it clean.

In particular, I was horrified by the memory of the voice I'd heard: it had been an educated man's voice, but there was violence underlying the veneer of civility, even in addition to its liquor-cured coarseness. It had been the voice of a man whose rage was normally kept on a very short chain like a murderous animal, the voice of no man I had ever known, least of all my father. And I was quite sure it had been a real voice.

All of this I pushed away, as much for my own sanity as anything else.

It had to have been a nightmare, nothing more. It had nothing to do with me except for the fact that I had been the nightmare's vessel. None of it had happened. I recalled Scrooge's words in *A Christmas Carol* as he dismissed the appearance of Marley's ghost as something imaginary: *"You may be an undigested bit of beef, a blot of mustard, a crumb of cheese, a fragment of an underdone potato. There's more of gravy than of grave about you, whatever you are!"*

I pulled the quilt around me and curled myself into a semi-foetal crouch, longing for daylight and for the sound of the city—any city—waking up and coming to life.

Sleep eluded me that night as I lay on a divan in front of the fireplace in the parlour, but I must have nodded off again at some point, because when I opened my eyes again, the sun was shining through the panels of stained glass above the shuttered windows along the wall opposite the hearth.

I went to the window and opened the shutters just a crack. The fresh air that blew in off the lake was soft and cool and magnificently clean after the rain. When I pushed them open all the way, light flooded in, utterly transforming the room. Whereas last night I had seen only shadows and smothered opulence in a Victorian mausoleum, this morning the room was gracious, even welcoming.

Further, I felt it welcoming *me*. Where the sunlight touched the ancient white paint, the old furniture, and the dark hardwood floors, there was now depth and dimension and the promise of actual beauty in the offing. And it was all mine.

What had that lunatic Fowler woman said? *The house and everything in it.*

This morning, in this sunlight, there was nothing sinister in her words. I had made an extraordinary real estate investment. For the first time since buying it under such unorthodox circumstances, I saw Wild Fell as a home— *my* home—not just a house or even a guest house; and certainly not the white elephant I had feared. I walked to the front door and opened it, letting the light into the front hallway. I felt the cool fresh breeze on my face from outside, smelled water, good fresh earth, and wildflowers. When the sun touched the rich mahogany, the grain seemed to pulse with a sumptuous crimson radiance all its own.

I put on my shoes and stepped onto the veranda, then down the great concrete steps to the gravel driveway. In the darkness of the storm last night, I had only seen the exterior of Wild Fell in flashes of lightning through the rain.

In the morning light, however, I saw that my house was more than just a house. It was a masterpiece of gothic revival architecture on par with any manor house I'd ever seen in books or magazines. The old stone exterior walls were shades of grey and taupe. They had acquired a patina over the decades, one that blended perfectly with the surrounding natural palette without challenging it. From where I stood on the driveway, I could clearly make out the complex silhouette of turrets rising from what could only be some sort of anterior wing. I walked the perimeter of the house, feeling ludicrously lordly as I surveyed it and the acres behind it, the wildly overgrown formal gardens that spread out across the acres to the place where the fields sheared downward and became the granite cliffs I had seen from the lake on arrival.

As I came around the part of the house that I knew would lead me back to the veranda and the portico, I noticed that one of the clapboard-sided porticos had fallen into a state of complete dereliction. There had obviously been a fire there at some point. The intact timbers showed signs of having been charred. The other wall had been taken out completely and its burned boards had collapsed. There had been no structural damage to the wing to which it was attached. The porch had a sealed doorway to the rear of the house and its flanking walls were concrete. If the fire had spread, I would be looking at a ruin right now, so perhaps the house was blessed in some ways other than its apparent agelessness.

I allowed myself to imagine Wild Fell with additional furniture, modern furniture, and the all the amenities of a modern guest house, all of which I could afford. I saw new paint, new wallpaper, paintings bought or maybe discovered in the attic, new beds, the gardens restored—if not with the doomed Queen Mary's black roses, then at least with the best rosebushes money could buy.

An adventure waiting to happen. The loathsome cliché be damned, my heart felt as though it could soar right up into the blue sky—*my* sky, over my house and my island.

Back inside, I opened the shutters in the library, as well. The effect was the same; the light transformed the room. There were more books than I had noticed last night. The shelves were deeper than I had first surmised and many of the volumes were pushed back against the farthest recesses of the shelving, which was why I hadn't seen them in the gloom, thinking the bookcases more or less empty. I brought a handful of books closer to the edge of one of the shelves, aligning the spines. It turned out to be a five-volume 1825 leather bound set of *The Poetical Works of Edmund Spenser*, magnificent, if a little dusty.

On the shelf immediately adjacent, I noticed three or four rows of books that seemed far older than the works of literature I had perused on the first shelf. These were outsized, the bindings hand-tooled. I read the titles on the spines. Some appeared to be in Latin, but without any real proficiency in ancient languages, I could only guess.

Here then was what appeared to be an actual sixteenth century edition of *Malleus maleficarum, maleficas, & earum haerisim, ut phramea potentissima conterens* by Henricus Institoris and Jacobus Sprenger, the famous *Hammer of Witches* published in Cologne in 1520. I recognized the title from a paper I had written in my second year at university on the European witch burnings of the seventeenth century. Also here was Jean Bodin's *De la demonomanie des sorciers* from 1586; Pierre Le Loyer's *A Treatise of specters or strange sights, visions and apparitions . . . also of witches, sorcerers, enchanters and such like; Daemonolatreiae libri tres* by Nicholas Remy. It would have cost a fortune to assemble a collection of first edition antique books and folios of this calibre.

There were other titles here too—some in English, others in French and German, all of them apparently pertaining to the history and practice of witchcraft. While many appeared to be genuine first editions from the sixteenth to seventeenth centuries, others appeared to be from the eighteenth and early nineteenth centuries, published in English, with titles like *To Call the Ancients*, *Grimoire of the Nine Stars*, *The Eye of Horus*, and *Lore and Summoning of the Bridge-Builders of Time*.

I frowned. In my newly minted role as proprietor of an ancient library, I took one of the newer volumes off the shelf to buff it gently against my shirt to try to clean it.

As I did so, something fluttered out from its pages and landed lightly on the faded Oriental carpet at my feet. I laid the book on the trestle table and bent down to pick it up.

Holding it up to the sunlight from the window, I saw that it was a faded sepia-toned nineteenth-century photograph of an imperious-looking young woman. A rip in the emulsion ran halfway across the surface of the image, cutting across the woman's mouth and neck. Oddly, the effect of the rip, which technically obscured the woman's mouth, was to stretch her smile in a way that stopped just short of the grotesque without any compromise to her beauty.

Her hair was gathered in a loose knot behind her head, tendrils of which tumbled with contrived casualness down the back of her neck. The dress she wore was modest in design, the under-sleeves trimmed with lace, the bodice buttoned, and flaring out into a wide skirt. Though relatively plain, it was obviously the garment of a woman of significant wealth. From the way the photographer had highlighted the folds of the dress, I took it to be organza or some other expensive silk that caught the light and held it.

Her head was inclined slightly, as though barely deigning to acknowledge the camera—indeed she seemed not to acknowledge any imperative to be pleasing at all, though her beauty was such that she couldn't be anything less.

When I looked closer, I made a discovery that astonished and delighted me.

The woman had been posed regally, at a three-quarter angle with her hand on the back of an elaborately carved chair in the classic Victorian style, but I saw that the image was a clever optical illusion.

While she was indeed posed against a photographer's seamless backdrop, the photograph wasn't of a woman in front of a backdrop; it was a photograph *of the reflection* of a woman standing in front of a backdrop, as recorded in the glass of an ornate mirror, the frame of which I could see at the frayed edge of the photograph.

I turned the photo over. There was writing there in violet-coloured ink, now long faded: *To my dearest brother Malcolm from his best-beloved only true love, Rosa, Wild Fell, Alvina, autumn 1872.*

I reached for the book on the trestle table and opened it. Inside the cover was another of the floral bookplates I'd found yesterday in the small book of Wordsworth's poetry, *Ex Libris Rosa Blackmore*. I felt a thrill of proprietary detective excitement. The woman in the photograph was Rosa Blackmore, daughter of Alexander Blackmore, the man who had built Wild Fell. I looked closer at the bookplate. There was a diamond-shaped lozenge in the lower centre of the design. Inside the lozenge was a heraldic griffin holding what appeared to be a Scottish thistle.

I carried the book out into the hallway and retraced my steps backwards from my arrival last night. I looked up at the archway at the carved coat of arms. The shield was the same as the design inside the lozenge on the bookplate.

The coat of arms on the archway was clearly that of Alexander Blackmore. As his daughter, Rosa would use her father's arms in a lozenge, as befitted a lady born into the antiquated traditions that Alexander Blackmore had clearly intended to perpetuate here in what must have been rough, rude country.

"Well, my lady," I said out loud. "It appears we've found each other."

The sound of my own voice startled me in the stillness, and I realized that I had already grown accustomed to the general silence that lay over Wild Fell, the same silence that had doubtless blanketed it during the entirety of its lonely untenanted century. I was struck yet again by the house's bizarre apparent agelessness, especially as I knew that it had lain vacant and shuttered for so many decades in a raw northern environment. This had been one of the selling points of the house, and I counted myself surreally fortunate that it fell into my hands under these circumstances, but I was still baffled by the *how.* There was no trace of mice, let alone birds or raccoons or any other of the wild fauna that made nests for themselves in old abandoned houses in the middle of nowhere. Aside from the dust that had obviously accumulated between the last departure of the cleaning crews and my arrival last night, there was nothing to indicate that the house was uninhabited.

It occurred to me that I was exhibiting a pathetic case of insecurity, a form of reverse narcissism that made it impossible for me to picture myself as extraordinary—even lucky—*ergo* there must be some sort of "catch," some sort of downside to my good fortune. I could probably trace that insecurity back to my childhood—to the bullying I had endured as a frail child, to my mother's disassociation and emotional distance—but I had always resisted that sort of pop psychiatry, finding it unbearably maudlin. I had been able to bury it by becoming useful: an athlete, a friend, a lover, and eventually a caregiver. Still, the existence of the exact insecurities I was feeling now as a property owner were undeniably entrenched. They hadn't come from nowhere.

When I'd asked Mrs. Fowler about a "catch," she had been offended, pointing out that the house had been inspected and been found structurally sound, even of superior condition. If the inspector had shared my questions about the how the structural integrity had been maintained, he hadn't shared them in his report. Too, I reminded myself that the house had not come *cheap.* Not only had I never written a cheque of that size, I'd never dared to imagine having that amount of money in my bank account in my lifetime.

And now the house was mine, and I was a lucky man. It was that simple. It was time I made friends with that notion and moved on. If the house was extraordinary, then perhaps it had chosen me; perhaps becoming one with Wild Fell would make me extraordinary, too.

In any event, there would be a great deal of work to do to get the house ready for next year's guests at the Happy Ghosts Bed and Breakfast. Mrs. Fowler might be half a bubble off of plumb, but that was a damn good name for a B&B. Maybe I'd use it after all.

I suddenly realized that I was famished. I remembered the protein bars in my suitcase upstairs in the yellow bedroom. Involuntarily, I felt my stomach contract at the thought of going back up there. Moving from room to room downstairs this morning had buoyed my spirits immensely but the memory of that terrible dream came back to me in a wave. I shoved the memory away, annoyed with myself for lapsing back into self-indulgent melodrama so soon after deciding that I would no longer yield to such things. As the sun had risen outside, the wood inside the house had begun to warm, releasing its particular perfume into the air. I was standing in a shaft of dazzling jewel-toned sunlight from one of the two stained glass windows in the hallway, and it was beautiful. More, it was mine. Again, I felt Wild Fell gather me in its century-old embrace, and this time I yielded to it willingly.

There was nothing for me to be afraid of anywhere in this house, my house. I would sleep wherever I chose, or walk wherever I chose. That decided, I mounted the stairs to the upper hallway. In the soft morning light, the Oriental carpet runner on the staircase revealed its rich patterns of burgundy, navy blue, and gold. It, too, would have been there for at least as long as the house had remained empty, if not longer. But like so much of the rest of the house, it had somehow retained its integrity. Though worn in places, the weave was tight and lush, the colours still vibrant, if low-burning, like the finest examples of carpeting of its type.

I proceeded down the hallway and stopped outside the yellow room. The door was closed, exactly as I had left it last night. I sighed with exasperation at my own reluctance to open it, then turned the handle and stepped across the threshold. I took the room's measure.

Everything was exactly as I'd left it: the mess of sheets on the floor, the suitcases, the t-shirt I had been wearing under the flannel shirt when I went to bed, the t-shirt I hadn't put back on when I went downstairs after the nightmare. I still smelled the smoke from the fireplace, but I was delighted to see that there was no ash on the floor, nor had the smoke blackened the room's walls.

The windows. I stood very, very still. *The windows were closed.*

Last night I had left them open to air the room out and now they were closed. More than that, they weren't closed the way the wind might have blown them shut; rather they were closed with the latch in place, something that could only be accomplished deliberately, from *inside* the room. I closed my eyes tightly, then opened them. I repeated it, blinking quickly, trying to clear my head.

Had I closed them before I went downstairs and simply forgotten? It was late. I was disoriented and terrified from the nightmare. There had been smoke everywhere and visibility was reduced to the moonlight outside and only that much once I'd been able to throw the shutters open and let in the cold night air. But I was sure I hadn't closed them. I could have sworn to it in a church, or in a court of law.

And yet there they were, shut tightly, the latch in its place.

I walked over to the windows and tapped the glass lightly, half expecting to feel someone, or something, tap back. Nothing did, of course.

I felt no fear. There was no sense at all that I was anything but alone in the old house, even with having thought I'd seen the human figure on the lawn yesterday. I'd dismissed it as the result of last night's nervous fantods. There was only one possible explanation, the same explanation I had used to dismiss the nightmare: all of the stresses leading up to my arrival on Blackmore Island were causing my mind to play tricks.

I heaved my suitcase onto the bed and unzipped it, rummaging around the interior for the protein bars I had tucked away just in case. I found them there among the socks and t-shirts. Ravenous, I tore the wrapper off one of them and devoured it in three quick bites. The chocolate taste of it stimulated my hunger and I ate a second one, only slightly more slowly than I had the first.

When I had swallowed the last bite, I wadded up the wrappers in my hand and automatically looked around the room for a wastepaper basket of some kind. It was a reflexive thought, one that people who live in normal houses have several times a day. It didn't occur to me that there was no reason for there to be waste, or somewhere to put it, in a room that had not been slept in for over a hundred years. And yet, there it was, on the ground next to the white ash vanity table, a small wastepaper basket covered in embroidered fabric. Again, the pattern was roses and violets of the kind that had been enwreathed on the bookplates belonging to Rosa Blackmore.

Last night I had deduced that this had been the bedroom of Alexander Blackmore's daughter, but until my discovery of the photograph downstairs in the library and the lozenge of the shield of her father's coat of arms, she hadn't had a name, or an identity. This wasn't just "the yellow bedroom," this had been the bedroom of Rosa Blackmore of Wild Fell, who had been born, lived, and died in this house.

As I walked over to throw the wrappers out, a glimmer of gold in the tangle of sheets on the floor caught my eye when the sun struck it. When I bent down to pick it up, something sharp jabbed into my thumb, piercing the skin and drawing blood. I inhaled sharply and drew back. Hanging from a pin in the soft meat of my thumb-pad was a cameo brooch, obviously very old, with a gold filigree aureole. I pulled the pin out of my thumb and pressed my thumb tightly to my forefinger to stop the bleeding. I held the brooch in my other hand and examined it closely.

Unlike most cameo brooches, which featured women's faces, either in profile or head on, this brooch was a fine rendering of a bearded man with a noble brow, holding a trident over his shoulder like a royal sceptre—probably Poseidon, the Greek god of the ocean. When I held it up to the window, the sunlight through the shell turned the image from white to radiant, glowing pink. The gold looked genuine. It had clearly been an expensive piece of jewellery in its day, and even now it would likely fetch a good price. I was not a jewellery connoisseur, by any means, but Ame had inherited a cameo from her grandmother—the "something old" part of her wedding ensemble—and it had been half the size of this one, and much less delicately carved, yet Ame had said it was worth a great deal.

I checked my thumb to see if the bleeding had stopped, relieved to find that it had. I placed the brooch in the marquetry box on the mantelpiece, then sat down on the bed. The cameo had obviously gotten caught on the inside of the quilt when the cleaning crew had made the bed. I hadn't felt it in the bed last night when I went to sleep because I had been dressed, but after all, I had been so exhausted that I'd even managed to undress myself under the covers without waking up, instead weaving it all into a horrible dream about Ame and my father.

Also, it was becoming more and more apparent that the isolation from people, a new experience for me, was beginning to fray my imagination. I needed supplies in town anyway, so I decided to take the boat across Devil's Lake early that afternoon to the beach where my car was parked, then drive into Alvina. I could do some grocery shopping and perhaps stop at the Alvina library to see if there was any material in the stacks pertaining to Wild Fell or the Blackmore family history.

But first I wanted to continue the exploration of my house.

I had yet to set foot in the servants' wing on the third floor, and I knew that there was some sort of basement beneath the kitchen, because I'd seen the doorway to it last night.

The servants' wing was bare except for some ancient single beds made of cheap pine and chests of drawers of the same wood. The Blackmore family clearly either had remarkably loyal servants, or else—more likely—they didn't care about their comfort. In the class-stratified years of the British-inflected Canadian 1800s, the men, women, and children who toiled for next to nothing in the service of the grand families were required to be hardy and Spartan in their expectations of what was owed them in the way of comforts. No plush Oriental carpets here, just hard, cold floors.

I left the windows as I'd found them, shuttered and with weak light shining through the slats, and walked back through the upper hallways and down the staircase. I paused at the yellow bedroom, finding the door closed, as I had left it. Then I descended to the main floor and made my way into the silent kitchen and the doorway I had seen last night.

I discovered there was no electricity in the cellar. Since I hadn't brought a flashlight with me, I found some candles in one of the kitchen drawers and fitted one into a silver candlestick I'd taken from the dining room. Holding the lit candle in front of me, I made my way carefully down the stone stairs.

I felt the draft almost at once, the earthy cold of dirt floors and old, old stone. The cellar was actually not one room, but a sort of subterranean antechamber with doorways leading into what seemed to be three separate storage rooms, each with its own thick wooden door. Two of the doors opened easily, but the third was locked tight and no matter how hard I leaned into it with my shoulder and rattled the handle, it was immovable. When I realized that opening it without a key was a lost cause, I explored the two rooms that were unlocked.

The first one was filled with rubbish—rusted garden furniture, rakes and hoes, smaller gardening implements, and a low, rough wooden table with a shelf over it lined with clay pots and jars containing God only knew what. It had clearly been used as an underground gardener's shed in the heyday of Wild Fell, but it looked like when the gardens went fallow, this room did, too.

In the second room, however, I made a remarkable discovery.

Amidst the piles of old books and various trunks and suitcases, I found a crate containing the framed oil portraits of the Blackmore family—probably the portraits whose outlines I had seen on the walls of the parlour. There were four in total, each one framed in gold leaf period frames.

Bringing the candle as close to the surface of the paintings as I dared without accidentally singeing the canvas, I tried to make out the faces.

I recognized Rosa immediately from the print I'd found in the library. She was dressed in a similar fashion as in the photograph: a modest but rich-looking gown of what looked like brown velvet, though in this painting the dress had a high collar. Pinned at the throat was the very cameo brooch of Poseidon I had found upstairs in my bed. In this portrait, Rosa appeared no less regal, but there was a softness in her eyes here that hadn't been present in the photograph. I realized that she was younger in this portrait, likely by a good ten years, though this might merely have been a painterly device to achieve an effect for vanity's sake, or even a trick of my candlelight.

I carefully placed her portrait against the side of the crate and took out the next.

This one was a painting of an older woman dressed entirely in black. Her thick white hair was elaborately styled, piled on top of her head and set with a pair of jewelled tortoiseshell combs. I took it be a portrait of Rosa's mother, Alexander Blackmore's wife, though there was no plaque affixed to the frame indicating the identity of the subject. Her face was severe and angular, and while the artist had obviously tried to flatter his subject, there was something frail, even sickly about her in spite of the imperial tilt of the head.

When I compared the two portraits side by side, I saw that there were echoes of the older woman in Rosa's face, but whereas Rosa's lips were full and lush, her mother's were thin and pinched in an expression that hinted at pain so long suppressed and hidden that in hiding from the world, the pain had become second nature. As if to smooth away traces of whatever illness the painter was trying to camouflage, the older woman was ornately jewelled: against the black velvet of her dress shone a necklace of diamonds and pearls, and she wore a pair of diamond and emerald earrings. The effect was almost perfectly achieved. At a distance, there was nothing of the portrait that would have been out of place in a baronial hallway in any great house anywhere. It was only upon close scrutiny that the woman's face hinted at secrets, or pain, or private grieving.

I withdrew a third portrait from the crate, and here I met Malcolm Blackmore, Rosa's brother. Her *twin* brother, judging by his face, which was nothing less than a masculinized version of his sister's.

I found myself surprised, not only by their close resemblance, as if they were mirrored selves, far beyond what linked either his sister or himself to their mother, but by the man's sheer physical presence. To call Malcolm Blackmore merely handsome was to do him a great injustice, especially in the context of the era of the portrait—an era when well-to-do men were usually portrayed as voluptuous and spoiled-looking, red lipped and full-fleshed. By contrast, the young man in the portrait looked as though he had been carved from the very granite of the island that bore his family name. His thick hair was dark brown, almost black. It tumbled from a high, intelligent forehead. The nose was strong and straight, the jaw consequential.

Malcolm Blackmore's eyes were the same clear charcoal grey-green as Rosa's, and he looked out at the world through the painting with a similar aristocratic distance, but the similarity in their expressions ended there. There was a warmth and humour in Malcolm Blackmore's face that was entirely absent in Rosa's. That and—in spite of his obvious virility—a suggestion of gentleness, perhaps even weakness, in the turn of his mouth.

The final portrait stunned me even more than the one of Malcolm Blackmore, though not for any reasons associated with the portraiture, which was, again, excellent. Judging by the indecipherable signature in the lower right-hand corner of the painting, the same artist had painted all four paintings.

But if the artist had taken pains to flatter Mrs. Blackmore and her children, even his consequential skills as a flatterer had met their match in this instance.

The portrait showed a man in the colder years of late middle-age: hair iron-grey and still thick, eyebrows still dark, the nose and jawline as strong as his son's—for this was clearly Alexander Blackmore, the patriarch. But here the resemblance to either of his children ended entirely. Aside from everything else, they had obviously inherited their mother's pellucid eye colour. The eyes of the man in the portrait were almost black. More dramatically, there was an arrogance and a venal cruelty in Alexander Blackmore's face that chilled me. It was the face of a conqueror that took no prisoners and cared little or nothing for the carnage he left in his wake.

I had encountered this expression often enough in photographs over the course of my history studies at university, particularly one course that dealt with the phenomenon of North American robber barons—the men who imposed their will on an unyielding landscape with their sheer implacability. In some cases, this strength manifested itself in photographs and paintings as a sort of forced *noblesse oblige*, one that never entirely succeeded in masking the reality that the titan in question was the son of a butcher, or a fishmonger, or a tailor, or merely that his was generic Victorian masculinity—strength, albeit more often than not a bully's strength.

But in this case, by candlelight, in spite of the veneer of ducal *hauteur* in this portrait of the laird of Wild Fell, the face rendered here was the face of a monster.

The surface of the painting had been slashed with some kind of long, sharp instrument. There were no jagged edges; rather the cuts appeared to have been made almost lovingly, as though the vandal in question had taken his or her time and profoundly enjoyed the sensation of carving Alexander Blackmore's face into strips.

I shuddered and turned the portrait away from me, facing it against the side of the crate. At that moment, a cold draft wafted through the basement, and I distinctly heard a soft sigh from the darkness behind me. The flame of my candle flickered, then went out. I heard something behind the locked third door, something that sounded like a piece of furniture being dragged across a stone floor.

I didn't wait for the scraping sound to repeat itself. I turned tail and stumbled as fast as I could back through the basement. When I found the stairs, I took them three at a time, as though the light from the kitchen windows was oxygen and I had been buried alive in the dark.

Chapter Six

THE TOWN LIBRARY

The Bass Tracker was full of water. I'd forgotten the tarp and hadn't turned it upside down when I'd landed just as the storm came. It had collected water all night, and now the water swished around inside as though it were a child's wading pool.

Though tied to the dock, it had drifted back onto the beach. I was horrified. My knowledge of boats was purely practical. I had no idea if the Tracker was constructed to withstand that much water without the engine shorting out. Although common sense told me that there wouldn't be much point to a motorboat that was sensitive to water, I was acutely conscious of the fact that I was looking at my only method of leaving Blackmore Island. If the Tracker went down, that would be that. The boat was my sole access to the other side of Devil's Lake, and only possible source of transport to my car and town. I could probably swim across if I had to, but the water was very, very wide, as I discovered on the boat ride across yesterday.

Oh God, if you're there, was the prayer of my hitherto irreligious self, *please let the boat start. Please, please, please let it start.*

I turned it over and watched the rain water gush onto the rocky beach, making little river trenches that swept around the small rocks, creating islands out of them in their turn. Once it was drained, I gently pushed the boat out again into deep enough water, then climbed in, using the paddle under the starboard seat to guide it out into deep enough water to lower the motor. I inserted the key into the ignition and turned it. A sputter, then nothing. Again I turned the key. Again it sputtered.

"Fuck you!" I shouted. "*Start*, you fucking bitch!"

The third time proved to be the charm: the fucking bitch started. The engine turned over and the boat rumbled to life. I pointed it in the direction of the opposite shore and revved it. The tracker shot across the water leaving a deep V-shaped wake in the grey water. I looked back at Blackmore Island growing smaller and smaller every minute, though I continued to see the gabled roofs of Wild Fell through the trees.

Whatever had happened in the basement, whatever the sound had been, it had frightened me badly. Whether it was the cumulative effect of all the odd things that had occurred in the last twenty-four hours, climaxing in the discovery of the four portraits hidden away in a stone chamber under the house, or just a very natural nyctophobic reaction to the sudden darkness, my previous coolheaded awareness that I needed to go into Alvina for supplies had turned into an all-encompassing desire to get out of the house and see other human beings—see them walk, hear them talk. To feel *life* around me instead of the seemingly borderless silence of Blackmore Island and Wild Fell. What had felt like an adventure this morning was, at least a bit, beginning to seem like a possible mistake.

On the other hand, even though the impulse to return immediately to Toronto, to what was familiar, had occurred to me once I was out of the cellar, I'd already dismissed the thought. Standing by the kitchen windows, it was obvious that what I'd heard was a squirrel, or a raccoon making a nest behind the door. What had blown the candle out was nothing more than the breeze I'd already felt wafting up from the basement when I had opened the door before going downstairs.

Above everything else, the house belonged to me. I had bought it and paid for it. It was my responsibility now. It had been immensely beautiful in the early morning light, beautiful and full of promise. I remembered my fantasies of enriching and modernizing it. Giving all that up because I had noisy raccoons in the cellar would be pathetic. I would look like a fool, even to myself. What I needed was an afternoon in town, some provisions, and a visit to the library to learn something about my house. Perhaps understanding the lives of the people who had lived there, even a bit, would smooth my own transition.

I felt for my car keys in the pocket of my jeans; they were there. I felt the hard plastic contours of the key ring and the jagged edge of the keys, modern and *real*.

Not surprisingly, the wind on my face had an immediate calming effect on me, the same effect a cool washcloth might have on a fevered face.

The closer I got to the mainland shore, the calmer I felt. By the time the water became shallower and I cut the engine, my heart rate had returned to normal and I was fully in control of myself again. I tied the boat up to the dock and climbed the hill to where the Volvo was parked. The sight of its boxy stolidity cheered me. I fished my keys out of my pocket and opened the driver side door. I started the car up, then realized I didn't have the faintest clue where I was, let alone how to get back to Alvina. I had followed Mrs. Fowler's car to this spot without paying much attention, and I'd left her folder of directions and instructions back at the house. I swore under my breath.

Then I remembered I had a portable GPS in the glove compartment. I hadn't needed it when I was following Mrs. Fowler and hadn't thought to turn it on for the sake of getting a route registered.

With the car still running, I punched in *Alvina, Ontario*. Nothing happened. I tried again, with the same result. The GPS was lighting up and everything seemed to be working, but it wasn't receiving a satellite signal from where I was parked on the promontory. *Perhaps it's the trees*, I thought. *Or the rocks. Maybe farther up the road I'll get a signal.* I backed the Volvo up, then turned it around and proceeded down that curious alleyway of trees that led to the main road.

As if by magic, when I'd passed through that corridor, the GPS lit up again. This time when I punched in *Alvina, Ontario,* the GPS requested a street. I didn't remember Mrs. Fowler's office address, and in any case, I had no desire to stop by her office, let alone see her, so I punched in *10 Main Street*. Every town had a *10 Main Street*, so that was as good a place as any to start.

The GPS took me into Alvina, but it guided me into a different part of Alvina than I'd been in yesterday. This part of town was newer, even a bit garish compared to the mid-century civility of the streets around Mrs. Fowler's office. There were no boxes of geraniums lining the street, and the lampposts were the ordinary garden-variety ones that were commonplace in small towns everywhere. I had definitely driven down Main Street yesterday but perhaps there were two ends of Main Street—a historic district and this more modern, commercial one.

At a rundown-looking supermarket two streets down, I picked up some non-perishable supplies. I regretted not having checked to see whether or not any of the appliances in the kitchen were in working order. I bought canned goods, soups and stews, and sugar for coffee. I bought a small carton of milk and one of cream, not wanting to waste larger cartons in case the refrigerator was hopelessly beyond repair. I also bought a flashlight and some batteries.

At the checkout counter I asked the cashier if there was a library in town. She wore a pin on her red polyester smock that said *Ask me! I'm JANICE*, and she had the ready smile and plump red face of someone who was born believing that the world was just bursting with new friends she hadn't yet met.

"Why, there *sure* is," she said. "You new in Alvina?"

"Yes, I am. I'm just getting the lay of the land. Where's the library?"

"Well, I'm *Janice*. Welcome to town." She beamed. "Okay, the library." She frowned. "You take a left on Main Street there." She waved a plump hand in the direction of where I'd come. "Then you turn left on Nickle Street, then right onto Jesse Skelton Road. The library is right there."

"You mean this end of Main Street, right?" I said, wanting to be sure. "Not the historic section?"

"There's only one Main Street, honey. I guess it's historic. Old, anyway. But I've never heard it called 'historic' before. Nice, though. Kinda ritzy."

I thanked Janice, then left the store and loaded my purchases in the back of the Volvo. At the library, which was not, in fact, on Jesse Skelton Road, but one street over on Hymers Street, I asked about reference materials pertaining to a family called Blackmore who had lived in the area in the 1800s and had owned a large property on an island that likewise bore their name.

The librarian frowned. "That doesn't ring a bell," she admitted. "Let me look it up on the computer." She tapped on the keyboard and stared at the screen. "Nothing yet."

Trying to be helpful, I added, "I believe the owner, Alexander Blackmore, was in local politics. His house was called Wild Fell."

The librarian looked up at me, her expression nonplused. "Oh," she said. "How interesting." She glanced back down at the screen. "Let's just see . . . well, yes. There he is." She tapped a few more keys. "Alexander Blackmore, elected to the Canadian House of Commons in the mid-1800s. Tory. Not very much on file here, I'm afraid." She frowned. "That's odd. I would have thought there would be more, unless he was a very minor politician. But still, elected to the Commons, there ought to be a bit more biography at least. Hold on, let me ask one of my colleagues if we have anything in the back. When the new library was built, a lot of the older material went to the historical society. They've got a more comprehensive archive there. After all, the past is all they *do*. I'm trying to convince people around here to modernize." She sighed and stood up. "But I'll just check, if you'll excuse me."

"Absolutely," I said. "Thank you very much for the effort."

She smiled wryly. "There's not a lot going on here, as you can see. I'll be right back."

When she returned, she was in the company of an older woman of perhaps sixty-five who had the authoritative air of a senior librarian, or supervisor of some sort. She peered intently at me through round eyeglasses. She carried a manila envelope in her hand, but to me it looked woefully thin.

"This is the gentleman." The younger woman indicated me with a nod. To me she said, "I asked Mrs. Beams, my colleague, about the politician you mentioned."

Mrs. Beams said, "You're researching the Blackmores?"

"Yes," I said. "I'm trying to learn something about their life here in the nineteenth century. I've seen some portraits of the family, and I was curious."

"To be clear, you are researching the *Blackmore* family. Of Blackmore Island, in Alvina?"

I was confused. "Yes, that's right. Is there something odd about that? Forgive me, I'm not sure I understand. Is something wrong?"

Mrs. Beams paused before answering. When she did, her tone was neutral, though I had the impression that the neutrality was forced, as though she were answering under duress. Not rude, but far from inclined to elaboration. "No, far from it. Nothing wrong at all. Unfortunately we don't have a great deal of information about the Blackmores aside from the barest information about Mr. Blackmore's political career. But most people in Alvina have heard something or other about Blackmore Island over the years."

I kept my voice light, thinking of Mrs. Fowler and her happy ghosts. "That sounds ominous."

"Not ominous," Mrs. Beams replied. "Just sad, in some ways. We had some deaths here in town in the sixties. It tore apart the town. I guess most people of my generation associate the name Blackmore with that tragedy. Forgive me, I didn't mean to sound melodramatic. I was just curious."

"I heard something about that. The drowning? A young couple, apparently?"

"Yes," she said. "Brenda Egan and Sean Schwartz. I was in school with them in 1960. I was a year ahead of Brenda. It was very hard on everyone."

"I'm sorry. It must have been. But I'm really only researching the family—the Blackmore family."

"So you said." Mrs. Beams smiled, if a touch grimly. "Well, the past is past, isn't it? Nothing to do with the present, especially for strangers. No, it's not really important unless you lived through it." She handed me a thin folder. "This is all we have, unfortunately. They're photocopies of some photographs of the family that were saved when the old Methodist church in town burned down in the thirties. The Blackmores were generous supporters of the church, apparently. Pillars of the community, so to speak. Not very lucky folks, from what I've heard, but there you have it." She handed me the envelope. "Please feel free to peruse these. *Here*," she said pointedly. "They aren't to leave the library. We're not sure where the originals got to, and we'd like to hang onto these, if you don't mind."

I thanked the two women and assured them that I wouldn't steal anything, then located a table far enough away from the main desk for privacy.

I opened the envelope, to which was affixed a sticker that read *Blackmore, A./ Methodist Church Fire of 1932*, and withdrew the sheaf of papers. As Mrs. Beams promised, the images were poor-quality photocopies of nineteenth century photographs that were likely already faded when they had been photocopied in the first place.

Several appeared to be church events, with the easily recognizable Alexander Blackmore presiding in his role of town squire, cutting ribbons and handing out prizes to a group of children.

In one, the banner behind the podium at which he stood read *Dominion of Canada Day Children's Poetry Recitation Competition*. Blackmore's eyes were in shadow, almost invisible, but his mouth was stretched in a wide politician's smile as he handed out what appeared to be a Bible, or a dictionary, to a small girl in a pinafore, and a boy in plus-fours and a flat cap. In another, he was seated onstage at a Christmas pageant, posing with the boys playing the shepherds and Joseph.

The little girl who was obviously playing the Virgin Mary was seated on his knee. His arm was around the child in a gesture that struck me as oddly intimate and proprietary, especially given the church setting. I frowned. Surely that couldn't be Rosa playing the Virgin Mary? And, no, it was not: in the next picture, clearly taken on the same night, a young, unsmiling Rosa, perhaps thirteen, posed beside her father. Alexander Blackmore's hand was clamped on her shoulder. While not actually leaning away from him in the picture, Rosa's body language suggested tension, even constraint, as though at that moment she would rather be anywhere else than standing next to her father.

The last photograph was a formal portrait of the entire Blackmore family in the nave of the church. Alexander and his wife were seated in high chairs like the lord and lady of the manor. Behind them, Rosa and Malcolm posed stiffly, Rosa standing behind her mother and Malcolm behind his father. I was struck that in this picture, while Rosa was still not smiling, in this case, very likely due to the formality of the pose, something about her proximity to her brother seemed to relax her. The set of her shoulders was less rigid and, in spite of the degraded quality of the reproduction, the expression on her face seemed markedly less severe.

"Excuse me."

I felt a hand on my shoulder and turned around to see an old man in a flannel shirt and a tweed jacket that had obviously seen better days. He wore baggy cotton trousers and ancient running shoes. But when he smiled, it began in his bright blue eyes and lit up his whole face—the kind of smile in the presence of which it was impossible not to smile as well.

"Hello," I said. "May I help you?"

"Actually, I was hoping to be able to help *you*, sir. My daughter"—he indicated the librarian's desk where Mrs. Beams stood watching with an expression I could only read as disapproval, though it was unclear which of us she was disapproving of—"told me that you're researching the Blackmore family. She told me not to bother you, but I couldn't resist stopping by an introducing myself. I wondered if I could be of any assistance. My name is Clarence Brocklehurst. I'm retired now, but I ran the Alvina Historical Society for many years. I was born and raised here. I'd be happy to answer any questions you might have. The Blackmores are an odd subject, but as a former teacher, I can't help but be pleased when young people take an interest in local history."

"That's very kind of you, Mr. Brocklehurst, but I don't want to put you out. Also," I said, *sotto voce*, "I don't want to get you into any trouble with your daughter for talking in a library. I don't think she'd appreciate that at all."

"Oh, I'm in here every day, Mr. Browning. I drive my daughter crazy. I've read all the books in my own house, and now I'm working my way through these here."

When he laughed, it was the open, full-throated laugh of a much younger man. Like his smile, his laugh again lit up his face and I suddenly wondered how old he was. He could be anywhere from sixty to eighty, though with the morose Mrs. Beams as his daughter, I leaned more toward the latter figure.

"Quite so, quite so," he said. He laughed again, more softly this time. "They can be a bit martinet-like in here, can't they? I have a proposal to make, young man. Do you have a car?"

"Yes, I do."

"I walked here from my house," he said. "And I'm feeling a bit worn out. If you would be so kind as to drive me home, I would be pleased to offer you a cup of home-brewed tea and share any information and stories I have about the Blackmore family."

I was surprised by the invitation from a stranger, albeit an apparently harmless stranger. "Mr. Brocklehurst, I'd be happy to give you a lift home, but you don't need to give me tea. I wouldn't want to impose."

"Oh believe me, Mr. Browning, it's no imposition at all. I would appreciate the company. It gets lonely around here sometimes, especially with my wife gone. Please rest assured I don't run around inviting strangers over to my house, but when my daughter told me you were researching the Blackmores, I just knew we had to talk." He beamed. "My father, you see, used to play chess with the Blackmore family butler, and he was a bit of a raconteur. The butler, I mean. Well, also my father, to tell the truth. And I seem to have inherited his garrulousness." He chuckled again.

"At Wild Fell? Your father played chess with the butler at Wild Fell?"

"Yes, at Wild Fell." Mr. Brocklehurst looked at me with evident surprise. "You know of it?"

"Actually, Mr. Brocklehurst, I bought it."

He shook his head slightly in confusion. "You bought what, exactly?"

"I bought Blackmore Island," I said. "I bought Wild Fell."

He gaped at me with unambiguous shock. "You bought *Blackmore Island*? From whom?"

"It was offered for sale. Apparently, the property reverted to a family in England who are related to the Blackmores somehow. I bought it a short time ago. I bought the island *and* the house."

"Good Lord," he said. "Good Lord. You must have very deep pockets, Mr. . . . I'm sorry, but I don't think I got your name. How rude of me."

"My name is Jameson Browning, Mr. Brocklehurst. It's nice to meet you."

"And you, too, Mr. Browning. Well," he said. "This puts an entirely new complexion on the matter. Perhaps you can enlighten me, as well, rather than just listening to an old history teacher give a lecture." Mr. Brocklehurst favoured me with a conspiratorial wink. "Were you interested in taking me up on my offer of a cup of tea? If so, we should probably go. And don't mention it to my daughter. She gets a little bit tense when the topic of Blackmore Island comes up. I believe she mentioned poor Brenda Egan to you, and what happened in '60?"

"She did, yes. Very sad. I'd heard about it before, but I'd never spoken with anyone directly connected to the drowning. I'm afraid I may have upset her a bit. I'm sorry about that."

"Don't worry," Mr. Brocklehurst said, patting my arm. "It's her way. It's all our way, really. Small towns, you know. These things get written into our DNA, almost. Collective consciousness or something like that. The farther you get from the city the stronger that experience is. Something can happen in a small town fifty, a hundred years ago and, in some cases, folks who weren't even born yet will share in some part of it. Does that make sense to you, or is it terribly quaint?"

"It makes sense to me," I said, thinking of the Blackmore family portraits in the cellar. "I could see how the past would live on in a small town. It's likely inevitable."

He rubbed his hands in excitement. "Oh, you *are* a wonderfully intelligent young man," Mr. Brocklehurst said with delight. "I'm looking forward to our talk very much. Intelligent conversation in Alvina is so rare. Shall we go?"

"My car is outside," I said. "After you, Mr. Brocklehurst."

Chapter Seven

THE HISTORIAN'S TALE

Clarence Brocklehurst's house on the outskirts of Alvina was an educated man's house, a teacher's house. Every available wall was occupied with either floor to ceiling bookshelves overflowing with books of British and Scottish history— as well as a significant number of volumes on Canadian history and works of classic English literature—or antique maps of Canada and the British Isles.

Next to the living room fireplace there was an easy chair with a neatly folded dark green crocheted afghan draped over the back. It was obviously his favourite, regular chair. Behind it was a long-necked lamp with a dusty rose shade that still likely provided more than enough light for reading. It was here that Mr. Brocklehurst repaired after making a pot of tea and carrying it into the living room, placing it on a low coffee table between us.

He explained that he'd been a widower for twenty years now, and that he still couldn't make proper tea like his wife had. It didn't taste the same when he made it, he said by way of apology. "That's my Bella," he said, pointing to a silver-framed photograph of a slender older woman with fine, kind features. "Isn't she beautiful? Cancer. We'd been together thirty years. When it happened, I didn't want to go on living. But then one day I remembered how she'd pushed me out of my shell when we were dating. I was a regular wallflower and Bella was the prettiest girl in Alvina. One day about three months after she passed, I realized I'd spent almost a week wearing pyjamas all day. I kept telling my daughter and son-in-law not to bother me and that I had the flu, or some such lie. Well, that day I was sitting here in this chair and I looked at her photograph. The light fell on it just so, and it was almost like she was in the room. I practically heard her say, 'Clarence, get off your G.D. fat *duff* and get out of those ugly pyjamas and brush your G.D. *teeth*. Your breath *stinks*." He laughed again, and at that moment, right on cue, the sun shone into his living room. "That's just the sort of thing she would have said, too," he added softly. "Well, that was the day I got my life back on track, got involved with things like the curling league. And of course, the historical society. Which," he said, "brings us to the subject of your visit."

"Yes, Mr. Brocklehurst."

"Please, call me Clarence," he said kindly. "Shall I call you Jameson? Or do you go by something else? James? Jamie?" In that moment, Clarence Brocklehurst reminded me so much of my father before the illness took him away that I felt my heart clench.

"Please call me Jamie, all my friends do."

"I will. Now," he said. "You say you bought Blackmore Island. First, if I may—and please forgive me in advance for my vulgarity—are you very rich? Or are you crazy?" His blue eyes danced. "The land alone must have cost a fortune. And the house is a ruin. It would take a fortune to renovate. What were you thinking?"

"Actually, the house is in remarkable shape. As for how I was able to afford it, I came into a rather large sum after an accident. My father is in an Alzheimer's clinic in Toronto. The money provided for his care and left me enough for an investment property. When the real estate agent sent me the photographs, I realized that Wild Fell had some potential as a vacation property, or guest house."

"Well, you must be a very enterprising young man. It's been a lot of years since I've been near Blackmore, but it was pretty run down. Frankly, it would take a lot of money to fix up, in my opinion. And I'm very sorry about your father," he added. "Alzheimer's is a filthy bugger of a disease."

"Thank you." I paused, waiting for him to continue. When he didn't, I said, "What can you tell me about the Blackmore family, Mr. Brocklehurst?"

"Clarence, please."

"Clarence."

He paused. "What do you know about them, Jamie?"

"Not much," I admitted. "I know that Alexander Blackmore was a local politician who apparently had deep pockets. The house must have been particularly striking back in its day. It's still impressive, but I can only imagine how it must have looked to the townspeople. Blackmore must have set himself up as a minor king out here."

"Wild Fell was like no house ever seen in this region," Clarence began. "The source of Blackmore's wealth was never actually established. It may have been inherited. You know, second sons were often sent out to the colonies to establish themselves in those days, but wherever it came from, he spared nothing when it came to that place. The stone was all local, of course, but I'm given to understand that entire rooms were deconstructed in Europe and reassembled inside Wild Fell. Tremendous art and furniture. Exquisite panelling for the walls."

"It's very impressive," I said. "I've never seen anything quite like it."

He paused, glancing at me strangely. Then he went on.

"As I was saying, why he ever picked Alvina as a place to settle, no one really knows. But even then, millionaires from as far away as America were building these palaces along Georgian Bay. It was almost as though Alexander Blackmore wanted to top them all. He married a woman from Montreal— old money. Well, whatever 'old money' meant in Canada in the early 1800s, anyway. All of the money was pretty new, but they loved to give themselves aristocratic airs. Her name was Catherine Agnes Russell. According to what I've heard, he didn't build Wild Fell for *her*. He built Wild Fell for *himself*, then married her because he felt it needed a chatelaine. Also, he obviously had political ambitions, and he needed a wife and family."

"There's a portrait of her in the house," I said. "I found it this morning."

Mr. Brocklehurst raised his eyebrows. "Really? A portrait of Catherine Russell? Good *Lord*, what sort of condition is it in?"

I shrugged. "Excellent, I'd say. I found portraits of all of them. They'd been hidden away in the basement. I don't know why. They're beautifully done and they must be worth a great deal of money."

Again, that strange look. "Well, if you've found portraits of them, you must at least know that he had two children, twins. Rosa and Malcolm. Of the two, apparently Rosa was the intellectual. She was a voracious reader, according to my father's friend, the butler. She wrote poetry, she painted. And she was supposed to be something of a dedicated lepidopterist—she collected moths, of all things. From what I've heard, her parents indulged her by ordering specimens for her from all over the world."

"I found a framed display of them in one of the bedrooms at the house," I interrupted. "I suspected it was probably Rosa's bedroom. And there was a box on the mantel with an odd inscription—'Moths for Forgetfulness' or something."

"The Victorians loved that sort of thing," Clarence said. "The phrase likely refers to the Cornish superstition that moths were harbingers of forgetfulness. That they actually carried away memories, or dreams. I can't remember exactly. And she was quite a beauty, apparently."

"Yes, she was quite beautiful. And he was a very handsome man—Malcolm, I mean, judging by the portrait."

The old man hesitated. "Do you know anything about . . . well, about the family dynamics? You see, I don't mean to be presumptuous. I don't want to tell you things you already know. What I know is a mixture of history and second-hand stories passed along by my father, who in turn heard them from Beckett, the butler at Wild Fell. As you can see, it's a bit of a broken telephone, historically speaking. On the other hand, frankly, the facts of record are fairly dry. Catherine died in 1847 of what we would now call cancer; she was only forty or so."

I nodded, remembering the pain in the woman's eyes in the portrait, her preternatural thinness, and what I now realized was premature aging from illness.

"Alexander Blackmore never remarried. He retreated to the house and raised Rosa and Malcolm as a single father, which was pretty unusual in those days, let me tell you. He died under fairly gruesome circumstances in an accident in 1883. The children—well, they were grown by then, of course—were extremely close. They lived on at Wild Fell till they were very old."

"I'm sorry, you said 'gruesome circumstances'?"

"Yes," Clarence said. "He was stung to death. By wasps."

I felt lightheaded. "What did you say?"

"Wasps."

"*How* . . . ?"

"He was out riding. In those days the Blackmores maintained a secondary stable manned by a groom at the edge of the point of land where their boathouse used to be. The ferrying place. If you've been there, you know the place I'm speaking about, am I correct?"

I nodded mutely. "I think so."

"He was on his way into town on some errand or other," Mr. Brocklehurst said. "The children were on the island. Well, hardly *children*, really. At that point, they must have been sixteen or seventeen, but no older than that. Blackmore had left them in the care of the servants that morning. He mustn't have gotten very far because apparently they could hear his screams—and the horse's—from across the lake. The groom had to put the horse down on the spot. By the time they managed to ferry Alexander Blackmore back to the island, he was dead. Ghastly way to die."

"Oh my God. What a horrible story."

"Well," he said. "That part of it isn't a story, it's a matter of historical record. He's buried in Carlton Cemetery up on the hill. The gravestone is very impressive. After you leave this afternoon, you should stop by and take a look, if you really want to get a sense of the kind of monuments people like Alexander Blackmore built for themselves to be remembered after they were dead. Gravestones, you know, they last forever. Not like houses."

"You said, 'that part of it.' Is there some other part?"

"Ah," Clarence said. "Well now, that depends."

"Depends on *what*?"

"Well, it depends on where you draw the line between history—the kind that's documented and written down by journalists and historians—and oral history that may or may not be entirely factual, or at least is unproveable."

"You said your father played chess with the butler at Wild Fell. Did he tell your father these . . . well, these *other* stories? The unproveable ones?"

"Quite so," he said. "Would you like some more tea?"

"No, thank you, Mr. Brock . . . *Clarence*. I'm fine. But please, go on. What did the butler tell your father?"

"You understand, Jamie, that some of this is going to sound ridiculous, don't you?"

I repeated, "Please, go on."

"The 'other part' is that she killed him. Rosa killed her father with the wasps. She sent them to him. To stop him . . . well to stop him—" Here Clarence actually blushed and lowered his voice. "To stop him from . . . interfering with her. Molesting her."

"What are you saying? That you believe Rosa Blackmore was some sort of *witch*?"

"No, I'm not saying that, Jamie," he said. "I'm just telling you what the butler told my father. Me, I don't believe in witches. Or magic. But the butler swore to my father that her relationship with her father was never 'natural,' as he put it. Not on Rosa's part, you understand. He was quite clear that if there was abuse— and I'm not saying there was, because this is all hearsay—she was an unwilling participant. But in those days, cut off from everyone on that island, in that house . . . well, anything was possible, especially something that unspeakable."

"Of course she was," I said. "No child is ever a willing participant in abuse. No wonder she was obsessed with moths, if that was the superstition—that they took away memory. Her memories must have been nightmarish. But why did anyone think she was a witch? I can't imagine anything crueller than spreading that sort of rumour about a victim of incest."

"Oh, believe me, if there were rumours spread, I never heard them," Clarence said quickly. "And I certainly wouldn't be spreading them about any child, living or dead. As far as I know, the only person who ever spoke of it was the butler and he only told my father, then swore my father to secrecy. But I don't think any of the servants would have begrudged her if she *had* killed her father with witchcraft."

"But why? Why did they think that?"

He waved his hand dismissively. "Oh, stories," he said. "We're not talking about an educated class of people, Jamie—servants in those days. It wouldn't take much for an old book to be considered a 'strange book.' Rosa's apparent obsession with mirrors might also have inspired superstition. Another story was that she had some sort of 'secret chamber' in one of the basements of the house, and that she used it for casting spells. According to my father, after Alexander Blackmore died, Rosa grew obsessed with the idea of escaping him in the afterlife by 'bending time' as she apparently called it, whatever that means, and ensuring that he could never come back to hurt her again."

"It sounds like she had a nervous breakdown." I thought of the bestial nature I had seen in the portrait of Alexander Blackmore in the cellar of Wild Fell. "It would hardly be surprising, considering what she went through."

"But at the end of the day, her father was dead and she was free. She was already close to her twin, but according to what I've heard, they grew even closer. In any case, they lived together till the end of their lives."

"Didn't either of them marry? Leave the island, ever?"

"As far as I my research went, Malcolm got engaged when he was thirty or so. Her name was Ailsa Crane. He'd met her in Toronto when he was there attending to some sort of family business. She was the daughter of a prominent lawyer, E.W. Crane."

"Malcolm was engaged? Did he marry?"

"No," Clarence said. "They didn't marry. His fiancée apparently drowned in Devil's Lake in 1888. Malcolm had made a visit back home to introduce Ailsa to his twin sister. Presumably he was also going to tell Rosa that he and Ailsa would be setting up housekeeping elsewhere, either in Alvina, or back in Toronto. According to the story my father heard, Rosa and Malcolm quarrelled about his leaving Wild Fell. Rosa didn't fancy being left alone." He paused thoughtfully. "Ailsa drowned the following night. It seemed as though she had just sleepwalked into the lake. She was in her nightclothes; she wasn't dressed for any sort of swimming. God only knows why she didn't wake up, but apparently she didn't."

"Mother of God."

Clarence shrugged. "Malcolm was disconsolate, but he apparently never left Wild Fell after that night, not even for his fiancée's funeral. Ailsa's body was shipped back to Toronto unaccompanied. Her father was livid, threatened all sorts of things, but nothing came of it. The Blackmore name carried a lot of clout in those days. In any case, Rosa and Malcolm died within a day of each other. That," he said pointedly, "is another one of the very few historical facts in all of this mess. That, and the very sad reality that if the worst suspicions about the actual nature of the relationship between Alexander Blackmore and his daughter are true, then he and her brother are the only two men she ever knew."

I sat back in my chair. The double meaning of Clarence's "knew" was not lost on me. I was beyond merely speechless. I had been expecting some biographical sketches, not this northern gothic fairy tale.

Across the living room, Clarence took my measure. He regarded me sympathetically. "I'm sorry, Jamie. You asked. But maybe I should have minded my own business back there in the library."

"No, I'm grateful," I lied. "I'd heard a bit of this from the real estate agent when I went out there the first time. Nothing as detailed or graphic as this story. But still, it's the sort of thing I probably would have appreciated her telling me before I bought the house in the first place."

He sighed. "Well, in fairness, there isn't any real way a British real estate agent could have known these details. They're rather esoteric."

"No," I said. "I didn't deal with a real estate agent in England. I dealt with one here in Alvina. She should have warned me about this. It's hard to imagine going back there now. It's beautiful, but all the wood and silver and portraits in the world aren't going to make me forget what you've told me about the family, and what happened in that house."

Again, he looked confused, as he had in the library. "You dealt with a local agent? Who was it? I'm surprised I didn't hear about it."

"Her name is Velnette Fowler. She has an office off Main Street. I found her extremely odd. She told me she wasn't my agent, she was the house's agent." I forced myself to laugh. "After what you've told me, I can certainly see why the house would need its own agent."

He whispered, "Say that name again?"

"Fowler," I said. "Velnette Fowler."

Clarence Brocklehurst's face drained of colour. He stared at me with some mixture of horror, anger and, most inexplicably, a new, terrible hurt.

Almost whispering, he asked, "Who are you? Why did you come to my house?"

I was stunned by this sudden turn of the conversation. "Why? You invited me. To talk about the Blackmores, remember? Your area of expertise."

"I remember," Brocklehurst said coldly. "At that time I was under the impression you were serious about researching Alvina history. I repeat, what are you doing here?"

When I didn't answer, he pointed to the door. "Please leave, Mr. Browning, if that's even your name. I had my doubts about you when you pretended to have bought Wild Fell, which you patently did not—if you had, you wouldn't be talking about what fine condition it's in. The house is a wreck. I've been there. But you seemed to be a nice fellow, and I imagined that your interest was harmless, even if you were lying. But to . . . to . . . use *Nettie* in your lies, especially after we told you what the drowning did to us all, and what happened to her. What I'd like to know is why you did it. What were you after? Just cruel kicks?"

"Sir, I have no idea what you mean."

He stood up abruptly. "Get out of my house, you sick, *sick* bastard. Coming here under false pretenses, getting me to talk like a lonely old fool. Who are you? What's wrong with you? Get out now before I call the police. I'm warning you. Get out. Coming to a town like this and . . . and manipulating people? Is this how you get your kicks in the city?"

I stepped toward him and reached out with open hands. He flinched and stepped back from me.

"Mr. Brocklehurst, what's wrong. Are you all right?"

He shouted, *"Get out of my house! NOW!"*

"What's wrong? What did I do?"

He reached for the telephone on the table next to his chair. He picked up the receiver and said, "I'm giving you to the count of three. If you're not out of here by then, I'm calling 911. Leave, and don't come back."

I put up my hands and backed away toward the door. "I'm leaving," I said. "Please calm down. I'm going. And again, I'm sorry to have upset you. But I still don't understand what you mean by any of this. But I'm leaving."

Standing outside on the front steps, I heard the sound of a teacup shattering on the other side of Clarence Brocklehurst's slammed front door.

Outside, a light fog was beginning to blow in from the direction of Devil's Lake.

I drove for twenty minutes, trying to calm myself and make some sense of what had happened, but if there was a method to Brocklehurst's bizarre mood swing, it entirely eluded me. This had been the third surreal encounter I'd had with one of the Alvina locals since my arrival—the first was Mrs. Fowler and her refusal to take me out to the island to show me my house. The second had been the librarian, who spoke of the drowning of Brenda Egan and Sean Schwartz as though it had happened yesterday. And now her father had thrown me out of his house and accused me of being a vindictive fraud.

I pulled the Volvo over to the side of the road and phoned Hank's number. I needed to speak to her, to tell her what had happened since I'd been here, and to hear her tell me that everything was going to be fine, that I was, as usual, making something out of nothing. I knew I wasn't, but I needed to hear her tell me I was. After the seventh or eighth ring, Hank still hadn't picked up, but neither had I been connected to her voicemail. Ten rings, eleven, twelve, all unanswered. I snapped the phone shut and placed it on the seat beside me, resisting the urge to throw it on the floor. I wanted to go home. I wanted to be back in the city, with my father and everything that was familiar.

My instinct was to turn the car around and find Highway 401 without delay. I didn't want to return to Wild Fell; I just wanted to forget that I'd ever come to Alvina at all.

On impulse, I hit the speed dial key that connected me to the switchboard at the MacNeil Institute. I had planned to call Nurse Jackson in the next few days to check on my father, but at that moment I needed to hear a familiar voice. Again, the phone rang, but no one picked up. I frowned. The switchboard at MacNeil was manned twenty-four hours a day.

It's an Alzheimer's clinic, for God's sake. Someone is always there to pick up the phone.

I continued to let it ring. Fifteen, seventeen, finally twenty rings. After the twenty-first ring I gave up.

I stepped out of the car, intending to try again in the open air in case the signal was being jammed in some way by my location, or more likely by my distance from a powerful enough cell tower.

Across the road, I saw the tall iron spikes of what could only be Carlton Cemetery, the graveyard that Brocklehurst had identified as the location of the tomb of Alexander Blackmore and his wife, Catherine Agnes Russell.

In spite of everything I'd heard that afternoon, and in spite of my own discoveries, I was seized by a powerful need to see the grave—if only perhaps to assure myself that Alexander Blackmore was dead and in the earth here, far from the island, far from the house I'd purchased that bore his name. It might, I felt, remove some of the revulsion I carried with me since finding his slashed portrait hidden away in the cellar. There was no doubt in my mind now about who had done the slashing, or why—or what she had been trying to say with it. Rosa Blackmore may have been a victim, but she had not been a mute one.

Once inside the gates, the Carlton Cemetery was larger than it had first appeared from the other side of the wrought iron fence. A small chapel stood opposite the entrance. It appeared to have been constructed using the same local quarry granite as had been used in the construction of Wild Fell, but it had been designed in a more modest variation of the same gothic revival style.

The stone path leading deeper into the cemetery was overgrown, and littered with fallen leaves and pine needles. The surface of the majority of the gravestones were worn nearly smooth, but I was still able to make out enough names and dates to recognize that the cemetery was very old—older than any cemetery I had ever been in.

Some of the stones dated back to the early 1800s and marked the final resting places of families with Scottish and English names—MacIsaac, Kilbride, McKitrick, McDermid, Hungerford, Weaver, Weatherly, Cartwright, Foley, Barrs.

The trees shielding the graves were mostly old growth white pine, interspersed here and there with the ubiquitous oak and maple and elm; here, as elsewhere in Alvina, the leaves had turned and fallen in earnest, carpeting the ground in yellow, red and brown. Squirrels scampered and chased each other around the tombstones like unsupervised children at play.

All in all, the effect was not one of neglect, the age of everything notwithstanding. Rather, it seemed to be a place of rest—obviously, for the dead, but also for the living. However unlikely, it was not inconceivable to imagine families picnicking here after visiting the graves of departed loved ones, or of walking dogs in the more convivial seasons.

In short order, I found the Blackmore mausoleum. It was a far cry from a mere tombstone, a far cry even from a cenotaph. It would have been impossible *not* to find the last resting place of the Blackmores, which clearly was the intention of the man who commissioned its construction before he died.

The tomb itself featured a four-sided roof with stained-glass dormer windows. The glass was too dirty to clearly identify the design, but it looked to be ecclesiastical in nature. Carved marble lions slumbered on pillars next to the wide stairs leading to the door. Four Greek revival marble pillars supported the roof, the peak of which was blazoned with the name BLACKMORE cut into the marble. I walked around the side of the tomb and read the inscription grandly carved into the wall of the tomb, below the coat of arms:

In Memory of Alexander Samuel Blackmore
Master of Wild Fell
A native of St. Juliot in Cornwall
Died 13th September 1883
In the 50th year of his Age
ALSO
Catherine Agnes Russell
Wife of the Above
Died 20th January 1847
In the 37th year of her Age

I walked around the entire tomb and searched the immediate grounds, but I couldn't find the graves of Rosa and Malcolm Blackmore. Even though there was a clearly designated vacancy beneath Alexander and Catherine Blackmore's epitaph where Rosa and Malcolm's epitaphs were meant to be inscribed—and, given the size of the mausoleum, someday *their* children, grandchildren, and great-grandchildren—there was no mention of the Blackmores' son and daughter carved anywhere on the mausoleum.

That in itself—the sharp, abrupt end of a dynasty that had barely begun—whispered its own mysterious, poignant tale, one that suggested much but offered nothing by way of explanation.

None of it was surprising, of course, given what I now suspected about the Blackmores. It seemed likely that in their old age, Rosa and Malcolm Blackmore had left instructions to be buried elsewhere in the cemetery, perhaps as far from their father as possible. Still, I decided to make at least one cursory attempt to find their graves before leaving the cemetery.

In short order, I found myself in the newer section of the cemetery—"new" being a relative term, as some of the graves dated from the 1930s and 1940s, though most were much newer than that, and dated from the 1960s and later.

In the shade of a large oak beside a stone bench, I came upon what was obviously a family plot. The graves were arranged in a circle around a small, delicate gravestone clearly a young girl's. At the upper curve of the stone was perched a tiny stone angel, hands folded in prayer and mourning. After the ostentation of the Blackmore tomb, I found this marker poignant in its simplicity. I leaned down and read the name on the stone.

BRENDA LOUISE EGAN
1944–1960
Beloved daughter and niece, taken too soon
The Sky is Brighter Tonight

I had found the grave of the girl who had drowned in Devil's Lake, near Wild Fell in 1960. Next to her stone was a larger, plainer one engraved *Thomas Egan*, with the dates of his birth and death, and next to it was the grave of *Edith Austin Egan, Wife and Mother*. The grieving family was gathered around their daughter, finally reunited in death. Farther behind were two more gravestones, these obviously belonging to Brenda Egan's grandparents.

As I turned away from the Egan plot to resume my search for Malcolm and Rosa Blackmore's graves, a squirrel skipped past my feet. Startled by the sudden movement, I followed its grey trajectory across the ground toward the trunk of the oak tree up which it scampered.

In doing so, I noticed that there was one more grave in the plot. I hadn't noticed it before because, unlike the others which had been upright, this one was a flat stone set into the earth face-up.

What I read on the tombstone, I read twice. Then I read it a third time. Then a fourth time. But even when I'd read it a fifth time, the initial chill I'd felt remained. The stone read, *Velnette Audrey Fowler (1935–1962), Beloved Wife of Arthur Wallace Fowler and Devoted Aunt of Brenda Egan*. And below that, *Vengeance is Mine Sayeth the Lord*.

What kept my knees from buckling—the *only* thing—was the knowledge that what I was seeing must be a mistake, or a coincidence, or some sort of prank.

When rational sense told me that there was no possibility of a "coincidence" like this in a town as small as Alvina, and that no one could be playing a joke on me with a gravestone that had lain undisturbed in a country cemetery for almost half a century, I shut rational sense down and instead focused on the details of Mrs. Fowler's appearance: the distinctive way she drove her Chevy at a snail's pace along the road to Wild Fell; the way she'd thrown the keys at my feet.

Perhaps she had a sister who now ran the office? And yes, I *had* been in that office. Mrs. Fowler had handed me papers with written instructions on how to get to Wild Fell. I *had* the papers—where? Were they in the car? No, I had left them back at the house. I felt in my pocket for the iron keys. I located them easily enough. And yes, the iron ring was there. When I pulled the keys out of my pocket, it took me a moment to realize that the whimper I'd heard had come from my own throat.

I did not buy Wild Fell from a ghost. No, a million times over. Ghosts were not real. People were real. Fathers were real and their love was real.

Houses are real. Wild Fell was real.

And yet, this grave.

It was Mrs. Beams who came to the door in answer to my banging this time. Not her father. When she saw it was me, her face went white with rage. Her father might have been afraid of me, but she was not. She pushed herself into the doorway, elbowing me out of the way, onto the front step, using her own body to block the entrance to his house.

"Get the hell out of here," she said in a voice that was remarkably flat and calm, diametrically opposed to the protective fury blazing in her eyes. "Get the hell off this property or I'll call the police. You may have conned my father into letting you into his house, at least before you sent him into hysterics, but you won't con me. I'm not a lonely old widower desperate to talk to someone he isn't related to. What are you, some sort of freak? Do you enjoy taking advantage of old men? Are you queer? Do you want to try taking advantage of *me*? *Do you?*"

I heard the shrill whine in my own voice when I answered her, but I was powerless to speak any other way. "I don't know what happened. We were talking fine, then I mentioned my house and the real estate agent who sold it to me. Mrs. Fowler—"

Mrs. Beams slapped me across the face as hard as she could. My head snapped back as though it were on hinges. I heard the crack of her hand on my cheek even before I felt the heat and pain. I stumbled back from the force of the blow and nearly fell down the stairs. I stumbled backward down the steps, only righting myself on the banister just in time to keep myself from falling.

"Stop it," she hissed. "Stop it, you bastard. Stop saying her name!"

I stared at her blankly. My cheek throbbed. "Stop what? Whose name? What did I do? I don't know what I did!"

"Do you know how badly you upset him? That you would use *her* name—to him—for whatever con game you're playing . . . you're disgusting. We *loved* her, all of us. She was like a second mother to Brenda. We all called her Aunt Nettie. She was the kindest woman in Alvina." The fury in Mrs. Beams' eyes was annihilating. "How did you get her name? The Egan family kept it out of the papers when it happened. How did you find out about Velnette's accident?"

"When *what* happened? I have no idea what you're talking about. What accident? Please, this is like a nightmare. She's not dead! I spoke with her yesterday. I want to understand. What's going on? Please tell me."

"As if you don't know!"

"I *don't* know! I don't know what's going on!"

"You told him 'Mrs. Fowler' sold you Wild Fell, and that you were staying up there? Well, as you already know, that's not a very believable lie. Aside from everything else, Wild Fell is a dilapidated wreck. And do you know how I know, Mr. Con Man from the city? Because I've been out there and seen it with my own eyes. I went there to put flowers on the place where . . . where she . . ." Tears came to Mrs. Beams' eyes, but she stared me down through them. "It's a wreck. It's *uninhabitable*."

"No," I insisted. "It's *not* a wreck. The house hasn't aged a day since it was built, apparently. Mrs. Fowler said so herself. If it was a ruin once, someone fixed it up. It's a beautiful house. Mrs. Fowler"—here I flinched, but she didn't strike me again—"said that a cleaning crew had worked on it. They must have worked very hard, especially if it was ruined, like you say. You have to believe me. There are candles, and paintings, and furniture. I slept in one of the bedrooms last night, in clean sheets. I slept in Rosa Blackmore's bedroom. Look!" I took the iron key ring out of my pocket and jangled it in front of her. "These are the keys to the house. I'm telling you, you're mistaken. Please, if I was lying, why would I have these keys?"

At the sight of the keys, some of the fury left her face. She looked at the keys with confusion, even mild curiosity, then back at me with something not unlike pity. Her regard was still cold, but the hatred and loathing of a few moments ago had disappeared.

"Mr. Browning," Mrs. Beams said. "Look, I'm sorry I hit you. Truly, I am. I don't know who you are. I don't know what you want. I don't know what your story is. I frankly wish you'd go back to wherever it is you came from. You people from the city come out to places like Alvina and we must all seem like rubes to you, just a bunch of dumb hicks who keep your 'cottage country' ready for you to come back to every summer. But we're more than that, Mr. Browning. Things happen out here in these towns. People have lives. They are born here, they live here, and they die here. They suffer things, things you people never see. You throw around names like 'Brenda Egan' or 'Mrs. Fowler' to my father like they were nothing but plot points in a novel. Well, sir, they were more than that to all of us. They were people we loved."

"I saw the grave." I was pleading, though I wasn't sure what I was pleading *for*. Confirmation I was the butt of some monstrous joke? That I wasn't insane? Even confirmation that I *was* insane would have been welcome just then. Anything real would have been. "I saw her gravestone in the Carlton Cemetery. But it's not possible. I *saw* her. I *spoke* with her. She handled the sale of Wild Fell to me. I'm *telling* you, I followed her to Blackmore Island in my car—"

"Just shut up, Mr. Browning." Mrs. Beams sounded tired now. "Shut up and listen to me, because I'm only going to say this once, and then I'm going to close this door. And if I ever see you around my father again, the police may not get here in time. Do we understand each other?"

I nodded dumbly.

She took a deep breath. "If you're running some sort of scam then I hope you rot in hell. If you're not, then you're the victim of a cruel prank at best, or a fraud. You didn't buy any house from any 'Mrs. Fowler.' There is a reason I know this: Velnette Fowler died in 1962." Mrs. Beams let that sink in, then continued. "She was indeed a real estate agent. She and her husband ran one of the oldest real estate agencies in Alvina. They'd taken it over from her husband's family. When he died, she tried to keep it up, but her heart wasn't in it anymore. So you're off by about fifty years." There was no humour in Mrs. Beams' smile. "Velnette had become deeply depressed after Brenda's drowning, especially coming so soon after losing her husband. He was the first love of her life. They never had any children, so Brenda was like a daughter to her. Brenda's drowning probably drove Velnette mad."

I was on the urge of blurting out *she's not dead!* again, but some inner compass of reason checked me before I did. I knew if I said that, Mrs. Beams would hit me again or, at the very least, stop talking to me at all.

Instead, I settled for, "How did she die?"

"She burned to death," Mrs. Beams said simply. "I know my father told you those ridiculous stories about the Blackmore family this afternoon. Well, unlike my father and I, Velnette actually believed them. She was convinced that, somehow, something in the ruin of that house killed Brenda and Sean. She believed all those stories about Rosa Blackmore being something other than completely human. She was sure that something on Blackmore Island wanted Brenda and Sean's souls."

"But Brenda Egan drowned," I said weakly. "It happens. It's a tragedy, but it's not—"

"Supernatural?" Mrs. Beams practically spat the word. "Is that what you were going to say? Well, I'm inclined to believe you, but many here in Alvina wouldn't. When they pulled Brenda's body out of the water, it was covered with moths. They say it was like she was wrapped in a sheet."

I had a sudden vivid image of the framed Lepidoptera display in the yellow bedroom at Wild Fell, and the marquetry box on the mantelpiece with the moth design, containing Rosa's cameo.

"Moths?"

Mrs. Beams ignored me and continued. "In any case," she said, "Velnette took a can of gasoline out there one afternoon in a boat. Her plan was to burn what was left of that house to the ground. But something happened. Maybe there was a sudden wind, or maybe she spilled some of the gasoline on herself by accident. In any case, her clothes caught fire. She and my parents had been close friends. My father is the one who found her that night—he knew where to look, because she'd spoken of almost nothing else in the week leading up to her death except 'getting revenge on that place.' When he found her, she was already dead. She had third-degree burns covering ninety percent of her body. Dad brought her charred body back to Alvina in his canoe."

"There's a burned spot," I said. "The beams are charred in one of the porticos off the main house. I saw it this morning. The wall is concrete. The fire couldn't penetrate the house—"

Mrs. Beams closed the screen door in my face. "Now please leave, Mr. Browning, or whoever you are. Or I *will* call the police. And don't come back." She was just about to close the main door, but something seemed to give her pause. Behind the screen, her face, backlit by the living room lamps, was indistinct and her voice was curiously flat when she spoke, as though she were deliberately masking any tonality that might alert me to what she was actually thinking. "Mr. Browning?"

I waited.

"Whatever you're trying to pull here, I don't know what it is, and I don't want to know. I just want you to stay away from my father, okay?"

I nodded. "I'm not trying to 'pull' anything, ma'am. Of course I'll stay away from your father, but I—"

Again she cut me off before I could continue, and I knew this would be the last time she and I ever spoke. "On the other hand, on the off chance you're the real victim here, the mark in some swindle, and you've been sold a Brooklyn Bridge here in Alvina through no fault of your own—and if you are, again, I'm sorry I hit you—there's something you should know. When they did the autopsy on Velnette, they found dead moths in her throat. Her throat was *packed* with them, just like Brenda's was when they found her in 1960."

"Why are you telling me this, Mrs. Beams?" Now *I* was angry, in spite of my own confusion and shock. I had made myself vulnerable by telling her my bizarre stories—not ghost stories, but stories of actual events, however unexplained at that moment—and she had chastised me for it. Now she was telling me stories of her own. "I told you the truth about everything that happened to me and you called me a liar! You told me you don't believe in any of this, but now you're telling me *this*? What kind of a game are *you* playing? What are *you* trying to say?"

"I'm saying it," Mrs. Beams said with suffocating patience. It was as though she were speaking to a recalcitrant fifth grader who refused to understand why he wasn't allowed to talk in her library. "*Listen* to me say it, Mr. Browning. I don't believe in witches—alive or dead—or ghosts. I believe in terrible accidents like the one that killed Velnette. I believe that teenage girls out swimming with their boyfriends get cramps, and drown in cold water. But the fact is, what they found in Velnette's throat had no business being there. Maybe whatever Velnette went to Blackmore Island to kill didn't *want* to be killed. Maybe it stopped her from killing it, and it punished her for trying to kill it." She paused again, carefully marshalling her words. "I'm not saying that's what happened, or even that it's what I believe happened. But if you're involved with some swindle to do with that place, even if you're the mark, maybe you should think twice about what you're playing around with. Now, get off my father's property. Leave us alone. Last warning."

"I don't believe in ghosts, Mrs. Beams."

She shut the main door. I heard the lock turn, and the porch light was switched off. I stood on the sidewalk in front of Clarence Brocklehurst's home and watched the lights turn off in the living room until the house was blind.

I spent an hour cruising slowly through Alvina's darkened streets searching for the place I'd turned off the highway and onto Main Street—the mid-century Main Street I'd seen yesterday afternoon, the one with the brass lampposts and the boxes of geraniums, not this new Main Street of convenience stores and souvenir shops.

At one point I was sure I recognized the corner down which I'd turned to Mrs. Fowler's office. But when I found what I thought was the place, there was only an office machine repair shop. The storefront was dark; the door locked tight, the street empty.

Later in the bright moonlight on the edge of town, I pulled over to the side of the road and tried to call Hank again. The line rang and rang, but again, no one picked up. There was likewise still no answer at the MacNeil Institute. The mechanical whirring of the ringtone in my ear seemed to go on forever.

Then, already knowing what the outcome would be, I stood in the road beneath the moon—that bright autumn moon which shone on everything but illuminated nothing—and dialled again.

Chapter Eight

JAMESON IN THE MIRROR

If necessity really is the mother of invention, then perhaps desperation is the father of memory.

The only proof of my sanity was back at Wild Fell, in Rosa Blackmore's bedroom—the manila envelope from Mrs. Fowler with her handwritten list of services and contractors, and her written instructions on how to drive between Alvina and Blackmore Island. When I went to turn on the GPS to find my way back to Wild Fell, it refused to boot up. As I had neither instructions nor a working GPS, I would have to find my way back to Wild Fell relying only on my own memory and the moonlight, which was now, at least, very bright. The place at which the road leading to Blackmore Island began, was at the turnoff near the supermarket where I'd bought supplies this afternoon.

I found the turnoff and began to drive back toward the house.

In the light of the moon, the roads were easy to follow and I was able to navigate them with relative ease. One road led to the next in an organic way. My subconscious had clearly recorded more in the way of recognition than my conscious mind would ever have thought possible.

As I drove, I replayed the events of the past twenty-four hours in my mind trying to make sense of them, but of course, none of it made sense. There was only one way it would ever even begin to make sense, and it was the one thing on which I pinned all my hopes for sanity.

I realized that even if I left Alvina that night and never came back, I would still need to see and touch Mrs. Fowler's envelope. I'd left it in my bag, on the floor of the yellow bedroom. I needed it. When I had the folder, I would leave and never come back. It was that simple.

That the house had been repaired and tended was not a question: I had been there. I had built fires in the fireplaces. I had slept in the yellow bedroom. I had gone downstairs to the cellar and I had seen the oil portraits of the family—portraits whose likenesses had matched the photocopies I had seen in the bright daylight of the Alvina Town Library.

Photocopies I had been handed in a file folder by Mrs. Beams herself.

This last thought cheered me immensely. Whatever was in question here, it wasn't my sanity. If all of this had been in my mind, if I had been suffering some sort of psychotic break or other, I would not have recognized the faces of the individual members of the Blackmore family in the copies of the photographs retrieved from the burned church. But I needed the file folder. It was the only concrete evidence I could show Clarence Brocklehurst that proved I had met and spoken with Velnette Fowler or, at the very least, someone pretending to be Velnette Fowler with the intention of swindling me out of a great deal of money.

I had to speak with Mr. Brocklehurst again. But if he still wouldn't speak with me, I would push the envelope through the mail slot in his front door on my way out of Alvina as I drove home to where I belonged: the city, with my father and Hank.

At the edge of Devil's Lake, I untied the Bass Tracker from the dock and climbed into the bow. I turned the key in the ignition and guided the boat back into deeper water. When I'd reached a good depth, I opened it up and pointed it towards Blackmore Island.

A full sturgeon moon had risen, large and low and red-tinged in the night sky behind Blackmore Island. As the Tracker swept to the rocky beach, I felt I could see every stone, every shimmer of the shallow water that had pooled around the larger boulders and recessed areas of the beach.

I tied the boat up, then found the stone staircase leading from the landing beach to the house and I began to climb, using the flashlight I'd bought earlier that day at the supermarket as secondary illumination, though it was a poor substitute for the moonlight.

A thought occurred to me as I climbed, a wild thought. It was not a thought that would have occurred to me yesterday, perhaps not even as recently as this afternoon.

At the summit, I crossed the overgrown tangle of ruined lawns and trees, playing the flashlight across the copse of pine I'd seen struck by lightning last night, searching for the branch I'd watched burn and the place where I'd seen the figure of the woman standing in the rain. I kept my light trained on the ground until I found it, found what I realized I knew I'd find there.

Two gravestones, each the twin of the other, rose out of the flinty soil of Blackmore Island in the protective shelter of the white pine grove. I shone the light on the first stone and read *Malcolm Alexander Blackmore 1833-1928.*

The second stone, his sister's, read *Rosa Amanda Blackmore 1833-1928.* Inscribed beneath it was the motto, *I will always find you.*

Rosa Amanda Blackmore. Rosa *Amanda* Blackmore.

"Amanda," I said aloud, suddenly nine years old again. "Amanda."

The front door stood open.

I walked up the wide cement stairs of the veranda, and then crossed the threshold of Wild Fell. *My* house. Of *course* it was my house. Of course it was real; of course it was solid. This was no ruin. I felt the hardwood floors and Oriental carpets beneath my feet, the wood panelling beneath my fingers. I could even smell the house: mahogany, silver, camphor, and dried violets.

Ruin, my ass. Fuck you, Mrs. Beams.

When I flipped the light switches back and forth, nothing happened. I waited for my eyes to grow accustomed to the dark. Once they had, I turned the flashlight back on and walked slowly down the hallway. I played the light on the carving of the Blackmore coat of arms on the soaring archway. From outside, the full moon lit the stained glass windows in the hallway, casting it into a lurid jewel-toned diorama.

I climbed the stairs to the yellow bedroom.

Now and then came the fluttering of moths. When I shone my flashlight in the direction of the sound, they descended in small clouds, attracted to the light. Then they fluttered away to the higher, darker recesses of the house.

Like the front door had been, the door to the yellow bedroom—a door that I'd closed before leaving the house that afternoon—was wide open.

The moonlight through the windows was bright enough that I didn't need the flashlight to see the contours of the room. I could clearly make out the furniture: the dressing table, the bed, and the full-length mirror reflecting the room behind it. It was in the glass of that mirror that I was able to see that the marquetry box, which I'd replaced on the mantelpiece that afternoon, was now sitting open in the middle of the bed.

I walked slowly to the edge of the bed and sat down. I placed my hand inside the box to see what latest gift I'd been offered by my invisible hostess. I found something cold and dry, like finely dressed leather.

From inside the box I withdrew the torn and mangled body of a tiny midland painted turtle. In the light of the flashlight, I was able to make out the yellow plastron with the butterfly markings. Two of the turtle's legs had been torn off. Its carapace was punctured with deep bites and the neck dangled from a greenish tendon, or perhaps just a stringy strand of the turtle's neck. It had been dead for a very, very long time.

Since 1971, I guessed.

It was Manitou, of course, the turtle I'd stolen from its home and brought back to the city, to its brutal death in the jaws of the neighbour's dog—a death that had been aided and abetted by my mother. All of which was shown to me on that terrible night when I had been nine and had returned to my bedroom from emptying my bladder only to find a candle lit beside my bed and Amanda, my secret friend, the little girl who lived in the glass, ready to show me any manner of horror, to threaten any manner of violence. That is, until I'd smashed my mirror, driven her away and erased the memory of an entire part of my childhood in the process.

Like everything else I could now remember, I recalled Amanda's parting words to me, the same words I'd found carved into the grave of Rosa Blackmore almost a century before I was born: *I will always find you.*

From the shadows of the yellow bedroom I heard, or imagined I heard, a soft, cruel giggle.

My hand stank of pond carrion. I dropped the turtle's tiny body on the floor. It landed on the carpet with a soft, tragic little *thud,* and lay there in the moonlight beside my bag. Furiously, I wiped my hand on my thigh, desperately trying to scrub away the stench.

Then I saw the edge of Mrs. Fowler's manila envelope extruding from the unzipped opening.

The relief I felt at that moment wiped away every other fear and made my senses swim. *Oh, thank God,* I thought. *Proof!* Whatever the rest of this madness was about, here at last was proof that someone real had sold me this house and brought me here to this island. At that moment, I didn't care if I'd been the victim of a world-class real estate swindle. I would have paid the money a hundred times over for the relief of knowing I was not insane. Nearly weeping with joy, I plucked the envelope out of the bag and shone the flashlight at the papers I had withdrawn. Then I looked closer and tried to make sense of what I was holding.

It was a sheaf of perhaps twenty closely handwritten pages tied with purple ribbon, a sprig of dried violet tucked beneath. The flower was so old that the very act of bringing the paper up into the light of my flashlight caused it to crumble away to dust before my eyes. The paper was likewise ancient, parchment-thin, browned with many, many decades of exposure to the air. The ink had likely been deep blue once, but it was now pale and faded. I tugged at the ribbon; it, too, turned to powder at my touch.

The document was written in a feminine hand, the letters small and beautifully formed in the way young ladies from good families had been taught to write a hundred years ago.

I want to teach you about fear.

I want to tell you a ghost story. It's not a ghost story like any ghost story you've ever heard. It's my ghost story, and it's true. It happened here in the house on Blackmore Island called Wild Fell, in the inland village of Alvina, Ontario on the shores of Devil's Lake. Like any ghost story, it involves the bridges between the past and the present and who, or rather what, uses them to cross from the world of the living into the world of the dead.

But I'm getting ahead of my story. I did say the bridge is between the past and the present. Although I'll tell you this story in the present, I would be remiss if I didn't start with the past—specifically my past. Time is, or ought to be, linear. Sometimes it's anything but linear, which brings us back to ghosts.

I shook my head. What I was reading was gibberish. There was nothing here about Alvina Power, or the phone company, or the names and numbers of any of the contractors or cleaning companies that had been engaged by Mrs. Fowler in the preparation of Wild Fell for sale. There were no directions to and from Alvina. Furthermore it was *old* gibberish. These pages must have been written in the heyday of Wild Fell, in the nineteenth century.

Why had Mrs. Fowler—or whoever was pretending to be her—taken the time to put them in a folder she'd claimed was full of practical information, only to have it be the preamble to an elaborate practical joke involving what appeared to be a fledgling nineteenth-century authoress's attempt at a ghost story—an attempt that had somehow survived almost a hundred years, likely in some drawer or trunk in this old house?

And then, in the trembling light of my flashlight, I saw my own name in the ancient violet handwriting, and I felt my heart shudder in my chest.

My name is Jameson Browning. In the summer of 1971, when I was nine, I went to Camp Manitou, the summer camp deep in rural eastern Ontario where edges of towns yielded to woods and marshes and rolling farmland hills.

I hadn't wanted to go at all. I deeply distrusted boys of my own age, all of whom had proven themselves to be coarse and rough and prone to noise and force. It would be tempting for anyone reading this to imagine a socially isolated, lonely boy with no friends—a loner not so much by choice, but by ostracism or social ineptitude. But the conjured image would be an inaccurate one. I wasn't a lonely boy at all, not by any stretch.

I read the words again.

"No," I said aloud, reasonably. "No, no." I read the paragraph twice more, then laid it down on the bed beside me. "Not possible. This is not about me. I am not in a ghost story written a hundred years ago. This is a trick. Someone is tricking me."

The hysteria felt like jubilation, as though the fact that someone would take such an enormous amount of care in setting up this elaborate ruse to drive me insane was a proof of love beyond anything I had ever experienced in my life. Perhaps I really was extraordinary at long last, extraordinary enough to warrant the time it had taken to execute this cruelty.

"*GREAT TRICK!*" I screamed into the darkness of the house, laughing at the echo that skipped across Wild Fell like a stone.

And then I heard the most welcome sound in the world: the one sound that represented any possible chance I might have at salvation. I heard the front door open with a bang and the heavy tread of work boots on the hallway floor.

"Jamie!" Hank's voice blasted up from downstairs. "Jesus fucking Christ! Jamie! Where are you? You scared the shit out of me! I got your message from yesterday and I came right away. I've been driving all night!"

I shouted, "Hank! I'm up here! Stay there! I'm coming down!"

I swayed on my feet when I stood up, dropping the flashlight to the floor. It rolled beneath the bed, the light vanishing beneath the dust ruffle, then winking out altogether.

I'm going to pass out from sheer relief, I thought giddily. *Sweet God in Heaven, thank you.*

I laughed as I stumbled out of the yellow bedroom into the darkness of the hallway, high on narcotic relief and thundering adrenaline. In the air above me, I heard the fluttering of the moths. They circled my head; they brushed against my face and hands with fairy skeleton bones of legs and wings like strands of milkweed in the wind. They alighted on my forehead; they caressed my eyes, their touch like dry snowflakes against my skin. I brushed them away, pinwheeling my arms in the air and swatting frantically to keep more from landing.

At the edge of the hallway I looked down over the banister and shouted,

"Hank! Where are you? It's so dark—shout so I can follow your voice!"

Hank yelled something encouraging in reply as I continued to descend the staircase, feeling my way in the feeble light from the moon behind the stained glass windows, but Hank's voice was fainter now, as though she had moved deeper in the house. I heard a door slam—*the kitchen door?*—and I staggered down the hallway toward the sound. There were brief bursts of moonlight through the windows as I passed the empty library and the parlour.

"Hank!" I shrieked. "Where the fuck are you? I can't find you!"

I heard another crash, this one coming from the dining room.

Oh Jesus, finally, I thought as I ran down the hallway. Then a dreadful thought followed that one. *What if she's hurt? Maybe she hurt herself coming here to save me, and now she can't call out anymore. Oh please, God, let her be all right. Let us both be all right, and let us both get away from this place tonight.*

Hank was not in the dining room, either, but I saw the door of the servants' entrance slowly swinging back and forth. The sound I had heard must have been Hank crashing into it on her way to . . . the kitchen? I ran through the doorway into the kitchen.

It was empty. But at its far end, the doorway to the cellar stood ajar. No, not ajar. It was wide open.

In a voice not much louder than a whisper, I called out, "Hank? Are you there? Where are you? Answer me," I pleaded. "Please, Hank."

And then from the cellar, I heard Hank's voice. It was clear and wonderfully calm and strong—the most calming voice I knew.

"Jamie, I'm here. I'm downstairs. Come on down."

"Hank, can you come up?"

"Jamie, come on," came the mocking-but-still-loving-bro voice in the cellar. "Don't be such a goddamn *girl!* You've got to check this out! Then we'll go. I've got a boat on the beach. I'll take you back to the city. We'll drive all night and make it a road trip. I'm going to need a Timmy's double-double before we hit the highway. Come on, hurry up!" It was Hank's warm, joyful laugh—the essence of all things Hank—which finally made my decision for me.

Whatever had happened at Wild Fell in the last twenty-four hours, my best friend was here and no problem was, or would ever be, a match for her ability to solve it and triumph. Everything would be all right. We would be on our way home to the city within the hour. I crossed the floor to the open doorway at the far end of the kitchen. Then, careful not to slip, I climbed down the stairs to the cellar where Hank was waiting.

As I descended the steps, I felt the cold drift of air I had noticed that morning. I became aware, too, of a weird flickering glow emanating from somewhere in the basement's depths. The glow grew brighter as I descended farther into the subterranean part of Wild Fell, as did the chill and the aroma of dirt and wintry rot.

When I reached the foot of the stairs, I paused in the antechamber and tried to let my eyes grow accustomed to this deeper darkness, but also to locate the source of the weird flickering pinprick of light. Finally, I did. The doorway to the third room—the farthest room from the entrance to the cellar, the room that had been locked tight that afternoon, but from behind whose door I had heard things moving—stood open.

It was the latest in the series of doors that had been open tonight—the front door, the yellow bedroom, the servants' door to the kitchen, the cellar door in the kitchen, now this one far beneath Wild Fell—none of them by me. In a voice just past louder than a whisper, I said, "Hank? Where are you? I can't see anything down here."

This time there was no reply. Then the cellar door to the kitchen slammed shut in the darkness above me, sealing me underground.

Because I was likely insane by that point, I believed entirely that it was still logical to conclude that Hank was in the third room in the basement, that Hank had lit the candles whose light I could now see, that Hank would be the one waiting for me as I made my way along the hallway, feeling my way along the rough stone walls of the cellar.

I passed the portraits I'd left stacked in front of the doorway to the second room. The portrait of the predatory Alexander Blackmore was where I'd left it: turned like an errant schoolboy forced to face the wall after misbehaving in class.

"You miserable cocksucker," I said to the back of the portrait. "You fucking child molester. Yeah, *you*, you rapist piece of shit. I know what you did here. The whole town knows now, you prick. I hope you burn in hell."

The light beckoned me, growing brighter and brighter with each step of my progress, until finally I stood in the open doorway of the third room. It was empty.

Hank was not there. Hank had never been there.

The walls were thick with dust, so thick in fact that the candlelight seemed to be absorbed by it. Yes, someone had indeed lit candles, two to be exact, each rising out of a floor-standing hammered-silver pillar candlestick.

In the centre of the room, flanked by the two candles, stood a large full-length mirror whose glass, latticed with webs of tiny cracks, looked almost dark blue in the candlelight.

My eyes were drawn to the mirror's frame, the thick gold scrollwork, and the ornate design. When I stepped closer to better examine it, I saw that what I had initially taken to be flowers carved into the gold were in fact runic symbols, interspersed with tiny, exquisite renderings of carved moths. I realized then that I *had* seen this mirror before, if only the edge of it.

This was the mirror from the photograph I'd found in the library, the photograph of Rosa Blackmore posing in the glass more than a hundred years before.

I turned my back to the glass and said, "Amanda? Are you there?"

There was silence. And then that familiar voice seemed to come from everywhere and nowhere. Yet as I had when I was a child, I still felt my mouth form the words—her words.

Yes, Jamie. I'm here. Turn around.

"Amanda, why? Why have you done all of this? What could you possibly want from me?"

Jamie, look into the mirror.

I moaned and covered my face with my hands. "No, Amanda, I won't look into the mirror. Go away. You're not real. None of this is real."

Jamie, look into the mirror. Look in the mirror and all of this will be finished.

"No. You're still making me see things that aren't real, that aren't there, just like you did when I was nine. My name is Jameson Browning," I began, reciting the basic facts of my life like a mantra to ward off evil spirits. "I am a middle-aged man with a father in an Alzheimer's hospital. My father is a kind, loving man. And I am the owner of Wild Fell and Blackmore Island. I bought them from Mrs. Fowler with money from my accident. You're not real."

Jamie, you're behaving like a child. Don't you want to understand why you're here?

I squeezed my eyes shut. "You are not real, Amanda. I reject your existence. You have never been real, and you have nothing to explain to me about why I'm here. I'm here because I bought this house. I own it. Wild Fell is mine."

Oh is it? This time there was humour in the voice. *How interesting. We'll have a long, long time to discuss the proper ownership of Wild Fell. But in the meantime tell me—haven't you ever wondered why you've always believed your father was perfect, Jamie? I always knew mine wasn't. Do you really think that's normal? Do you think that's how normal boys, or men, think of their fathers? That they're perfect?*

"He *is* perfect." Even to my own ears my voice had acquired a childish singsong *na-na-na-na* quality. "He was kind to me every day of his life. He was kind to everyone. Why are you talking about my father?"

Because I'm going to kill him tonight, Jamie, that's why. I failed that night on the bridge when the policeman saved him. But there's no one to protect him now. I will visit him again tonight while he sleeps. You have no idea of the dreams I send him, Jamie. Terrible, terrible dreams. I torture him with them. Tonight I will have his last breath.

"Why, Amanda? Why do you keep hurting people? Why do you keep hurting *me*?"

Touch the glass, Jamie.

And then because there was nothing left to do, no other way to make the voice stop, no way to bring an end to the terrible lies it whispered, I looked into Rosa Blackmore's mirror and placed the tips of my fingers against the cold glass one last time.

This time there was no shock, no violence to my body. I felt nothing pass through me. For a nanosecond, I caught a glimpse of my own shape in the dark blue glass.

Then the surface of the mirror rippled and shimmered beneath my touch, reflecting not the underground room beneath Wild Fell but rather the night-contours of the bedroom in my old house, the house in which I had grown up, the bedroom in which I was nine.

The bedside lamp had been switched off, but I could make out the dark hulk of my father's body looming over mine, my own body curled in on itself, hugging the pillow to my midsection. My back shook with the force of my sobbing. As I watched, my mirror-father traced his fingers along my spine, lingering at the place where my lower back met my waist. When he spoke, there was no love in this voice, no tenderness, only shame.

"Jamie, don't cry," my mirror-father said. "I'll just stay here with you here for a little while. Until you fall asleep. What's wrong? There's nothing to be scared of. Are you upset about the bike? We'll get it back. You shouldn't have gone out of our neighbourhood, but what happened wasn't your fault. Is that what this is about?"

"No, Daddy, I'm not upset about the bike. Please daddy no . . . it hurts too much. No more. I'll do anything you want. Please, daddy, I love you. I'll be good. I won't tell, I promise. But no more."

"Hush, Jamie," my father crooned. He began to rub my shoulders. "I'll just stay for a little bit. Just until you fall asleep." Then he lay down beside me on the bed and put his arm around my shoulders and pulled me in close, spooning his body around mine, locking my nine-year old body to his in an implacable grip.

Beside my narrow bed, the wall mirror. Innocuous looking, perhaps, but not empty. It had never been empty. It had always been a doorway, all through the lost years of my now-remembered childhood, a childhood in which every mirror in every room I had ever stepped had been a doorway.

"No!" I screamed. "That never happened! You made me see that. That's *not* what happened! He *never* hurt me! You were the one who hurt me, Amanda . . . Rosa . . . whoever you are! You killed Manitou; you killed that little boy who stole my bike with your wasps, just like *you* killed *your* father, because *he* hurt *you*. My father would never hurt me! Never!"

We'll kill him, Jamie. Amanda's voice was implacable. He has always hurt us, and we have always killed him. When we sent the wasps that day when our father was out riding, our father died terribly. If we had succeeded that night on the bridge in the city, our father would have died quickly. In this life, he has sought to escape our vengeance through oblivion, through forgetfulness. But we found him, anyway. We will always kill him and he will always die, no matter how hard he tries to forget what he did to us.

"THERE IS NO *WE!* YOU ARE NOT ME! THAT IS *YOUR* STORY, NOT MINE! THAT HAPPENED TO *YOU*, NOT ME!"

Her voice was the tauntingly cruel voice of a sadistic child impersonating a vastly patient adult woman, an adult woman with all the time in the world for torture.

Are you sure *it never happened, Jamie? Don't be stupid—I just showed you what your father did to you. How do you know it didn't happen? Haven't you always wondered why your mother really left him, Jamie? Do you not wonder if, perhaps, your mother was jealous of the attention your father was paying you?*

I turned my back on the mirror. "You're making me see things that aren't real, Amanda. It's your trick. You're not real. None of this is real. None of this happened. You're a liar—you always were. You're a sick, evil liar."

How do you know they aren't real, Jamie? How do you know he didn't hurt you and you didn't just forget about it when you smashed your bedroom mirror, like you forgot about everything else? You forgot about me, didn't you? What else have you forgotten?

"Shut up, Amanda! Shut up!"

Who did you really buy Wild Fell from, Jamie? Mrs. Fowler? How could you have? She's dead. You saw her grave. Everyone you've spoken to swears this house is a ruin. But you see furniture and paintings and rugs and silver. You see walls and doors and windows. Are they real?

"They're real, Amanda. I'm standing here in the basement of Wild Fell. The floor is real. The walls are real. The house is real. I've touched it. I slept in your bed. The only thing not real here is you."

Then why are you talking to me, Jamie, if I'm not real?

"Shut up! Shut up! Get out of my head!"

She was pitiless, relentless. *And if they are* not *real, what else is not real? Are* you *real, Jamie? Do you exist? How do you know you're not just a character in a ghost story I wrote one evening to amuse myself?*

"SHUT UP! SHUT UP! SHUT UP!"

No one believes in Wild Fell, Jamie. No one believes in you. *Where do you think you really are? Who do you think you really are?*

I looked wildly around the room to find something that I might use to smash the glass into a million pieces—to stop the lying voice I now knew had never been the voice of a little girl, but had always been Rosa Blackmore's voice, across time and through the doorways of any number of dimensions in between. She said she would always find me. She'd had it carved onto her own gravestone.

I reached for one of the silver candlesticks to swing at the glass, to shatter it and banish this creature forever by destroying her main portal into the world of the living.

But as I picked up the candlestick, the walls of the room trembled and shivered and I realized that I had been wrong about something else, as well—the walls were not coated with thick dust.

What I had at first taken for dust were thousands, perhaps millions, of tiny white moths. They clung to the wall, they clung to each other, three, six, nine layers deep. And now, disturbed by the movement and the sound of my voice, they began to stir.

Jamie, look into the mirror again, just one more time. Tell me whose reflection you see there. Look into the glass, Jamie. It will show you the shape of your true soul. And it will show you what else you've forgotten about who you are.

And I looked. God help me, I looked.

My face and body in the mirror had become the face and body of a woman of forty-five, a woman with a high, intelligent brow and eyes of the purest grey-green, the eyes of the portrait in the cellar. My long hair, chestnut brown now, was gathered in a loose knot behind my head, tendrils from which cascaded down the back of my neck. When I moved my hand across the glass, my hand moved there, too, with fingers that were long and white and slender.

"This is not real," I cried, my voice now a high, light musical contralto. I pointed my finger at the woman in the mirror. She pointed back with a slender index finger. My voice, her voice—Rosa Blackmore's voice—formed my words in the glass. "This is not my reflection. My name is Jameson Browning. I am a man, not a woman. You're still lying, Amanda. You're still hurting me."

Her mouth—my mouth—formed a perfect oval of horror and agony as she—*I*—screamed and screamed. I tore at my—*her*—face with those lovely white hands with their fine sharp nails until the blood began to flow; the reflection in the mirror was that of a keening, raving madwoman staring into her mirror, watching her own sanity flow away like water while she wept and gibbered and bled.

My mother, Catherine Blackmore, always said you could tell a lady by her hands. On those hot days of my girlhood summers here on the island that bore our name, Mother said it while forcing my own hands into white lace gloves to ward off the sun as I played. Malcolm had never been forced to wear gloves.

Boys don't have to, Mother said. *They're boys.*

Even before my father's vile, beastly depredations—depredations for which he paid with his life, at my hands and the hands of . . . certain *friends* of mine—the world had seemed woefully unfair to me. I hated the gloves and refused to wear them after I turned thirteen.

By that time, my mother was dead, and my father didn't care if my hands were white, only that they were soft. But my hands *are* white and lovely, and they *are* soft.

In time, Jameson's friend, the girl, Hank, will come to Blackmore Island. Her hands are not white, nor lovely, nor soft. Her hands are hard and rough, the hands of a man. She is possessed of a man's soul. I can *smell* it on her. She will come to find him, of that I have no doubt. I will ensure it. I will visit her tonight in her dreams and I will give her such a taste of his death that she will make haste to reach Blackmore Island even before the sun rises, in fear of his life. She won't find him, of course. No one will. But I will be waiting for her, here in my house.

When I find her, I will flay her alive and peel that male soul of hers like a grape.

And if I find that her soul is sheltering and disguising my brother Malcolm, I will discover it and I will make him suffer for having tried to escape me through death.

I heard the sound of Jameson Browning's harsh crying on the other side of the mirror—a clumsy, indelicate masculine braying that hurt my ears to listen. I put my hands to the side of my head to block out the sound. Men forget how to cry for the most part, don't they? And when they *do* cry, the sound is hoarse and crude, undignified and difficult to listen to. Jameson may have had a woman's voice when he wept, but I heard his own voice.

Still, I did feel a kind of pity for the body that was making the sound as it remembered and acknowledged whose soul it harboured, whose soul occupied it (whatever vanity it may have concocted about its own identity), and most of all, whose soul would now reclaim and recycle that body's life-force, devour it, in fact, for regenerative sustenance.

My sustenance, to be exact. I seeded his body with my soul while he slumbered in his mother's womb; now was the harvesting time. In truth, I had and always would find my own soul's corporeal host wherever she—or he—had been reborn.

Jamie, I said, gazing at his rent face on the other side of the mirror, *it's not* my *ghost story. It's* our *ghost story. We* are the ghost.

From this side of the glass, I opened my arms to him. From his side of the glass, the storm of moths surged off the walls, a dry white squall of wings and dust, erasing what was left of Jameson Browning's light, carrying off all traces of him as he pitched forward into the mirror.

I said I wanted to tell you a ghost story. I said it wasn't to be a ghost story like any ghost story you'd ever heard. I'd said it was *my* ghost story and that it was true.

Like any ghost story, it involved the bridges between the past and the present and who, or rather *what*, uses them to cross from the world of the living into the world of the dead. As I said earlier, time is, or ought to be, linear. Sometimes it's anything *but* linear. Certainly it has never been linear to me, not in life, certainly not in death, nor any of the time afterward.

Which brings us back to ghosts. One ghost in particular: me.

As you may have surmised, I do not acknowledge time. I do not abide temporal borders. Life or death is all the same to me. I walk those bridges with ease now, and their guardians call me by my Christian name.

I will bring pain to anyone who trespasses here on my island and I will make the trespassers see and feel terrible things before they die. I am the queen of wasps and moths. I am the enslaver of lesser spirits. I am the authoress of agonies barely yet conceived.

I am Rosa Blackmore. I am eternal.

I live in your mirror. And I will always find you.

Wild Fell House
Blackmore Island
29th April, 1890

Author's Note

Although Wild Fell and Blackmore Island are fictional locales, as is the town of Alvina, it was inspired in part by The Corran, the nineteenth-century estate of Alexander MacNeil of Wiarton, Ontario, which lies in ruins in a forest on the outskirts of that town, on a cliff above Colpoys Bay. I visited the ruins in January of 2012 with a friend in order to get a sense of the locale, and how it might possibly play into the novel I was writing. I was able to take two or three quick pictures of the ruins before my camera shut down completely and I lost the use of my cellular phone. While I do not ascribe any supernatural influence to either of those two things, I was relieved that both the camera and the phone promptly resumed their proper functions when we left the site of the ruins and returned to town.

Acknowledgements

Once again, first and foremost, my deepest thanks to Sandra Kasturi and Brett Savory for their patient, respectful nurture of this, my second novel—an experience that reminded me once again why accolades continue to be showered upon ChiZine Publications, the finest dark fantasy publisher in the business. And special thanks to Michael Matheson, for reasons he knows well.

Thank you to the supremely gifted two-time Aurora Award-winning artist Erik Mohr for the elegant cover he designed for *Wild Fell*. And thanks to my friend, writer and essayist Stephen Michell, who once again lent me his time and skill as a researcher.

Thanks to Sam Hiyate and Kelvin Kong of The Rights Factory literary agency for their work on behalf of both *Wild Fell* and *Enter, Night*.

I will be forever indebted to my friend of more than twenty years, novelist David Nickle, who generously read early drafts of *Wild Fell* and offered not only insightful and concise thoughts on its structure, but also proved an unflagging and tireless cheerleader and supporter for both the book and its author during the course of its creation.

I'm grateful to the real Sean "Moose" Schwartz for agreeing to guest-star in the opening section of *Wild Fell*. I'm pleased to report that he's still alive and kicking, and hasn't fallen at the hands of any woman, alive or dead—but it's early yet.

Again, I would like to acknowledge the support of the women of my writers' group, the Bellefire Club: Sèphera Girón, Helen Marshall, Nancy Baker, Gemma Files, Halli Villegas and Sandra Kasturi. It's astonishing how many spirits can be raised after gallons of Earl Grey tea, barrels of red wine, entire forests of paper, and meetings of gorgeously twisted minds.

Many thanks also to Denis Armellini and Jesse Skelton for listening to me babble about ghosts and missed deadlines on our daily dog walks; to Kaley O'Neill and Chuck Gyles for sharing their practical knowledge of certain technical events in the story; to my friend Julian Russell, the youngest reader of *Enter, Night* for his unvarnished enthusiasm for that book, enthusiasm which carried me through the writing of this book; to John Toewes and Chadwick Ginther and the staff of McNally Robinson in Winnipeg, my favourite indie bookstore in North America, for the kind of personal care and attention that novelists almost never receive any more in this day and age; to Eliezenai Galvao for once again keeping the home fires burning during the writing of a novel; to my boon companion of many journeys, Scott Bramble; to Steward Noack, my longtime muse, who always makes New York feel like home and who continues to inspire me on too many layers to list; and to Christopher Rice, whose unparalleled generosity, grace and kindness is a rare wonder to behold.

If I've missed anyone here, please feel free to give me a bang on the ear the next time you see me.

To my family, chosen and otherwise—my father Alan Rowe and my stepmother Sarah Doughty; Shaw Madson; the Bradbury-Kus family; the Gyles family; the Davidson-Hymers family; the Braun family; the Oliver family; Nancy and Jay Bowers; Barney Ellis-Perry; Christopher Wirth; and especially Ron Oliver—I'm so glad we're on this journey together.

And lastly, my husband Brian McDermid—none of this would make any sense without everything the last thirty years has been for us, and I thank him most of all.

About the Author

Michael Rowe was born in Ottawa and has lived in Beirut, Havana, Geneva and Paris.

An award-winning journalist and essayist, he is the author of several nonfiction books including *Other Men's Sons*, winner of the 2008 Randy Shilts Award for Nonfiction. He is also the editor of four anthologies of original fiction including the Lambda Literary Award-winning *Queer Fear* anthologies. His political and cultural essays have appeared in numerous journals, magazines and reviews in Canada and the United States. His first novel, *Enter, Night* was a finalist for both the Sunburst Award and the Prix Aurora, and will be published in Germany by Random House in 2014. *Wild Fell* is his second novel. He is married and lives in Toronto, and welcomes readers at www.michaelrowe.com.

ENTER, NIGHT
MICHAEL ROWE

Welcome to Parr's Landing, Population 1,528 . . . and shrinking.

The year is 1972. Widowed Christina Parr, her daughter Morgan, and her brother-in-law Jeremy have returned to the remote northern Ontario mining town of Parr's Landing, the place from which Christina fled before Morgan was born, seeking refuge. Dr. Billy Lightning has also returned in search of answers to the mystery of his father's brutal murder. All will find some part of what they seek—and more.

Built on the site of a decimated 17th-century Jesuit mission to the Ojibwa, Parr's Landing is a town with secrets of its own buried in the caves around Bradley Lake. A three-hundred-year-old horror slumbers there, calling out to the insane and the murderous for centuries, begging for release—an invitation that has finally been answered.

One man is following that voice, cutting a swath of violence across the country, bent on a terrible resurrection of the ancient evil, plunging the town and all its people into an endless night.

AVAILABLE NOW
978-1-926851-45-7